What Readers Are Saying about 86 Bloomberg Place

"Melody offers Chick Lit readers a bouquet of colorful characters. Kendall and her Bloomberg roommates are guaranteed to brighten up your reading hours. Lovely!"

Robin Jones Gunn, best-selling author of the Sisterchicks® novels and *Peculiar Treasures*

"Melody Carlson is a master storyteller who deftly captures the heart and yearnings of young women. Readers will connect with the ladies of Bloomberg Place as they strive to find their place in this big world."

Rachel Hauck, author of *Sweet Caroline*

"This fun romp with the Bloomberg Place girls has it all—snappy dialogue, complex relationships, and a fantastically diverse cast of characters that kept me reading nonstop!"

Camy Tang, author of *Only Uni* and *Single Sashimi*

"As the 'Bloomberg Girls' weather the challenges of friendship together, they discover the joys of forgiveness and restoration."

Melanie Dobson, author of *Together for Good* and *Going for Broke*

three weddings and a bar mitzvah

Melody Carlson

86 Bloomberg Place

David C Cook®

transforming lives together

THREE WEDDINGS AND A BAR MITZVAH
Published by David C. Cook
4050 Lee Vance View
Colorado Springs, CO 80918 U.S.A.

David C. Cook Distribution Canada
55 Woodslee Avenue, Paris, Ontario, Canada N3L 3E5

David C. Cook U.K., Kingsway Communications
Eastbourne, East Sussex BN23 6NT, England

David C. Cook and the graphic circle C logo
are registered trademarks of Cook Communications Ministries.

This story is a work of fiction. All characters and events
are the product of the author's imagination. Any resemblance
to any person, living or dead, is coincidental.

LCCN 2009929972
ISBN 978-1-58919-108-2
eISBN 978-0-7814-0347-4

© 2009 Melody Carlson
Published in association with the literary agency of Sara A. Fortenberry

The Team: Andrea Christian, Erin Michelle Healy, Amy
Kiechlin, Jaci Schneider, and Karen Athen
Cover Design: The DesignWorks Group, Charles Brock
Interior Design: The DesignWorks Group
Cover Illustration: Rob Roth

Printed in the United States of America
First Edition 2009

1 2 3 4 5 6 7 8 9 10

062909

One

Megan Abernathy

"Okay, then, how does the *second* Saturday in June look?" Anna asked her housemates.

Megan frowned down at her date book spread open on the dining room table. She and Anna had been trying to nail a date for Lelani and Gil's wedding. Megan had already been the spoiler of the first weekend of June, but she'd already promised her mom that she'd go to a family reunion in Washington. Now it seemed she was about to mess things up again. "I'm sorry," she said, "but I promised Marcus I'd go to his sister's wedding. It's been scheduled for almost a year now, and it's the second Saturday too. But maybe I can get out of it."

Lelani just shook her head as she quietly rocked Emma in her arms, pacing back and forth between the living room and dining room. The baby was teething and fussy and overdue for her afternoon nap. Megan wasn't sure if Lelani's frustrated expression was a result of wedding planning or her baby's mood.

"Is it possible you could do both weddings in one day?" Anna asked Megan.

"That might work." Megan picked up her datebook and followed Lelani into the living room, where she continued to rock Emma.

"Or we could look at the third weekend in June," Anna called from the dining room.

5

"Shhh." Megan held a forefinger over her lips to signal Anna that Emma was finally about to nod off. Megan waited and watched as Emma's eyes fluttered closed and Lelani gently eased the limp baby down into the playpen set up in a corner of the living room. Lelani pushed a dark lock of hair away from Emma's forehead, tucked a fuzzy pink blanket over her, then finally stood up straight and sighed.

"Looks like she's down for the count," Megan whispered.

Lelani nodded. "Now, where were we with dates?"

"If you still want to go with the second Saturday," Megan spoke quietly, "Anna just suggested that it might be possible for me to attend two weddings in one day."

"That's a lot to ask of you," Lelani said as they returned to the dining room, where Anna and Kendall were waiting expectantly with the calendar in the middle of the table and opened to June.

Megan shrugged as she pulled out a chair. "It's your wedding, Lelani. You should have it the way you want it. I just want to help."

Anna pointed to the second Saturday. "Okay, this is the date in question. Is it doable or not?"

Lelani sat down and sighed. "I'm willing to schedule my wedding so that it's not a conflict with the other one. I mean, if it can even be done. Mostly I just wanted to wait until I finished spring term."

"What time is Marcus's sister's wedding?" asked Anna.

"I'm not positive, but I think he said it was in the evening." She reached for her phone.

"And you want a sunset wedding," Kendall reminded Lelani.

"That's true." Anna nodded.

"But I also want Megan to be there," Lelani pointed out.

"That would be helpful, since she's your maid of honor," said Anna.

Megan tried not to bristle at the tone of Anna's voice. She knew that Anna had been put a little out of sorts by Lelani's choice—especially considering that Anna was the sister of the groom—but to be fair, Megan was a lot closer to Lelani than Anna was. And at least they were all going to be in the wedding.

"Let me ask Marcus about the time," Megan said as she pressed his speed-dial number and waited. "Hey, Marcus," she said when he finally answered. "We're having a scheduling problem here. Do you know what time Hannah's wedding is going to be?"

"In the evening, I think," Marcus said. "Do you need the exact time?"

"No, that's good enough." Megan gave Lelani a disappointed look. "I'll talk to you later, okay?"

"You're not thinking of bailing on me, are you?" He sounded genuinely worried.

"No, but we're trying to pin down a time and date for Lelani."

"It's just that I really want my family to meet you, Megan. I mean all of my family. And I want you to meet them too."

"I know, and I plan to go with you."

"Thanks. So, I'll see you around six thirty tonight?"

"That's right." Megan told him good-bye, then turned to Lelani with a sigh. "I'm sorry," she told her. "That wedding's at night too. Maybe I should blow off my family reunion so that you—"

"No." Anna pointed to the calendar. "I just realized that the first Saturday in June is also my mother's birthday."

"So?" Kendall shrugged. "What's wrong with that?"

Megan laughed. "Think about it, Kendall, how would *you* like to share your wedding anniversary with your mother-in-law's birthday?"

Kendall grinned. "Oh, yeah. Maybe not."

"How about a Sunday wedding?" suggested Megan.

"Sunday?" Lelani's brow creased slightly as she weighed this.

"Sunday might make it easier to book the location," Kendall said. "I mean, since most weddings are usually on Saturdays, and June is a pretty busy wedding month."

"That's true," agreed Megan.

"And you gotta admit that this is short notice for planning a wedding," added Kendall. "Some people say you should start planning your wedding a whole year ahead of time."

"Marcus's sister has been planning her wedding for more than a year," Megan admitted. "Marcus says that Hannah is going to be a candidate for the *Bridezillas* show if she doesn't lighten up."

They all laughed.

"Well, there's no way Gil and I are going to spend a year planning a wedding." Lelani shook her head. "That's fine for some people, but we're more interested in our marriage than we are in our wedding."

"I hear you." Kendall laughed and patted her slightly rounded belly. She was in her fifth month of the pregnancy. They all knew that she and her Maui man, Killiki, were corresponding regularly, but despite Kendall's high hopes there'd been no proposal.

"I really don't see why it should take a year to plan a wedding," Megan admitted. "I think that's just the wedding industry's way of lining their pockets."

"So how much planning time do you have now anyway?" Kendall asked Lelani. "Like three months?"

"Not even." Lelani flipped the calendar pages back. "It's barely two now."

"Which is why we need to nail this date today," Megan said. "Even though it's a small wedding—"

"And *that* remains to be seen," Anna reminded her. "My mother's list keeps growing and growing and growing."

"I still think it might be easier to just elope," Lelani reminded them. "I told Gil that I wouldn't have a problem with that at all."

"Yes, that would be brilliant." Anna firmly shook her head. "You can just imagine how absolutely thrilled Mom would be about that little idea."

Lelani smiled. "I actually thought she'd be relieved."

"That might've been true a few months ago. But Mom's changing." Anna poked Lelani in the arm. "In fact, I'm starting to feel jealous. I think she likes you better than me now."

Lelani giggled. "In your dreams, Anna. Your mother just puts up with me so she can have access to Emma."

They all laughed about that. Everyone knew that Mrs. Mendez was crazy about her soon-to-be granddaughter. Already she'd bought Emma all kinds of clothes and toys and seemed totally intent on spoiling the child rotten.

"Speaking of Emma"—Kendall shook her finger—"Mrs. Mendez is certain that she's supposed to have her on Monday. But I thought it was my day."

"I'm not sure," Lelani admitted. "But I'll call and find out."

"And while you've got Granny on the line," continued Kendall, "tell her that I *do* know how to change diapers properly. One more diaper lecture and I might just tape a Pamper over that big mouth of hers. Sheesh!"

They all laughed again. Since coming home from Maui, Kendall had been complaining about how Mrs. Mendez always seemed to find fault with Kendall's child-care abilities. In fact, Mrs. Mendez had spent the first week "teaching" Kendall the "proper" way to do almost everything.

To be fair, Megan didn't blame the older woman. Megan had been a little worried about Kendall too. But to everyone's surprise, Kendall turned out to be rather maternal. Whether it had to do with her own pregnancy or a hidden talent, Megan couldn't decide, but Kendall's skill had been a huge relief.

"Now, back to the wedding date," said Lelani.

"Yes," agreed Megan. "What about earlier on Saturday?"

"Oh, no," Anna said. "I just remembered that I promised Edmond I'd go to his brother's bar mitzvah on that same day—I think it's in the morning."

Lelani groaned.

"Edmond's brother?" Megan frowned. "I thought he was an only child. And since when is he Jewish?"

"Remember, his mom remarried," Anna told her. "And Philip Goldstein, her new husband, *is* Jewish, and he has a son named Ben whose bar mitzvah is that Saturday." She sighed. "I'm sorry, Lelani."

"So Saturday morning is kaput," Megan said.

"And Lelani wanted a sunset wedding anyway," Anna repeated.

"So why can't you have a sunset wedding on Sunday?" Kendall suggested.

"That's an idea." Megan turned back to Lelani. "What do you think?"

Lelani nodded. "I think that could work."

"And here's another idea!" Anna exclaimed. "If the wedding was on Sunday night, you could probably have the reception in the restaurant afterward. I'm guessing it would be late by the time the wedding was over, and Sunday's not exactly a busy night."

Lelani looked hopeful. "Do you think your parents would mind?"

"Mind? Are you kidding? That's what my mother lives for."

"But we still don't have a place picked for the wedding," Megan said.

"I have several outdoor locations in mind. I'll start checking on them tomorrow."

"We'll have to pray that it doesn't rain." Megan penned 'Lelani and Gil's Wedding' in her date book, then closed it.

"Should there be a backup plan?" asked Anna. "I'm sure my parents could have the wedding at their house."

"Or here," suggested Kendall. "You can use this house if you want."

Anna frowned. "It's kind of small, don't you think?"

"I think it's sweet of Kendall to offer." Lelani smiled at Kendall.

"I can imagine a bride coming down those stairs," Kendall nodded toward the staircase. "I mean, if it was a small wedding."

"I'll keep it in mind," Lelani told her. "And your parents' house, too."

"It might be tricky getting a church reserved on a Sunday night," Megan looked at the clock. "And speaking of that, I better get ready. Marcus is picking me up for the evening service in about fifteen minutes." She turned back to Lelani. "Don't worry. I've got my to-do list and I'll start checking on some of this stuff tomorrow. My mom will want to help with the flowers."

"And my aunt wants to make the cake," Anna reminded them.

"Sounds like you're in good hands," Kendall said a bit wistfully. "I wonder how it would go if I was planning my wedding."

"You'd be in good hands too," Lelani assured her.

"Now, let's start going over that guest list," Anna said as Megan stood up. "The sooner we get it finished, the less chance my mother will have of adding to it." Megan was relieved that Anna had offered to handle the invitations. She could have them printed at the publishing company for a fraction of the price that a regular printer would charge, and hopefully she'd get them sent out in the next couple of weeks.

As Megan changed from her weekend sweats into something presentable, she wondered what would happen with Lelani's parents when it was time for the big event. Although her dad had promised to come and was already committed to paying Lelani's tuition to finish med school, Lelani's mom was still giving Lelani the cold shoulder. Make that the *ice* shoulder. For a woman who lived in the tropics, Mrs. Porter was about as chilly as they came. Still, Lelani had friends to lean on. Maybe that was better than family at times.

"Your prince is here," Kendall called into Megan's room.

"Thanks." Megan was looking for her other loafer and thinking it was time to organize her closet again. "Tell him I'm coming."

When Megan came out, Marcus was in the dining room, chatting with her housemates like one of the family. He was teasing Anna for having her hair in curlers, then joking with Kendall about whether her Maui man had called her today.

"Not yet," Kendall told him with a little frown. "But don't forget the time-zone thing. It's earlier there."

"Speaking of time zones," Lelani said to Marcus. "Did I hear you're actually thinking about going to Africa?"

Marcus grinned and nodded. "Yeah, Greg Mercer, this guy at our church, is trying to put together a mission trip to Zambia. I might go too."

"Wow, that's a long ways away." Kendall turned to Megan. "How do you feel about that?"

Megan shrugged as she pulled on her denim jacket. "I think it's cool."

"Are you coming with us to church tonight, Kendall?" Marcus asked. "Greg is going to show a video about Zambia."

"Sorry to miss that," Kendall told him. "But Killiki is supposed to call."

"Ready to roll?" Megan nodded up to the clock.

He grinned at her. "Yep." But before they went out, he turned around. "That is, unless anyone else wants to come tonight."

Lelani and Anna thanked him but said they had plans. Even so, Megan was glad he'd asked. It was nice when Kendall came with them occasionally. And Lelani had come once too. Really, it seemed that God was at work at 86 Bloomberg Place. Things had changed a lot since last fall.

"So are you nervous?" Marcus asked as he drove toward the city.

"Nervous?" Megan frowned. "About church?"

"No. The big interview."

Megan slapped her forehead. "Wow, I temporarily forgot. We were so obsessed with Lelani's wedding today, trying to make lists, plan everything, and settle the date ... I put the interview totally out of my mind."

"Hopefully, it won't be out of your mind by Monday."

"No, of course not."

"So ... are you nervous?"

Megan considered this. It would be her first interview for a teaching job. And it was a little unsettling. "The truth is, I don't think I have a chance at the job," she admitted. "And, yes, I'm nervous. Thanks for reminding me."

"Sorry. Why don't you think you'll get the job?"

"Because I don't have any actual teaching experience." She wanted to add *duh*, but thought it sounded a little juvenile.

"Everyone has to start somewhere."

"But starting in middle school, just a couple of months before the school year ends? Don't you think they'll want someone who knows what they're doing?"

"Unless they want someone who's enthusiastic and energetic and smart and creative and who likes kids and had lots of great new ideas and—"

"Wow, any chance you could do the interview in my place?"

"Cross-dress and pretend I'm you?"

She laughed. "Funny."

"Just have confidence, Megan. Believe in yourself and make them believe too. You'd be great as a middle-school teacher."

"What makes you so sure?"

"Because I remember middle school."

"And?"

"And most of my teachers were old and dull and boring."

"That's sad."

"And I would've loved having someone like you for a teacher."

"Really?"

He chuckled. "Yeah. If I was thirteen, I'd probably sit right in the front row and think about how hot you were, and then I'd start fantasizing about—"

"Marcus Barrett, you're pathetic." Just the same, she laughed.

"What can I say? I'm just a normal, warm-blooded, American kid."

"Give me a break!" She punched him in the arm.

"Is that your phone?" he asked as he was parking outside of the church.

"Oh, yeah, a good reminder to turn it off." She pulled it out to see it was Kendall. Megan hoped nothing was wrong. "Hey, Kendall," she said as Marcus set the parking brake. "What's up?"

"Guess what?" shrieked Kendall.

"I have no idea what, but it sounds like good news." She stepped out of the car.

"Killiki just called."

"That's nice."

"And he asked me to marry him!"

Megan raised her eyebrows and looked at Marcus as he came around to meet her. "And you said yes?"

"Of course! Do you think I'm crazy?"

"No. Not at all. Congratulations, Kendall. I mean, I guess that's what you say."

"So now we have *two* weddings to plan."

Megan blinked. She walked with Marcus toward the church entry. "Oh, yeah, I guess we do."

"And I'm getting married in June too!"

"That's great, Kendall. I'm really, really happy for you. And Killiki seems like a great guy."

"He is! Anyway, we just looked at the calendar again. And we finally figured that I should just get married the same day as Lelani, only I'll get married in the morning. That way we'll all be able to go to both weddings."

"Wow, the same day?"

"Otherwise, you'll be at your reunion or Marcus's sister's wedding. Or Anna will be at the bar mitzvah. Or Lelani and Gil will be on their honeymoon."

"Oh, that's right."

"And I want all of you there!"

"Yes, I suppose that makes sense."

"It'll be busy, but fun."

"Definitely." Then Megan thanked Kendall for telling her, and they said good-bye. Megan closed her phone and just shook her head. "Wow."

"Kendall's getting married?" asked Marcus as he held the church door open for her.

"Yes. Can you believe it?"

"Good for her."

"And her wedding will be the same weekend as your sister's and the same day as Lelani's."

Marcus held up three fingers and wore a perplexed expression. "Three weddings in one weekend? That's crazy."

"Yep." Megan nodded. "Three weddings and a bar mitzvah."

"Huh?" Marcus looked confused, but they were in the sanctuary, and Megan knew she'd have to explain later.

Two

Kendall Weis

"I'm sorry, Kendall, but I find it a little hard to believe that you're actually going to—"

"Mom," Kendall protested, "I thought you'd be happy for me." Not wanting to wake Emma, who'd just fallen asleep in her playpen by the sectional, Kendall lowered her voice as she went over to the dining room.

"The last time you told me you were getting married turned out to be a great big hoax that your father and I footed the bill for."

"Yes, Mom, I realize I was a little confused about Matthew Harmon's interest in me, but are you going to hold that over my head for the rest of my life? People make mistakes, and hopefully—"

"Speaking of Matthew Harmon … and mistakes … have you done a paternity test yet?"

Kendall took in a deep breath and stared out the front window. Blossoms from the ornamental plum trees were blowing off the branches and littering the street with a layer of pale pink fluff. Kind of messy and pretty at the same time.

"Have you?" repeated her mother.

"No."

"May I ask why not?"

Kendall considered this. At one time she couldn't wait to get DNA results. At first it was because she felt certain that a DNA match would force Matthew to 1) take her seriously, 2) leave his wife, 3) marry Kendall, and 4) live happily ever after with her. Then she realized that was just her own delusional fantasy, and Matthew actually despised her. So she decided that if the DNA matched up, like she suspected it would, she'd simply slap a gigantic paternity suit on Matthew Harmon—make him pay. And then she'd met Killiki.

"Kendall?"

"Sorry, Mom. I was spacing."

Her mom cleared her throat. "So this new guy that you met in Maui ... why this sudden rush to get married?"

Kendall laughed as she patted her stomach. "Why not?"

"Because you haven't even dealt with one problem before you go leaping after another."

"What do you mean?"

"I mean your pregnancy, Kendall." Her mom was using that mother-of-a-five-year-old tone with her again. "And please don't tell me you want to get married so that your child will have a father."

"Why shouldn't I want my baby to have a father?"

"Perhaps because you may not even be ready to be a mother."

Kendall glanced over to where Emma was sleeping in the crib and frowned. "How can you say that, Mom? You haven't been around me. You don't even know—"

"I know that you haven't used good judgment for the past few years. Your life just seems to go from one disaster to the next. And now you want to marry someone you hardly know while you're pregnant with another man's baby. Isn't that like jumping from the frying pan into the fire?"

"Thanks for that vote of confidence, Mother."

"You don't have to get mad."

"I'm not mad. I'm hurt."

"I'm just being honest with you." Her voice softened. "And the truth is, I'm a little surprised by all this."

"I'm sorry I even called. But I thought you would be happy for me. Aren't moms usually happy when their daughters get married?"

"Usually. Although weddings are quite expensive these days."

"I don't expect you and dad to pay for any of it," Kendall said quickly.

Her mother just laughed.

"I'm serious, Mom."

"So how do you plan to pay for your wedding?"

"I'm making a little money watching Lelani's little girl and—"

"You plan to finance a wedding with babysitting money?"

Kendall took in a quick breath. "And I also have a little online business."

"Really?" Her mother's voice dripped with skepticism. "Doing what?"

"I sell things. On eBay."

"What do you sell?"

"Things I buy."

Her mother laughed again. "Oh, that must be lucrative. You buy things and then sell them again?"

"I find good deals on things at garage sales and I re—"

"You shop at garage sales?" She sounded incredulous.

"That's right, Mom. I shop at garage sales and I babysit for a living. Are you proud of me now?"

"Oh, Kendall."

"I'm sorry I bothered you, Mom. I just thought you'd want to hear the good news."

"So, tell me, Kendall, how is your little dog doing?"

"Huh?" Kendall knew her mom was just trying to change the subject.

"Cinderella? Or what was her name?"

"Tinkerbell."

"Oh, yes, that's right. So how is Tinkerbell?"

"She's fine," Kendall snapped. "But she's not my dog anymore."

"What? You got rid of her? And you had seemed so attached to her, Kendall."

Kendall heard the judgment in her mother's voice.

"Perhaps having a dog wasn't such a good idea after all?" she persisted. "Or perhaps you just changed your mind?"

"That's not what happened. Anna's mother watched Tinkerbell while I was in Maui. Then we came home from Maui and Lelani brought home her baby—"

"Another one of your roommates has a baby?" Her mother sounded scandalized. "What sort of place are you running there anyway? A home for unwed mothers?"

As tempting as it was to scream, Kendall did not want to wake up Emma. "No, Mother," she hissed into the phone. "In fact, Lelani and Gil are getting married soon."

"Oh, that's a relief."

"You don't have to be sarcastic." Kendall bit her lip and considered hanging up.

"So about your dog," persisted her mother. "What happened to it?"

"It turned out that Tinkerbell was not happy to share the house with a baby," Kendall said. "And I realized that Emma would be safer if I found another home for my dog. I didn't really want to get rid of her—" Her voice broke slightly. "But a friend of Anna's mother fell in love with her, and she promised that I could come visit and take Tinker for walks and"—Kendall was actually crying now—"and … that's … what … happened. Good-bye!" Then she hung up. And she turned off her phone too.

Kendall checked to see if Emma was still napping, then quietly sat down beside her. Why did Kendall let her mom get to her like that? And why had she even called in the first place? She should have known better. And yet she'd hoped that her parents would be happy for her. Kendall had been deliriously happy when Killiki proposed to her. In fact, she was still happy. She would not let Mom get to her.

In her mind, Kendall replayed Killiki's phone call.

"Aloha, my little mermaid," he had said, just like he always did. She loved that he called her his little mermaid and she hoped he never stopped. "I have a surprise for you," he had continued in a mysterious tone.

"What?" she asked him.

"Listen," he told her. And then some beautiful Hawaiian guitar music began to play. "I'm sitting on our beach, Kendall," he continued with the music in the background, which he later confessed was just his iPod, although she had felt sure there was a full Hawaiian band playing for them. "And I have a beautiful lei in my hand that I will send to my little mermaid today."

"Oh, that sounds lovely. Thanks, Killiki. What's the special occasion?" Even as she asked this, her heart was beginning to pound with anticipation.

"I would rather do this in person, Kendall, but I don't think I can wait that long."

"Do what?" Her hands were shaking.

"Kendall Weis, my little mermaid, will you do me the honor of marrying me?"

She sucked in a quick breath, then screamed, "Yes! Yes! Yes!" so loudly that she wondered if she'd damaged his ears. But he just laughed joyously, and then they began to make plans.

Kendall sighed happily as she curled up in a corner of the sectional. She was not going to let her mother get to her. All was right with the world. And nothing was more soothing than the even, gentle breaths coming from a sleeping baby. Before long, Kendall fell asleep too.

Kendall woke up to the sensation of something poking her shoulder. She opened her eyes to see Megan looking down at her and Emma standing up and peering over the edge of her crib. "Wake up, Sleeping Beauty," said Megan.

Kendall blinked and sat up. "Has Emma been awake long?"

"She just woke up as I came into the house," Megan told Kendall as she bent down and kissed the top of Emma's head. "I'd stick around and watch her, but I have to go to my interview at Madison."

Kendall nodded. "That's right. My car keys are in my bag over by the hall tree. Good luck. And if it helps to drop my name ..." She kind of laughed. "Not that it would, but feel free."

Megan smiled. "Hey, it couldn't hurt to mention that I live with an alumna."

"I was a Pirate and proud of it." Kendall reached down to pick up Emma, then wrinkled up her nose. "Smells like someone needs a change." Then she started dancing with Emma as she sang an old song. *"I think a change—a change would do you good—do you good—a change would do you good—I think a change ..."*

Megan laughed. "Maybe you two should put your act on YouTube."

Kendall smiled. "I think Sheryl Crow's got this one covered."

"Not with a baby, I'll bet." Megan held up Kendall's keys. "Thanks again for letting me borrow your car."

"Good luck!"

Kendall continued her song as she transported Emma into Lelani's bedroom, where a changing table was all set up and, thanks to her preplanning, a disposable changing pad was already in place. "Okay, let's do this the way Grandma Mendez has taught us," she cooed to Emma as she fastened the safety strap over Emma's middle. Not that the strap would confine Emma if she decided to squirm or roll. And not that Kendall planned to leave Emma unattended anyway. She knew better than that.

Kendall pushed up her sleeves and held her breath as, carefully, step by step, she peeled off the gross diaper, taped it into a neat albeit smelly bundle and dropped it in the waste basket, used lots of wipes, made sure Emma was really clean, rubbed on some diaper rash ointment, followed that with a conservative "sprinkle" of baby powder, and finally put on the fresh diaper—securely but not too tight. Kendall had learned early on that a toddler can worm her way out of a loose diaper.

"There you go, princess," she said as she lifted Emma up. "And some people think I don't know how to take care of a baby." She glanced at Lelani's bedside clock. "And if I'm not mistaken, your mommy should be here pretty soon."

Since the housemates' return from Maui, and thanks to Lelani's father's financial help, Lelani had switched over to part-time at Nordstrom and registered late for two classes at Portland State, where she planned to finish her medical degree. Today was a school day, and she should be home by three.

"Not that I'm trying to get rid of you, little darlin'." Kendall sat down with Emma on the living room carpet, watching as the baby crawled directly toward the coffee table, used it to pull herself up to a standing position, and then walked around the perimeter with a proud expression.

"Yes, you're going to be walking soon," Kendall told her as she moved closer in case she needed to spot a tumble. "But, really, there's no hurry, sweetie pie, you're not even a year old yet." She chuckled. "Trust me, you'll grow up soon enough. Enjoy your childhood while you can." Kendall remembered what it was like to be the youngest of five kids—all of whom were much older than she was. It was like she was always running to catch up, trying to measure up, hoping to be one of them, constantly wishing she were older. Was it possible she had hurried so fast that she'd missed a few things along the way? She was sure her mother would agree. Not that she wanted to think about her mother.

Kendall blocked the phone conversation from her mind as Emma sat down with a plop and immediately crawled under the coffee table in pursuit of her pink bunny.

"Watch your head," Kendall warned. But the nimble baby emerged with bunny in tow and a satisfied grin. Then she quickly discarded the bunny in exchange for a nearby ball, which rolled away as soon as she reached for it. Emma laughed and followed it. And Kendall followed her, thinking that this was probably how her mother saw her—as an infant who chased after one thing, got distracted, and then took off after something else. Maybe it was true, or had been true. But people could change. Besides, Kendall did *not* want to think about her mother.

She would much rather think about Killiki. *He had asked her to marry him!* She could hardly believe it, and yet she could hardly believe it had taken him this long. She had almost expected him to pop the question before she'd left Maui. After all, it had been love at first sight for both of them. But he had been thoughtful and careful and even prayerful, all qualities she appreciated about him.

"Let's play roly-poly." Kendall sat with legs spread and rolled the ball to Emma. She laughed as she caught the ball and clumsily pushed it back.

"Yay!" Kendall said as the ball slowly made its way to her. "I see a sports future for you!"

"Hello," called Lelani as she came in the front door. Without even taking off her jacket, she rushed toward Emma. "Hey, little sweetie, how's my girl?" She gathered the baby up and kissed her. "I missed you!"

Kendall used both hands to push herself onto her knees, then slowly stood with a grunt. "Man, this is getting harder all the time."

Lelani laughed. "Yeah, I remember those days."

Kendall picked up the discarded pink bunny and tossed it into the playpen.

"So was she a good girl?" Lelani asked.

"She's *always* a good girl." Kendall winked at Emma. "And if she wasn't, do you think we'd tell?"

"I wonder how Megan's interview is going." Lelani sat Emma down to peel off her jacket. "I even remembered to pray for her."

Kendall slapped her own forehead. "I forgot." Then she closed her eyes and silently shot up a quick prayer. "There. A quickie will have to do for now."

Lelani laughed as she picked up Emma again. "I'm sure God gets lots of quickies."

"So how was school?" Kendall asked as she flopped down onto the sectional and put her feet up.

"Okay. You know the classes I'm taking are pretty insignificant, just a way to get my foot in their door for next year."

"Maybe so, but you seem to be doing a lot. I mean being a mom, working part-time, going to school." Kendall shook her head. "I don't think I could do all that."

"But you watch Emma for me, and you're still doing your eBay business. Besides that, you're pregnant, and that can take a lot of energy." Lelani grinned at Emma. "Oh yeah, little girl, I remember how tired I got when you were in my tummy."

"Still, you have your life a lot more together than I do." Kendall frowned. "In fact, it seems like everyone does."

"Everyone's different." Emma was patting Lelani's face and laughing as Lelani changed expressions for her entertainment.

"Plus, you're planning a wedding," Kendall reminded her.

"So are you." Lelani set Emma back on the floor. "I'm so happy for you, Kendall. Killiki is really a great guy."

Kendall nodded. "I know. I knew it from the beginning. But I'll admit it was encouraging when you gave him your endorsement."

"He's been my friend for as long as I can remember. And I've always had the greatest respect for him. In fact, I think he and Gil are a lot alike. Both very responsible and mature."

Kendall made a face. "You'd think my mother would be happy for me. I mean, I finally fall in love with a good guy and—"

"Did you tell her?"

Kendall nodded. "But I wish I hadn't. I wish I'd just kept it a secret until Killiki and I tie the knot. Maybe I could put a note in the baby announcements, that is, if I send any to my family. Something like, 'Oh, by the way, I'm married.'"

"But don't you think your family will want to come to the wedding?"

"Not if they're thinking like my mom."

"How's that?" Lelani was playing peekaboo with Emma.

"My mom actually said that I'm jumping from the frying pan into the fire."

"Seriously?" Lelani peeked at Kendall from behind her fingers. "She said *that*?"

"She did." Kendall nodded. "And a lot of other things too. Like why haven't I gotten a paternity test?"

"She wants you to be tested while you're still pregnant?"

Kendall shrugged. "I guess so."

"Well, tell her that's not in the best interest of the baby. Prenatal tests are invasive and carry a risk of miscarriage. Admittedly, it's small, but it's a risk nonetheless."

Kendall rubbed her abdomen in a protective way. "Maybe I should wait until the baby's born."

"And besides the risk factor, a test won't prove a thing without Matthew's cooperation. My guess is that he won't cooperate, not short of a court order."

"So, really, there's no big hurry to be tested, then."

Lelani didn't respond.

"That whole paternity thing made me wonder about you and Emma." Kendall watched as mother and daughter continued with peekaboo. "Did you get her tested?"

Lelani put her hands down. "It's like I already told you, Kendall. Emma's dad has no interest in her and I have no interest in him."

"But what if something happened?" Kendall persisted. "Like what if he changed and wanted to know for certain that she was his daughter?"

Lelani's brow creased. "I don't honestly know what I'd do." She put her nose against Emma's nose. "But I don't think that'll ever happen."

"What if there was some kind of a medical need?" Kendall asked.

"You mean like if Emma needed a kidney or bone marrow transplant?" Lelani sighed.

"Yeah, something like that."

"Naturally, if Emma had a desperate medical need like that, of course I would contact her biological father. But it's not something I lie in bed worrying about every night."

"I know."

"Look, Kendall." Lelani gathered up Emma and stood. "How you handle your situation is totally up to you. I did what I felt was best for me and my baby. And as you know, I'm not terribly proud of all my decisions. You need to decide what's best for you—and at least you have Killiki to help you figure things out now. I was pretty much alone."

Kendall smiled. "You're a strong woman, Lelani."

Lelani just shrugged as she headed to her room with Emma. "I don't know about that. I just did what I had to do. But I'm not afraid to admit that it's a relief to have Gil in my life. Or that he helps me to be stronger."

"That's how I feel about Killiki," Kendall called out. "In fact, I'm going to phone him right now. If I'm lucky, he'll still be on his lunch break." But she wasn't lucky. Her call went straight to voice mail. As she left him a warm, loving message, she imagined him with his head underneath someone's kitchen sink, or perhaps he was setting a toilet. She knew a plumber's life (even in Maui) was not a glamorous one, but she also knew she didn't care. She loved Killiki for who he was, not for his occupation or net worth or real estate holdings, and not even for the kind of vehicle he drove, and that for her was something new. She had just finished her message to him when her phone buzzed and, hoping it was him, she eagerly answered.

"Kendall?" her mother's voice was shrill. "Good grief, girl, it's about time you turned your phone on. I even tried the house phone several times, but all I got was a busy signal. I was starting to get worried."

Kendall walked over to see that the landline receiver had been knocked off the hook. Probably Emma's doing. *Good girl!* She reluctantly set the phone back in place, then took in a deep breath. "What do you want, Mom?" she asked in a flat voice.

"Well, I told your father about your, uh, your situation."

"Which situation is that?" Kendall placed a protective hand over her stomach. "Being pregnant with a married man's baby? Or suddenly deciding to get married to a man I barely know? Or just the general jumping-from-the-frying-pan thing?"

"So, perhaps you *do* see my concerns."

"I was being sarcastic."

"Still."

"Look, Mom, I'm sorry I'm not your perfect child. I'm sorry I've made some stupid mistakes. I'm sorry I lied to you sometimes. But the only reason I lied was because I thought I was saying what you wanted to hear. If you'll recall, you were pretty thrilled when you thought I was going to marry a celebrity."

"Yes, but that was only because—"

"I'm sorry to be a disappointment to you, Mother. But this is my life and I'm the one who has to live it."

"And that's exactly what your father said."

"Well, tell him thank you for me. Better yet, put him on and I'll tell him myself."

"He just left for a golf date."

"It figures."

"And I wasn't calling you so that we could fight again, Kendall."

"Really?"

"No, I was calling to let you know that Dad and I are changing our travel plans so that we can return to Oregon and help you with your wedding. Isn't that wonderful!"

Kendall had vivid flashbacks to her three older sisters' weddings: how her mother had taken over every little detail and all the fights that entailed, and how Kate and her mom had nearly come to blows over menus and flowers, and how Kim ended up wearing the "poodle" dress, and how Kristen had gotten so fed up at the last minute that she called off her wedding entirely.

"I … uh … I don't know what to say."

"You don't have to say a thing, Kendall. Just know that Mommy is coming and that everything is going to be okay."

"Have you been drinking?"

She just laughed. "My daughter just asked if I've been drinking," she said to someone else. This was followed by ripples of feminine laughter.

"Seriously, Mom, it's a little early for martinis."

"You know what they say, Kendall, it's always happy hour somewhere."

"Obviously."

"So, don't you worry about a thing, Kendall, darling. Toodles!" And then she hung up.

"Right," Kendall said to nobody. "Nothing to worry about now."

Three

Anna Mendez

"It's only eleven more names," Anna's mother said in a pleading voice. "Surely, you can squeeze in a few more guests, Anna. It's not like I'm asking for the moon."

"You're not supposed to call me about this at work, Mama." Anna forced a smile for Edmond as he waited by her desk. "Besides, you've already squeezed in about forty more guests than Gil and Lelani wanted. At the rate you're going, the wedding's going to triple in size before the invitations are even sent."

"But these are family members, *mi'ja*, your family too."

"Not every single family member has to come to this wedding."

"But you know how it is. There are expectations … feelings will be hurt."

"They'll get over it. Just explain that it's a *small* wedding."

"But Gil is my only son."

"And I'm your only daughter, and I have a meeting that I'm going to be—"

"But you will talk to Lelani for me?"

Anna stood. "Talk to her yourself, Mama. Better yet, talk to Gil." Then she said good-bye, snapped her phone shut, turned it off, and rolled her eyes for Edmond's sake. "My brother is going to owe me big-time before this wedding is over."

He just chuckled. "Maybe Gil and Lelani should just bite the bullet and have a big wedding."

"They don't want a big wedding." She picked up her laptop and glanced at the clock. Fortunately they still had a couple minutes before the meeting.

"I thought all girls wanted big weddings."

"Not Lelani. Her ideal wedding would be to get married on a beach at sunset, probably in Maui."

"Why don't they do that then?"

"Lelani can't afford that. And, besides, she wants all of us at her wedding."

"How about an Oregon beach, then?"

"Not possible."

"Why?"

"Remember, that's a really busy weekend. Megan has a wedding to go to on Saturday."

Edmond nodded. "And we have the bar mitzvah."

"Plus there's Kendall's wedding too."

"Man, that's going to be one crazy weekend."

"Tell me about it."

"Hey, why don't Lelani and Kendall have a double wedding?"

Anna frowned at him.

"What's wrong with that?"

"Think about it."

He chuckled. "I guess Lelani and Kendall are about as different as two girls could be. But they do have Maui in common now."

"Besides that, my mother would probably throw a hissy fit if Gil's wedding had to be shared with anyone else." She almost added, "Unless it was me," but thought better of it. No way was she going to hint that she wanted to go down that road. Oh, sure, all this talk of weddings brought out some longings in a girl. It bothered her a little (although it obviously bothered her mother more) that Gil, the younger one, was getting married first.

"So, I guess my future as a wedding planner just hit the rocks," Edmond said.

"Better stick with publishing," she said as they went into the meeting room.

The meeting dragged on and on, and Anna tried to concentrate on the last thing on the table, a boring nonfiction book proposal from a friend of Edmond's mother, but she felt distracted by all the recent talk of weddings. She also resented the way her mother kept pulling her into the planning, even calling her at work. Why should the guest list be Anna's responsibility? After all, it wasn't her wedding, was it? And it's not like she was fulfilling the role of maid of honor. Why wasn't her mom calling Megan? Or Lelani or Gil?

Of course, Anna knew why her mother was acting like this. It was her way of rubbing Anna's nose in the fact that Gil was beating his older sister to the altar. Not that her mother was the least bit enthusiastic about the fact that both of her children were dating outside of their religion and their culture. Still, she seemed to be adapting. And really, perhaps Anna should be thankful that Gil was breaking this new turf on the home front. At least if (and when) Anna decided to get married, it should be easier.

She glanced at Edmond, who was trying to show interest in the book project although she knew he wanted it to be rejected. His sandy brown hair was a little shaggy, in need of a trim, but it actually looked rather attractive too. And had he changed his glasses lately? Anna tried to remember. Hadn't they been black frames before?

These were more of a dark tortoise shell. Still, they looked good on him. She smiled and, to her surprise, he looked at her in that same instant and smiled back. Fortunately, the meeting was coming to an end and no else seemed to have observed her flirting with him. Not that she was flirting actually. After all, he was her boyfriend, so she was allowed to flirt, right?

"Glad that's over," he said as they rode down the elevator together. "I was worried that Rick was going to push to publish that last one." He feigned a yawn. "We'd have to sell it with a complimentary packet of NoDoz."

She laughed. "Not a bad idea."

"So what're you doing tonight?" he asked as he helped her with her coat. "Want to go grab a bite to eat?"

"As tempting as that sounds, it's my night to cook. We're all trying to save a few bucks by taking turns in the kitchen."

He smacked his lips. "So, what does a guy have to do to get an invite?"

"Nothing, except that we all agreed to devote our evenings this week to getting the wedding plans solidified. There are still lots of decisions about when and where and whatnot and I need to get those invitations—"

"Yeah, yeah …" He held the door open for her. "And I'm guessing it's no guys allowed."

"It's distracting enough with four girls trying to agree on things," she told him as they went out to the parking lot. "Throw in a few guys and we'd never get any decisions made."

He stood by her car, waiting as she unlocked it and got in. "So, maybe all this wedding planning is good practice."

She frowned up at him. "What do you mean?"

He shrugged, then glanced toward the door, where the new intern was emerging with an armful of books. The girl was halfway out when the door swung back, knocking most of the precariously stacked books to the pavement.

"Looks like I better go give Lucy a hand," he said quickly. "See you tomorrow, Anna."

Anna smiled and waved as he closed the door to her car and hurried over to where poor Lucy was scrambling to gather up the books, dropping even more as she did this. Why hadn't the silly girl thought to have gotten a box? Edmond was gathering up the books as Anna backed out of her parking space. It was so like him to help others like that. Really, he was one of the good guys. Old-fashioned when it came to etiquette, honest, traditional, hardworking. Really, Anna's mother should be pleased that she was dating a guy like Edmond.

Anna replayed his words as she drove to the grocery store. *Maybe all this wedding planning is good practice.* He must've been talking about their relationship. But was he seriously considering marriage? Oh, she knew he liked her well enough. In fact, he'd been the one to do the pursuing. Even when she'd hurt him in her brief period of insanity by going back to her old boyfriend Jake (the Snake), Edmond had waited in the wings and eventually forgiven her.

Anna thought about this as she pushed her wobbly cart through the grocery store, gathering up the few things she needed for dinner. What if Edmond was thinking about popping the question? How would she feel about that? On one hand, Anna had never planned to marry young. Not that she was so young at twenty-six—at least by her mother's standards. Most of Anna's younger cousins had already married. Some of Anna's aunts (probably her mother too) called her the Old Maid when they didn't think she was listening. Not that it bothered her. At least it hadn't before … all of this wedding talk. She found herself thinking about marriage and weddings a lot more than she used to.

While growing up, all Anna wanted was to be a single career woman, at least until she hit her thirties. She wanted independence and freedom and, most of all, her own apartment. Living at Kendall's house was simply supposed to be the first step toward that goal. It hadn't been easy to convince her mother to let her move away from home. What may have appeared to be "one tiny step" for a young woman was "one giant step" for a traditionally raised Latina girl.

Anna parked her cart at the end of a line at the checkout stand and waited. She gazed blankly over the glossy magazines, absently scanning the covers until her eyes locked on a headline of a slightly cheesy woman's magazine. *Single and Over Thirty—Meet the New Spinster.*

Anna blinked and read the line again. What were they trying to say? That no one over thirty was going to get married? Someone needed to get a life. She resisted the temptation to pick up the magazine and skim the stupid article. Really, why should she give a stupid magazine like that a second thought? They were simply being sensational, trying to scare young women like her into buying their ridiculous magazine. Well, she was not falling for it.

The cashier began ringing up Anna's groceries—ingredients for enchiladas, which had been Lelani's request. "Looks like your family is in for a treat tonight," the woman said as she tucked the sour cream into Anna's reusable shopping bag.

"Actually, it's my roommates," Anna corrected.

"Lucky roommates." The woman waited as Anna handed her the cash. "But then I suppose roommates are a lot like family too."

Anna nodded, but she was thinking that her "family" of roommates would be dispersing in June, all going their separate ways.

"Have a nice evening," the woman said automatically as Anna gathered up her bags and thanked her. It was starting to drizzle as Anna hurried to her car. Suddenly, her mood seemed to be synchronized with the weather. She hadn't really given a whole lot of thought to what she would do after that second weekend in June. Kendall had said they could remain in the house until the end of that month and possibly even after that, unless her grandmother allowed her to sell the house, which was what Kendall was hoping to do.

"It would help me to get rid of my debt and give Killiki and me a fresh start," she'd told them last week.

As Anna drove home, she knew it was time to come up with a plan. Already her mother had dropped some hints that Anna might want to move back home. "To save money," her mother had said. Money for what? Anna had wondered. But she hadn't gone there, and she intended to do all she could to avoid moving back home. Because if being an unwed Latina at twenty-six was bad, it was far worse to be still living at home. If Anna was going to be able to afford an apartment on her own, she was going to have to start pinching pennies. And she would need to pinch them hard.

As Anna turned onto Bloomberg Place, though, she wondered if she was being shortsighted. After all, she and Edmond were compatible. She'd never had a guy who treated her so well, who seemed to love her so much. And yet ... she seemed to be always pushing him away, as if she needed to keep him at arm's length. Why was that?

She parked her car, gathered her things, and hurried into the house. As she was unloading her groceries and starting to prep for dinner, she began to imagine that she was fixing dinner for Edmond, and that they were newlyweds just settling into their first home. Instead of Kendall's pots and pans and dishes, Anna would be using her own things. She would be opening her own refrigerator, she would—

"Hey, Anna," said Kendall as she burst into the kitchen. "I've been thinking about your enchiladas all afternoon. Need any help?"

Anna was caught off guard, partly from the interruption of her daydream and partly because she still wasn't used to this side of Kendall—and, frankly, she wondered how long it would last. "Sure," she said. "Why don't you start grating cheese?"

While Kendall grated cheese, she prattled on about wedding plans and how Killiki was willing to live part-time in Maui and part-time in Oregon. "Just today he told me that if we could sell this house, we might be able to afford a condo. He was looking online, and there are some good deals right now."

"Wow." Anna nodded. "A home in Maui and a home in Oregon. This is sounding really good, Kendall."

She grinned and nodded. "I know. I'm starting to feel like a princess." She laughed. "I don't want to be the spoiled princess though. I am working on that."

"Oh, a little spoiling is probably okay." Anna smiled as she stirred the enchilada sauce. "I kind of like it when Edmond spoils me."

"How's it going with you and Edmond?" Kendall asked with sincere interest. "I haven't seen him around here for a while. You guys are still together, right?"

"Of course." Anna nodded vigorously. "In fact, he said something today." She sort of giggled now and wondered if it was even worth saying out loud.

"What?" Kendall asked eagerly.

"Oh, we were just talking about all this wedding planning stuff—and it's funny because Edmond keeps making these suggestions, which are sweet but totally won't work. Anyway, as I was leaving he said that all this wedding planning might be good practice." Anna waited for Kendall's reaction.

Kendall's eyes grew wide and she smiled knowingly. "He's thinking about proposing, Anna."

"Oh, I don't know."

"He is!" Kendall slapped Anna on the back. "And he's a great guy. You'd say yes, wouldn't you?"

Anna considered this, then slowly nodded. "Yeah, maybe I would."

"Oh, Anna, that's so—"

"But I would insist on a long engagement," Anna said. "So don't worry about a triple wedding in June."

"When would you want to get married?"

Anna thought about this. "I've always liked the idea of a winter wedding. But not this coming winter. That would be too soon."

"So you mean a really long engagement."

"Some couples wait two or more years."

"I couldn't do that." Kendall looked down at her midsection. "And not because I'm pregnant either. But when I know the guy I love and want to spend the rest of my life with, I don't see any reason to wait."

Anna felt the need to bite her tongue now. After all, it hadn't been all that long ago—six months—that Kendall was certain she was in love with Matthew Harmon.

"It's smelling good in here," said Megan as she came in through the garage entrance.

"Hey, how'd the interview go?" asked Anna.

Megan smiled hopefully. "It seemed like it went fairly well."

"Did you tell them that I was an alumna?" asked Kendall.

Megan laughed. "Actually, the subject never came up."

Kendall looked disappointed. "Well, maybe they'll hire you and I can come visit you and check out my old school. That would be fun."

"So when will you know?" asked Anna.

"They have more applicants, but the teacher I'd be taking over for is due to have her baby in just a couple of weeks, so there's a little bit of a rush." Megan snitched a piece of sliced chicken breast that Anna had just browned. "Need any help?"

"I think we've got it under control. But maybe you could tell Lelani that it'll be ready in about five minutes."

Before long, dinner was on the table, and the four of them were enjoying Anna's chicken enchiladas and a green salad, talking about weddings. Then Kendall said she had an announcement to make.

"I don't want to scare you guys," she began seriously, "but I have some not-so-pleasant news."

They all waited.

"My mother has decided to come and help me plan my wedding."

Megan actually laughed. "What's so horrible about that?"

"Are you kidding? My mother could have her own reality show—it would be *Mother-of-the-Bridezilla*." Then she launched into stories of how her mother's interference and obsessive need to control had seriously messed up her sisters' weddings. "And my sister Kim actually cancelled the whole thing."

"She cancelled her wedding because of your mom?" asked Megan.

Kendall nodded. "Oh, she eventually got married—and to the same guy—but they went to Las Vegas and didn't tell anyone until after the fact. My mom was more than a little ticked about that. But they've been speaking for a few years now."

"Maybe your mom has mellowed with age," suggested Lelani. "How long has it been since the last wedding disaster?"

"More than ten years. But when I heard the tone in Mom's voice today, I felt like history was about to repeat itself."

"But if your mom is planning the wedding, won't that mean that your parents are footing the bill too?" asked Lelani as she spooned some mashed peas into Emma's wide-open mouth.

Kendall brightened now. "Yeah, you're right."

"And you were worrying that you couldn't afford much," Megan pointed out.

"That's true. I was even thinking about just having it here at the house. And serving cake, not dinner, for the reception. But maybe I can pull out all the stops now."

"If you're willing to bite the bullet when it comes to your mom," said Anna as she reached for another enchilada.

Kendall seemed to be thinking about this. As much as Anna hated to admit it, she could relate to the mother dilemma. The fact was, if Anna were getting married, her mother would be much more of a headache than she was being with Gil and Lelani now. She would insist on inviting every single relative, even the ones still in Mexico, and she'd probably invite most of the restaurant customers as well. She would have strong opinions about dresses and who should be brides-maids (probably all of Anna's cousins), and Anna probably wouldn't get much of a say in anything. If Anna were getting married, her mother's involvement might be enough to drive Anna and Edmond to Las Vegas to get hitched. Not that Edmond had asked her. Not yet, anyway.

Four

Lelani Porter

"I've been thinking," Gil said on the phone later that evening. "Maybe we should consider moving the wedding to Maui."

"But we can't—"

"Hear me out, Lelani."

She rearranged Emma, who was almost asleep, to a more comfortable position in the crook of her arm, then leaned back on her bed, adjusted the phone, and prepared herself to listen. "Okay."

"Well, relations with your family are … sort of strained."

"At best."

"I mean your dad's been great, don't get me wrong. I have the utmost respect for him."

"I know, Gil, and he feels the same about you."

"But what if moving the wedding to Maui somehow, well, somehow helped your relationship with your mom?"

Lelani sighed and pushed a dark lock of hair away from Emma's forehead. "I'm not sure that's possible."

"But what if it was? What if this gesture … what if—"

"Give me a minute." Lelani set down the phone as she slowly sat up with Emma, now soundly sleeping. She eased her down into the crib, tucking the bunny quilt snuggly around her, then returned to the phone.

"It's really sweet of you to think of this," she said quietly to Gil. "But I'm just not sure it would make any difference."

"But what if it did?"

Lelani sat back down on her bed. "I guess that would be pretty amazing, slightly miraculous even."

"So, you'll think about it, then?"

"I'll think about it, but we don't really have much time to figure this out, Gil. I mean, if we want to have a June wedding here in town. Megan's really working hard to help me figure out the details. And Anna's ready to rock and roll on the invitations."

"But consider this," he said in an enticing tone, "not only would you have your dream wedding—on a Maui beach at sunset—you would also avoid having a huge wedding, which is what's threatening to happen if my mother gets her way."

"Yes, but I would also miss having our friends with us, and you know they can't afford airfare to Maui again. And we can't afford to cover it for them. Plus, there's Kendall's wedding now."

"You sound frustrated."

"I guess I am a little. Not at you, Gil. But just everything. I suppose if I could have my way, I'd say, 'Let's just run down to city hall.' Do they do that anymore? And then after we were married, we could send everyone an after-the-event sort of announcement."

He laughed. "Hey, that works for me."

"But it would hurt your mother's feelings."

"Yeah."

"You're being so thoughtful of my mom, Gil. And she doesn't even deserve it. So I should consider your mother equally."

"It's too bad that relatives think they have the right to participate in something as personal and important as a wedding."

"I know exactly what you mean, but maybe that's how it should be." Lelani held her left hand up, admiring the solitaire diamond in its simple-yet-elegant setting. Gil had presented it to her shortly after they returned from Maui, and she hadn't taken it off since. "I mean, we're making a big commitment, Gil. Shouldn't we want our loved ones to witness our vows so they'll understand how seriously we're taking it?"

"No one has to see me say my vows. Trust me, Lelani, I'm taking this seriously."

She smiled and closed her eyes. "I do trust you. Implicitly."

"So you'll think about Maui then? I have enough in savings to cover it—no debt incurred. And I was thinking it would be cool to honeymoon there anyway."

"Really?"

"Yes, but now I've spoiled the surprise."

"Okay." She sat up. "I will think about it."

"Thanks."

"Thank you," she said quietly. "For being so thoughtful about my family, I mean. I love you, Gil."

"I love you too. Good night and sweet dreams."

"You too." She smiled to remember her tormented dreams from before—before Gil had helped her to get her daughter back. Only once since they'd been home had she awakened suddenly, worried for her little girl, wanting her, feeling like a failure. But then she saw the Winnie the Pooh nightlight bravely glowing, and the shape of Emma's crib so close that Lelani could reach out and touch it. And then she slept peacefully—more peacefully than she had slept in several years.

She knew she had Gil in part to thank for that. And she knew that she would give his suggestion for a Maui wedding serious consideration. What if it somehow helped to heal something between her and her mother? Wouldn't that alone be worth a lot?

Emma was soundly asleep, and Lelani slipped out to make a cup of herbal tea and do some studying. Not that she was very concerned about her classes, but she wanted to make sure she pulled A's in both of them. Her transcript from Hawaii was in great shape, but it had been more than a year since she was enrolled.

Maybe she was making a mountain out of a molehill, but she wanted to be certain that nothing kept her from finishing med school. Not only for her own sake, and for her daughter's, but she wanted to make her dad proud. Maybe even her mother too. And perhaps she wanted to do it for Gil as well, although Lelani knew that he would love her whether she remained a salesgirl at Nordstrom or became head of pediatrics at the best Portland hospital. Perhaps most importantly, Lelani wanted to do this for herself. It was a journey she'd started long ago and intended to finish.

"Hey, I thought I was the only night owl tonight," Megan said quietly when Lelani emerged from the kitchen with her tea.

"I didn't even see you."

"I was lurking in the sun room."

Lelani sat down at the dining room table where her books were waiting.

"But I won't bother you if you need to study."

Lelani waved her hand. "No, it's okay. Actually, I'd like to talk to you about something."

Megan sat down. "Sure, is something wrong?"

"Not exactly." Lelani spilled Gil's suggestion about a wedding in Maui. "He thinks it might heal something between my mom and me."

Megan frowned. "What do you think?"

"That it would take a major miracle."

Megan nodded. "I'd have to agree."

"But I love that Gil is thinking about me and my family. It's so sweet."

"Especially considering the grief he'll get from his own family if you relocate the wedding to Maui."

"But his parents could easily afford to come."

"Yes, but not all the relatives that Mrs. Mendez is set on inviting." Megan rolled her eyes. "The guest list is about to hit two hundred."

"Seriously?"

"Uh-huh."

"Oh."

"Not that I want to tell you what to do. But I hope you'll get it figured out soon. We really need to make decisions. Anna is eager to get those invitations going."

Lelani ran her fingers through her hair and sighed.

"What do *you* want?" Megan asked.

"What do you mean exactly?"

"For your wedding. What do you really want? I mean hopefully you'll only have one wedding in your lifetime. What do you want it to be? Where do you want it to be? What would make you happiest?"

Lelani just smiled. "It would make me happiest to simply say 'I do' to Gil and then get on with our life. The truth is, when I had Emma I gave up on the old dreams of a perfect wedding. I honestly didn't think I'd ever get married."

"That was *then*." Megan's brow creased. "And I heard you saying you'd always dreamed of a beach wedding at sunset. In Maui."

"Of course, but *that* was then."

"Yes, yes, I understand. But if you could wave your magic wand, what would you do?"

Lelani considered this.

"I mean, aside from making everyone happy, which is what I'm guessing you would do. But you can't go that road. What would you, Lelani Porter, want in your wedding?"

"Gil."

Megan rolled her eyes. "You're killing me here."

"I'm serious. All I want is to get married to Gil. I don't need all the bells and whistles."

"So, you're saying a simple wedding?"

Lelani couldn't help but laugh. "That's what I've been saying since day one."

Megan nodded. "Yes, I do recall that."

"But everyone seems intent to keep me from it."

"Maybe that's just the nature of weddings."

"But a wedding is only one day." Lelani held up one finger. "One single day. And then you're married for the rest of your life. Why so much fuss for one little day?"

"Because it's a big day. And because you want to remember it always. You want to make it special. Like you said, it's only one day. But doesn't that make your wedding day a rarity? You'll have your whole married life to do what you want." Megan frowned. "Well, maybe."

"So, are you saying I should have a big overblown wedding that makes Mrs. Mendez happy? Or that I should have a Maui wedding that may or may not make my mother happy? Or what?"

Megan looked stumped. "I'm not sure what I'm saying. Maybe I'm just tired. It's been a long day."

Lelani chuckled. "Thanks for helping me to figure this out, Megan."

Megan rubbed her head. "Yeah, sure, anytime."

"Just wait until it's your turn," Lelani called out as Megan headed for her room.

Megan laughed in a way that sounded like she wouldn't be planning her own wedding anytime soon. Apparently she and Marcus were nowhere near that place yet. Good for them. No need to rush things. In fact, Lelani sometimes wondered why she and Gil felt like they were in such a rush. On the other hand ... she smiled to herself as she opened her textbook. Sometimes, like now, she wondered why they weren't in an even bigger hurry.

She tried to refocus her attention as she picked up where she'd left off in the early Pleistocene period. At one time she would've been extremely interested in archaeology. Now it was mildly intriguing, but more than anything, she just wanted to get on with her life, and finishing her degree had become an important part of that. Her dream to become a doctor seemed almost within reach. But, to her surprise, even more than finishing med school and starting her own pediatric practice, she wanted to marry Gil and to be Emma's mother. Okay, she wanted it all. Really, was that too much to ask?

Five

Megan

"So, tell me, how did your interview go?" Megan's mom asked as soon as they sat down at the Soup Pot to wait for their order.

"I feel hopeful." Megan dropped her teabag into the little ceramic pot. "Mrs. McCall, that's the principal, really seemed to like me. And she thought it was great that I'd been working in interior design."

"See, all experience is valuable."

Megan laughed. "In fact, she was so interested that she even asked me about helping her to redo her office."

"That sounds promising."

Megan nodded. "I'm praying God will open the door."

"Did you tell Cynthia yet?"

"Tell her what exactly?"

"That you may be leaving the design firm."

Megan shook her head. "No way. I don't want them to know that I'm even looking. Vera would probably use that as an excuse to give me my walking papers."

Her mom chuckled. "That Vera—I just don't understand what makes her tick."

"Probably a mechanical heart."

"Poor Cynthia. She suffers from Vera almost as much as you do."

"I'm afraid she'll suffer even more if I leave. I think I'm actually a buffer, like Vera takes her meanness out on me and then goes easy on the others. Honestly, I probably wouldn't be leaving if Vera were a little bit nicer."

"I think that God sometimes uses difficult people to get us to where he wants us to be."

"Kind of like how Pharaoh motivated Moses to look for greener pastures?" Megan joked.

"Actually, I think it was God who motivated Moses. But Pharaoh made it easier for him to want to leave."

Their soup arrived, and Megan's mom began to inquire about the progress of the wedding plans. Megan gave her the latest update—how Kendall's mom was likely to take over, and how Gil wanted Lelani to consider a Maui beach wedding after all.

"How does Lelani feel about that?"

"I'm not sure. Gil thinks it might help her relationship with her mom." Megan sighed and shook her head. "The more I hear about other people's mothers, the more grateful I am for mine."

Her mom smiled. "Well, thank you."

"Thank *you*!"

"If Lelani decided to get married in Maui, would you still be her maid of honor?"

"That's a good question."

"Well, just so you know, I'd be willing to help with your airfare. I know you're not making much at the design firm."

"And even if I get the teaching job, I'll still be unemployed by mid-June."

Her mom frowned. "I hadn't even considered that. Don't you think it's possible you might get hired for the following year?"

"Even if I did, my contract wouldn't be effective until September."

"Yes, of course. It looks like you'll have some decisions to make before summer, Megan. A possible change in job as well as where you live."

Megan just nodded. She'd been considering both things.

"If you want, you can always move back home." Her mom smiled hopefully. "I wouldn't mind a little company."

"I'll think about it."

"To be honest, I've been considering listing the house. I really don't need all that room, and I hear real estate is starting to warm up."

"Really?" Megan felt a flash of worry to think her childhood home, the very house her dad designed, might no longer belong to them.

"I thought I might get a townhouse. Something simple and small and where someone else gets to do the maintenance."

"I guess that makes sense." Megan sadly sipped her tea.

"I know it'll make you sad, Megan. At first anyway. But it's just part of growing up. You'll get used to it."

"I think I'm a little resistant to change right now. I mean, changing my job would be a relief. But having to move this summer, well, I'm not looking forward to that. And the idea of not being able to come home when I want." Megan sighed.

"Home is where the heart is. You're always welcome wherever I am."

"I know." *Still,* Megan wanted to say, *it won't be the same.* Except that she knew how selfish that sounded.

"How are things at your church?" her mom asked. "And Marcus, is he still thinking about selling everything he owns and moving to Zimbabwe or wherever it was?"

"Zambia actually. And he's still very interested. He's on board with a guy from church, who's organizing a mission to put in some wells over there."

"Would you go too?"

Megan shrugged. "Sure, I'd like to. The funny thing is that I thought I was the one who had the dream to become a missionary. And sometimes I feel almost jealous, like Marcus has stolen it from me. How juvenile is that?"

"Isn't it something you two could do together?"

"Marcus has kind of hinted at that possibility. The problem is that he's financially set. He could actually go and do something like that. I mean, he's been making a lot of money these past few years. I, on the other hand, am not exactly rolling in the dough. And my financial future will look even bleaker if I find myself unemployed this summer."

"But maybe your unemployment will be your ticket to Zambia," her mom said optimistically. "You wouldn't even have to ask for time off."

"I guess if I'm really supposed to go, God will provide, right? Maybe I just need more faith."

"Here's an idea, Megan," her mom said. "Suppose I do put the house on the market, and suppose it does sell. How about if I dedicate a portion of the sale toward the Megan Abernathy mission fund?"

"You'd do that?"

"Of course. Why not?"

"See!" Megan proclaimed. "You really are the best mom ever."

Her mom gave her a sly look now. "I don't know. When I hear about those other wedding moms and how they're acting, well, I'm not sure I'd be much better if it were your wedding. To be honest, it's one of those things I've looked forward to for a long, long time. You might be singing a different song about your mother by then."

"Tell you what, Mom. If I ever do get married—and that's so out there that I can't even wrap my head around it—I'll welcome your help in planning my wedding."

Her mom beamed. "And I'll hold you to that."

"Just don't hold your breath." Megan paused to taste her soup.

"What's that supposed to mean?" her mom asked.

"Just that Marcus and I aren't talking about marriage or anything. In fact, he's been so distracted with all he's doing in church that I'm starting to feel a little left out."

Her mom laughed. "Well, isn't that a change? I remember sitting in this very restaurant listening to you fretting over your *unsaved* boyfriend and telling me that you wanted to break up. Now you're complaining that he's too involved in ministry."

"I suppose I do sound pretty flakey."

"Actually, you sound like a young woman who's at a crossroads."

Megan considered that. "I like the way *crossroads* sounds more than the word *change*. Crossroads mean you're going somewhere."

"You are going somewhere, Megan." Her mom patted her hand. "I can just feel it."

❧

When Megan got home from work, Anna was extremely worked up. "I cannot believe Lelani and Gil want to move their wedding to Maui!" she exclaimed even before Megan had a chance to remove her coat. "Did you know about this?"

Megan slowly took off her coat, hung it up, then turned to Anna. "Why are you so upset?"

"Because my mother is going into hysterics."

"Hysterics?" Megan went into the kitchen and put on the teakettle.

"Apparently Gil mentioned it to her today at the restaurant. She called me at work at least a dozen times. She's had her heart set on this wedding, and she's already told most of our relatives and probably already bought her dress, and now she's totally bummed and doesn't care if she takes me down with her."

"Sounds like you've had a rough day."

Anna nodded as she sat down on the kitchen stool. "I tried to be understanding … at first. But then she just kept calling. She kept coming up with reasons they should have the wedding here and finally suggested they get married twice. Once on the mainland and again in Maui. Anything to have her way."

"Well, if it's any consolation, I feel kind of sad to think they'll be married in Maui."

"But you'll go to the wedding, won't you?"

Megan shrugged. "I don't know. Airfare, hotel … that's a lot of money just to go to a wedding."

"I'm going," Anna declared. "My mother told me that much."

"Maybe you'll be able to step into the maid-of-honor position." Even as Megan said this, she felt sad. She'd been so honored to be Lelani's choice. It wouldn't be easy to let it go.

"I don't know. Maybe one of Lelani's old friends will want to stand up with her."

"Maybe. By the way, has Gil decided on his best man yet?"

"I assumed he was going to go with his old best friend, Richard, but he hasn't said anything for sure. And he and Richard aren't all that close anymore. My mom is pushing him to invite one of our cousins. We have no lack of cousins to choose from."

Megan chuckled. "Must be nice."

"Sometimes nice. Sometimes a great big pain in the—"

"So this is where the party is," said Kendall as she carried Emma into the kitchen. "We just got up from a late nap, and Emma is hungry."

"Where's Lelani?" asked Anna. "Shouldn't she be home from work by now?"

"She's not at work." Kendall strapped Emma into the high chair, then reached for the box of Cheerios.

"Where is she, then?" asked Megan. Usually Lelani sprinted home from work, she was so eager to see Emma.

"She's with Gil." Kendall poured some Cheerios onto Emma's tray. "Apparently they have something very important to discuss."

"I'll bet it's about the wedding," said Anna. "Did you know that they may be moving their wedding to Maui?"

Kendall's eyes lit up. "I wish I could do that."

"Why don't you?" asked Megan.

Kendall poured milk into Emma's sippy cup, then put on the lid. "I considered it, but Killiki really wants to meet my family. And I have a big family." She handed the cup to Emma. "In fact, I was just adding them up on my guest list. Just my siblings, their spouses and kids— and some of their kids are married—and then there's my parents and my godparents and, anyway, I have twenty-four people and that's just my immediate family. By the time I include extended family and close friends, it won't be a very small wedding." She slapped her forehead. "And I forgot Nana!"

"Sounds like it's a good thing your mom is going to help out," Megan told her as she reached for the whistling teakettle.

Kendall nodded. "Yeah, I guess so. Because I think it's gonna get pretty crazy before this is over."

"I guess if Lelani has her wedding in Maui, we can help out more with yours," offered Megan.

"That'd be great." Then Kendall frowned. "But I can't believe we're going to miss Lelani's wedding. That's so sad."

"I won't be missing it," Anna told her. "I wouldn't be surprised if my mom's booking the flights and hotel and everything even as we speak. She's pretty upset about the whole thing, but she still plans to go."

"Hello to the house!" called Lelani from the living room.

"Sounds like Mama's home," Kendall told Emma.

"We're in the kitchen," called Anna.

Lelani joined them, going straight for Emma. "How's Mama's big girl?" she cooed and Emma's face lit up.

"We were just breaking your news to Kendall," Megan told Lelani.

"What news?" Lelani was extracting Emma from the high chair now, smothering her face with kisses.

"About the wedding."

Lelani nodded somberly. "Ah, that."

"So is it a done deal then?" pressed Anna. "You're really going to have it in Maui?"

"If Gil has his way."

"But what about what you want?" Megan asked.

Lelani shrugged. "Gil seems to think it's what I really want."

"But is it what you really want?" persisted Megan. "This is your wedding."

"Maybe the problem is that I'm not sure what I want. I mean I know I want to marry Gil. And it would be nice if there was a way to make everyone happy. But you know what they say about pleasing all the people all the time."

"You're sure not pleasing my mother," declared Anna.

Lelani gave Anna a worried look. "Is she pretty upset?"

"*Upset* is putting it mildly." Then Anna launched into the tale of her mother-interrupted work day, making this version even more dramatic than the one Megan had already been subjected to.

"Excuse me," Megan told them, "but I need to get into some comfy clothes, and then I'll start dinner, since tonight is my night to cook."

She listened to the music of their voices as she walked through the house—Anna's dramatic descriptions, Kendall's off-the-wall comments, Lelani's attempts to smooth over everything, and all this was topped off with Emma's random squeals of delight. It was funny how familiar and appreciated those sounds had become to Megan in less than a year's time. She knew she would miss all this when mid-June rolled around. Why did it seem that things were always changing? Sometimes Megan wished she had a magic wand that she could wave to simply freeze the present good times and delay the future. Oh, she knew it was childish and shortsighted, but sometimes …

As Megan changed out of her clothes, she told herself that it was probably for the best that Lelani and Gil wanted to be married in Maui. Really, it would've taken a major effort to pull off a classy wedding in such a short amount of time. Plus, Megan had been coming up blank on the perfect location. Not that she'd been ready to give up. If all else failed, she figured they could've had it at her mom's house. With the vaulted ceilings, massive windows that looked out over the river, and a spacious great room, it could've been quite nice. In fact, Megan often entertained fantasies of getting married there herself. Of course, her daydreams had always included her dad escorting her down the winding, open staircase that he had designed. His sudden death was just one more change in life that she had been unable to control.

As Megan pulled on her UGGs, she realized she had a hard time letting go of a lot of things, including the idea that she was going to plan and participate in Lelani's wedding.

Yes, it would've been a lot of work, but she'd really been looking forward to it. The artist in her had already started conjuring up ideas, trying to come up with ways to make their big event feel like it was taking place in a tropical paradise. She'd even toyed with the idea of creating some kind of a backdrop that resembled the setting sun over the ocean. If they'd be forced to have an indoor wedding, she imagined using king-sized white sheets and sunset-colored spray paint and some colored lights. She even considered bringing in beach sand and seashells and having it spread out around the altar. With Hawaiian music and food and leis and everything … well, it could've been fun.

As silly as it seemed, Megan could relate to Gil and Anna's mom. Oh, she wouldn't mention any of her personal feelings to Lelani. But she understood Mrs. Mendez's disappointment. As pathetic as it seemed, Megan had been excited about being Lelani's maid of honor and all that went with it. But it was time to "buck up" as her dad would say, be a big girl and not let Lelani see that she felt slighted. After all, Lelani had enough to deal with.

Kendall

"I really appreciate your help with this," Kendall told Lelani on the drive into the city. "I mean, it's going to be hard enough to do wedding-dress shopping with my fat belly, which seems to growing fatter by the minute, but if I wait to pick out a wedding gown with my mom ..." Kendall shook her head. "Well, that would be pure torture."

Lelani glanced at the backseat of Kendall's car. "I just hope Emma will cooperate. You know how she can totally lose it when she misses her afternoon nap."

"I told Emma that I expect her to be a big girl," Kendall said as she exited the freeway, "and I explained that if you were going to be around for my wedding, which looks unlikely, I will have her for my flower girl."

Lelani laughed. "She's not even walking by herself yet."

"She'll be walking by June."

"Hopefully we'll be able to come to your wedding. I told Gil that if we're really going to get married in Maui, we could at least set the date for the following weekend. It's not like it's that hard to find a free strip of beach for the ceremony."

"I can just imagine you guys barefoot and gorgeous with wind-tossed hair." Kendall sighed. "I told Killiki that I wouldn't mind if we repeated our vows, privately I mean, on a Maui beach sometime."

"That sounds romantic."

Kendall nodded. "And we'll do it when I'm not pregnant, and I'll get a really pretty dress and maybe have someone take our picture. I hate to even think what our wedding photos will be like with me as big as a house."

"You don't have to get married before the baby comes," Lelani pointed out.

"I know. That's what my mom said too. Call me old-fashioned, but I just want my baby to be born with a daddy." Kendall instantly regretted her words. "Not that it's that big of a deal. I mean you did what you had to do and I totally respect that. And, as we all know, Killiki isn't my baby's real daddy."

"No, Kendall, he will be your baby's real daddy. Just not his biological one. There's a difference."

"Yeah. And speaking of biological daddies, I've been thinking that my mom could be right."

"Right about what?"

"That maybe I should have Matthew Harmon do a paternity test."

Lelani didn't say anything.

"I mean, I know where you stand on that, and for the most part, I totally agree. And it's not like I have the slightest interest in getting together with Matthew." Kendall turned into the parking lot of the wedding gown outlet store. "But I wonder if he has the right to know."

"That's a tricky question, isn't it?" Lelani was already getting out of the car.

Kendall hoped she hadn't stepped on Lelani's toes about this. In fact, she wished that she'd just kept her big mouth shut. It wasn't as if Lelani should have all of the answers to Kendall's questions. Kendall eased herself out of her car, then got the stroller out of the trunk while Lelani unbuckled Emma from her car seat.

"She's sound asleep," Lelani said quietly. "If we're lucky, she'll sleep a while longer."

Kendall was arranging the quilt in the stroller, helping Lelani to gently lay the sleeping princess down, tucking the quilt around her, and hoping that she would continue to sleep while she and Lelani looked at wedding gowns.

"So far so good," Lelani said as Kendall held the door open for them. Kendall looked around the store and tried not to feel too disappointed. It hadn't been her idea to look at a discount store, but Megan had suggested it, and in light of Kendall's finances, it had seemed sensible. On the other hand, if she waited to get a dress with her mother, money might not be such a problem. And yet, if she did that, she could end up with 1) a dress she hated and 2) a great big fight with her mom. In the end, waiting was probably not worth it.

"Keep in mind that you're going to be a lot bigger by the time June rolls around," Lelani said as Kendall held up a fitted gown.

"I've been trying to decide whether it's better to go with something fluffy and full or something clingy that shouts out *pregnant bride alert*. Like, 'Get over it, Aunt Betty.'"

"Can I help you?" asked a young-looking salesgirl.

Kendall pointed to her rounded midsection. "Maybe so. As you can see, I'm pregnant, and I'll be even more pregnant two months from now."

The girl looked slightly uncomfortable. "Well, I'm kind of new here, but I know that we have some maternity wedding gowns somewhere."

"You do?" Kendall felt hopeful as they followed the girl toward the back of the store. "I did an online search and I found this satin number that I really liked, except that it was more than a thousand dollars and I need to economize."

"Here they are," the girl told them. "Unfortunately you're limited to the sizes on this rack. Because we're an outlet store, it's not like we can order anything special for you." The girl stared at Kendall's belly. "So, do you know what size you are?"

"I know what size I used to be."

"Let's just start there." Lelani was already looking at the gowns. "How about this one?"

Kendall frowned at the dress. It was satin, but it seemed kind of frumpy.

"Now, I don't think you can make any snap judgments," Lelani told her. "Not until you actually start trying them on."

Kendall nodded. "You're right. In fact, I felt kind of encouraged when I checked out the pregnant-bride Web site. I was surprised at how pretty those pregnant brides actually were."

"They were probably just models pretending to be pregnant," the salesgirl said.

"Some women are at their most beautiful when pregnant," Lelani said quickly.

The salesgirl nodded and stepped back. "Well, I'll let you guys look around. And when you're ready for a dressing room, just let me know."

Kendall giggled. "I'll bet I'm her first pregnant customer."

"There are some really pretty dresses here," Lelani said as she continued to peruse the rack. She pushed a couple more at Kendall. "Why don't you go get started trying them on, and I'll keep looking."

"Want me to take Emma with me?" offered Kendall.

"That's okay." Lelani glanced at Emma, who was still sleeping.

Kendall carried the gowns back to the dressing-room area and waited for the salesgirl to unlock one of the doors. Like everything about this store, the fitting room was barren and cold-looking, nothing like the bridal shops that Kendall had always dreamed of shopping in. Of course, those dreams had never included a pregnancy. "Thanks," she told the girl. "My friend is going to bring some more gowns back."

"We have a limit of only three gowns at a time," the girl told her.

Kendall chuckled. "Right, probably a lot of bridal-gown shoplifting going on."

"You'd be surprised." She closed the door.

As Kendall peeled off her T-shirt and maternity jeans, she tried to imagine how someone could possibly steal a wedding gown. Perhaps they wore a fake-pregnancy pack that was large enough to stuff a gown into. She tried not to look at herself in the mirror. No matter how many times she saw that belly, it was pretty shocking. For sure, she was not wearing a fake-pregnancy pack.

She slipped the first dress on, struggling to zip up the back. Fortunately it fit. Unfortunately, it was ugly, so bad that it seemed pointless to wait for Lelani's opinion. Kendall removed the dress, hung it up, and went for the second one.

"How's it going?" asked Lelani.

Kendall opened the door so that Lelani could see the second dress. It was an improvement on the first, but still not right. Kendall held her arms out in a hopeless gesture. "Maybe pregnant brides aren't supposed to be pretty."

Lelani shook her head. "You're pretty, Kendall. But the dress is all wrong. Who wants to wear puffy sleeves when she's pregnant?" She held up another one. "Try this."

After a while they narrowed the choices down to a couple possibilities: a semifitted satin dress that was low cut and sleeveless, and a lacy number that made her belly look smaller but also made her feel like she was going to Sunday school.

"Try on the satin one again," Lelani told her. "And I'll go have one last look on that rack. Maybe I missed something."

As Kendall removed the lacy gown, she heard Emma waking up. The little girl was clearly not happy. Kendall was not happy either. In fact, she was on the verge of tears. Maybe it had been a stupid idea to go shopping with a baby along. For that matter, with two babies along. But then, wasn't Kendall the Queen of Stupid Ideas? She hung up the lace dress and started to don her street clothes again. Enough was enough. Time to call it a day.

She was just emerging from the changing area when Lelani and a still-fussing Emma came toward her. It figured that Lelani had found another gown.

"Let's go home," Kendall said. "Emma shouldn't have to suffer for my—"

"She'll be fine," Lelani said firmly. "Here, you take this dress so I can pick up Emma."

"But I think we should—"

"I think you should try that one on, Kendall. Really, it seems perfect."

"But I'm already dressed and—"

Lelani shoved the dress toward her. "Please, just do it for me." She bent over to release Emma from her stroller, then scooped her up. "It's okay," she said soothingly. "Auntie Kendall is just going to try on one more gown."

Kendall couldn't help but smile at the *auntie* part. "Okay," she told Lelani, "but this is the last one."

"Yell when you're ready. In the meantime, Emma and I will look around." She laughed. "Maybe Emma would like to pick out her mommy's wedding gown while we're here."

Kendall reluctantly returned to the fitting room only to find the door was locked again. So she set out to find the salesgirl.

"I thought you were finished in there." She reached for her keys.

"I thought I was finished too," Kendall admitted. "Like stick-a-fork-in-her-she's-done kind of finished."

The girl scowled as she unlocked the door, acting like Kendall had inconvenienced her. "Here you go," she said with an impatient toss of her head.

Kendall wanted to tell her to lighten up—or grow up—or take a customer-service class, because if that girl ever wanted to work in anything higher class than an outlet store, she had better figure it out.

Kendall hung up the dress, which upon a second glance wasn't half bad, then slowly began to undress again. This time, instead of hurrying into the dress to avoid her image in the mirror, she really looked at herself. Okay, she was pregnant. Not fat, just pregnant. She ran her hands over the taut skin on her belly and for the first time thought it was actually kind of beautiful. Maybe it was a strange kind of beautiful, but it wasn't as horrible looking as she often told herself. Just last night, Killiki had said that he wished he could see her, that he thought pregnant women truly were beautiful, and that he looked forward to her next pregnancy when they could be together. She sighed and reached for the dress. Really, all that mattered about her wedding dress was that Killiki's eyes lit up when he saw her. Well, okay, she wanted to feel beautiful in it too.

"Need any help in there?" called Lelani from outside her door.

"Actually, I do." She opened the door. "The zipper seems to be stuck."

Lelani set Emma down on the floor and went to work on the zipper. Emma crawled beneath the full skirt and began to giggle.

"Whatcha doing down there?" Kendall asked. "Is it like a big white tent?"

"There," said Lelani as she zipped it up. "And it fits too."

Kendall lifted up her skirt and Lelani picked up Emma. As Lelani stood, her eyes lit up. "Wow, Kendall, this gown is really good. Well, other than your bra straps. Can you tuck those down?"

Kendall struggled to unhook her straps and push them below the strapless bodice before she stepped out to where the three-way mirror was situated. Once out there, she just stared at her reflection. "Wow, it is good." The empire-cut bodice fit well, and the full fluffy skirt actually disguised her midsection. Not that she felt the need to hide anything.

"You look beautiful, Kendall," Lelani said from behind her.

Kendall looked at Lelani in the mirror and nodded. "This is the one. Thanks for making me try it."

"Well, you've got those gorgeous shoulders and long neck, it just seemed like you should show them off some."

Kendall turned to see all sides of the dress. "It's perfect. Really perfect. I think even my mother might approve."

"Now, if you wouldn't mind, I found a dress that I'd love to try on."

"Sure, go for it." Kendall reached for Emma now. "I'll take care of the princess."

"Thanks!" Lelani ducked into Kendall's fitting room. "I'll hurry."

"Take your time," sang out Kendall. "We'll just be out here dancing." Kendall danced Emma in front of the mirror, watching the skirt of her gown and imagining that she and Killiki were dancing at their reception.

"So you found one?" asked the salesgirl as she led what appeared to be a mother and daughter into the fitting-room area.

Kendall smiled at her. "And it's perfect."

The girl shrugged. "Well, as perfect as it can be anyway. I mean for a *maternity* gown." She smiled at her other customers like this was funny.

Everything in Kendall wanted to scream at this stupid, insensitive girl, but that would just bring Kendall down to her level, which felt like middle school anyway.

"Here you go," the girl told the mother and daughter. "Let me know if you need anything."

Lelani emerged from the dressing room. Her gown was a dreamy tea-length confection of lace and ribbons and beads, perfect for a beach wedding.

"It's beautiful," Kendall told her.

The mother and daughter paused to look as well. "Very pretty," the mother said approvingly.

"You're both getting married?" the salesgirl asked in surprise.

Kendall looked directly into the girl's eyes. "Yes, we're both getting married. We've been roommates for a while and we're sharing our wedding day and we thought it was about time we gave our babies a proper home." She linked her arm with Lelani's as they both stood in front of the mirror. "You look lovely, dahling," she said to Lelani in a seductive voice. "Don't you think we make a stunning couple?"

The mother and daughter looked slightly taken aback as they disappeared into their fitting room with their arms full of dresses. Then the cheeky salesclerk made a forced smile and hurried on her way.

Lelani started to giggle. "What was *that* all about?"

Kendall grinned and began to belt out one of her favorite oldies in her best Bonnie Raitt imitation. "Let's give them something to talk about." Emma laughed with glee as Kendall danced her around the small dressing area singing with more enthusiasm than talent. "Love, love, love ..."

Lelani just shook her head. "Oh, Kendall," she said with her hand over her mouth to suppress her laughter. "You are something else, girlfriend!".

Just then Kendall pointed. "Look at Emma!"

Lelani looked down, then let out a happy shriek. "She's walking!" She clapped her hands. "Oh, Emma, you're walking!"

"She's not walking, Lelani." Kendall grinned. *"She's dancing!"*

Seven

Anna

Something about Edmond seemed different. Several days had passed since that comment in the parking lot, and Anna couldn't quite put her finger on it, but she knew something had changed between them. She hoped it didn't have anything to do with what she'd said to him in front of Felicia the other day. Surely, Edmond hadn't taken it seriously.

Anna sat at her desk, flipping through e-mail, as she replayed the scene in her head. They'd been at a marketing meeting, trying to hammer out some back-cover copy, when Edmond had made a thoroughly lame suggestion. Naturally, Anna had teased him about it. After all, they often teased each other. Really, it was no big deal. Or was it? Edmond's promotion from Felicia's assistant to head of publicity was still new enough that he could be worried about impressing everyone. And he fell quiet after Anna's comment. As it turned out, Anna came up with the best one-liner for the back of the book. When she apologized to Edmond later he'd been fairly nonchalant, like it was nothing. Really, Anna told herself, it probably was nothing. She was just making a mountain out of a molehill.

Perhaps Edmond had been hurt when they said good-bye on Tuesday. They were in the parking lot, and Edmond was getting a little friendlier than usual, and suddenly his uncle, Anna's boss, came out. Anna literally shoved Edmond away from her. Still, he should understand that.

69

She'd told him more than once that physical displays of affection in the workplace were taboo, at least where she was concerned. And he got that. She knew he did.

In fact, the more Anna thought about Edmond, the more she wondered if his quietness had to do with something else altogether. Perhaps something weighed heavily on his mind, maybe it had to do with his future—and hers. Oh, she tried not to dwell on what he'd said at the beginning of the week, about how wedding planning might be good practice for her. But it wasn't unlikely that Edmond might be giving the marriage idea some serious thought. Or maybe she was just daydreaming.

Because sometimes, like this morning when Edmond was particularly aloof, it seemed entirely possible that Anna had imagined the whole thing. She knew things like this could happen. She'd heard stories of otherwise perfectly contented single women who, being constantly exposed to "happily" engaged women and all the hoopla of wedding plans, eventually caught the disease. Wedding Fever. In fact, she'd seen this very thing in her cousin Elisa.

Elisa was just one year older than Anna. She'd been a little uncomfortable when her younger sister, Manuela, beat her to the altar. Now, up until this event, Elisa had always seemed a sensible girl. But something about her sister's wedding plans seemed to undo Elisa. And so poor Elisa jumped into a relationship with a guy she barely knew, married him just six months after Manuela's wedding (Anna remembered this because she'd been forced to wear a horrid lime green bridesmaid dress that made Anna and everyone else look like they had a bad case of the influenza), and within the year the "happy couple" separated and (to her mother's horror) eventually divorced. It was the first divorce in Tia Benita's family. To Anna it had seemed an obvious case of Wedding Fever. Elisa was still getting over the entire fiasco. The last Anna had heard, Elisa had sworn off men and dating for the unforeseeable future.

Anna *so* did not want to get the dreaded Wedding Fever. In fact, she would do everything possible to inoculate herself against it. Even if that meant acting somewhat chilly to Edmond occasionally. Not that he seemed to notice. And why would he? Most guys his age ran in the opposite direction when the topic of commitment and marriage came up.

And yet, Anna reminded herself as she saved and closed her document, it was Edmond, not her, who had made that bold statement about weddings. And it was Edmond, not her, who had been the pursuer in their relationship. At least to start with. For a while she had held him off, thinking he was just a young climber using whomever he could to find a better spot for himself in the publishing company. But when she discovered that his family actually owned the company and his job was secure, she began to see him differently. She realized that seemed a bit disingenuous. But the truth was, she'd let her guard down and found out that she honestly liked him. Then, following a complicated but short breakup, she'd been the one to throw him the white flag (or was it checkered?) and he gladly took it. Since that time, they'd been happy together—compatible, congenial, and even simpatico. Was it true love? Anna wasn't one-hundred-percent sure, but she had a feeling it might be. And why not?

"Have you proofed that thing I brought down here this morning?" asked Felicia's new assistant. Chelsea had been hired to replace Edmond. According to him, she was driving his aunt and most of the marketing department nuts with her lack of business savvy.

"Yes," Anna shuffled through the papers on her desk. "I don't see why you didn't just e-mail it to me, though. It would save time *and* trees."

"Because Felicia already printed it out," she said.

Anna nodded. "Right." She finally located the page and handed it back to Chelsea. "For the record, it's not *the thing*; it's called back-cover copy. I know it takes a while, but the sooner you learn to call things by their proper names, the easier it'll be for everyone." Anna smiled. "Including you."

"Thanks." Chelsea lowered her voice. "Is Felicia always this grumpy?"

"She's a perfectionist." Anna's smile grew even more stiff. "And she's part owner of this company, and she's not known for her patience."

Chelsea nodded. "I better get moving, huh?"

Anna looked at the clock and was surprised to see that break time had come, but Edmond hadn't come down to get her. That was different. She picked up her tea mug and headed for the break room. Maybe he was on a deadline. When she arrived, however, she saw that he was already there and seemed to be engaged in a very intimate conversation with the intern Lucy. Edmond didn't see Anna come in. He was sitting on the edge of a table with Lucy leaning toward him, eyes wide, and apparently talking about something terribly interesting, because Edmond seemed mesmerized.

Anna decided to pretend to ignore them as she made her way to the hot water and tea bags. But even with her back to them, she could feel her blood pressure rising. She wanted to turn around and demand to know what was going on. Of course, she would not lose her cool.

"Anna," called Edmond. "I was just on my way to get—"

"Oh," she said turning, "I didn't even notice you there. Don't mind me, I just wanted to grab a quick cup of tea and get back to work. I'm really behind on the Foster edits."

"But I thought you were—"

"You know how it goes," she said lightly, making her way to the door, "just when you think you're done, suddenly you have to start over."

"But aren't they due by the end—"

"Which is exactly why I need to run." And then she was gone. But her heart was pounding as she took the stairs, trying not to slop her hot tea as she went down. She hadn't wanted to wait for the elevator or chance Edmond's questions. Of course, the edits were finished. But what else was she going to say?

Anna took a deep calming breath as she sat back down at her desk. This was one of those times when a private office would have been most welcome. Maybe someday. She pulled the Foster manuscript back onto her computer screen, sipping her tea as she pretended to give it one final check before signing off and sending it to the printer. For all she knew, it might need a little tweak here or there. It wasn't unheard of for the proofers to miss something, or sometimes the designers made a change that created a new typo.

The harder she studied the pages, the more the words seemed to blur together. And then her phone rang. She grabbed up her desk phone and then realized it was her cell. Why hadn't she turned it off after lunch? She saw it was her mother and was tempted to send the call to messaging, but then she thought the distraction of her mother might be preferable to obsessing over Edmond and Lucy. Edmond and Lucy? *Edmond and Lucy!*

"Hi, Mom," she said. "What's up?"

"Oh, Anna," her mother began, "I don't know what to do."

"About?"

"The wedding."

Anna wanted to say "duh" but controlled herself.

"My travel agent is ready to book the whole trip—tickets, hotel, and rental car—but Gil isn't certain the wedding will be in Maui. And then he said that it might be the third weekend in June because Kendall is having her wedding the very same day that he and Lelani had picked. The same day! What is wrong with that crazy girl, *mi'ja*? Has pregnancy messed up her mind?"

"Kendall wanted a June wedding too, and she wanted Lelani and—"

"But the very same day?"

"It's a short month."

"So what do I do? Gil refuses to say yea or nay, and Lelani is at school right now, and the travel agent says this deal will not last for long."

"I suppose you should do nothing."

"Nothing!" Her mother switched over to Spanish.

"If you're going to swear at me, I will hang up," Anna threatened.

"Sorry, *mi'ja*. I know it's not your fault, but it is very frustrating."

"Just take a deep breath," Anna said. "And remember: When in doubt, *don't.*"

"When in doubt, don't what?"

"Don't make a decision. Just wait."

"But if I wait, I might miss out on this deal."

"But if you book this deal and they decide something different, you'll probably lose your money. When it doubt, *don't,* Mama. It actually makes sense. If you're not sure about something, don't make a move. Tell your travel agent to wait. I'm sure you can get a firm answer out of Lelani and Gil by tomorrow. I know that they gave themselves the week to figure things out, and today's Friday."

"I suppose you're right. That's what your father said too."

"See. Daddy and I agree. Just wait."

"So, how are you doing? Any special plans for the weekend? I'm making dinner for Tia Louisa and—"

"Thanks anyway, Mom, but I think I have plans."

"With Edmond?" her mother asked in a surprisingly hopeful tone. "I was just telling Tia Louisa what a very nice boy he is, even if he's not Latino. So what are you and Mr. Wonderful up to anyway, *mi'ja?*"

"To be honest, I'm not sure that he is Mr. Wonderful."

"What?" Her mother's tone grew sharp. "Has he done—"

"No, no," Anna said. "He is Mr. Wonderful. I think I'm just a little stressed with work. In fact, I need to go now."

"Well, if you change your mind about dinner on Saturday, you and Edmond are most welcome and—"

"Thanks, Mama. *Adiós!*" Anna closed her phone, then took in another deep breath. How stupid could she be? Nearly spilling the beans to her mother about Edmond and Lucy in the break room? What was she thinking?

It was not quite four thirty now, but Anna had put in enough comp time to know that she'd be fine to leave thirty minutes early. The sooner she got away from Erlinger Publishing, the happier she'd be. It was true that she had been a little stressed at work, and she was tired, and it was the end of the week. Surely she deserved a break. And right now she really did not want to see Edmond. She quickly finished up the last tasks on her desk, grabbed her coat and bag, and made a swift exit.

It wasn't until she was safely in her car and several blocks from the company that she realized something. She and Edmond usually went out on Fridays. Sometimes they made specific plans and sometimes not. But saving the day had long been an unspoken agreement between them. Well, she thought as she drove straight home, she'd let him wonder about her. Didn't absence make the heart grow fonder?

It was just a little before five when she got to the house. She decided it might help him to wonder even more if she turned off her phone for a while. Maybe he'd get worried and come over and apologize like a gentleman.

"You're home early." Kendall looked up from the pages of a fat, slick bridal magazine.

Anna made a grim face as she threw down her bag.

"Something wrong?"

Anna sat down on the sectional and folded her arms tightly across her chest. "Edmond!"

Kendall closed the magazine and leaned forward with interest. "What did Edmond do?"

Anna quickly recapped what she'd witnessed in the break room.

Kendall seemed to consider this. "It sounds pretty innocent. I mean, maybe Lucy was coming onto him. He's a cute guy, and let's not forget that his family owns the publishing company. It makes sense that female employees might find that an attractive package."

"Meaning?" Anna sat up straighter.

"Not you, Anna. Good grief, I remember how Edmond chased after you. I'm just saying this Lucy intern girl might think she'll be on the inside track if she hooks up with good ol' Edmond." Kendall laughed. "Not hook up as in … you know."

"Oh, please! I don't think that's likely."

"Because Edmond is a good guy."

Anna sighed. "Yes, but if you'd seen the look in Lucy's eyes. It was like Edmond was a rock star and she was so enchanted she was about to throw some undergarment at him."

Kendall laughed. "So why not be mad at Lucy and let poor Edmond off the hook this time?"

Anna considered this. For Kendall, the advice actually sounded pretty smart. "You could be right."

"Of course I'm right. I've seen Edmond look at you, Anna. If you ask me, that boy's pretty smitten."

Anna smiled. "Thanks, Kendall. I think I'm just a little stressed."

"You know what you should do?" said Kendall with enthusiasm. "Go and have a bubble bath. That always cheers me up. And believe it or not, the tub is clean!"

"Seriously?" Anna wasn't sure whether to trust her or not. She and Kendall shared a bathroom, and Kendall's housekeeping skills, while improving, still left a lot to be desired.

"Absolutely. I scrubbed it myself this morning. I thought I was going to take a bath, but now I think you'd enjoy one even more."

Anna stood. "Well, thank you, Kendall. I appreciate it." A bath really did sound good. She would soak and relax and read the paperback she'd gotten at the grocery store a few days ago, and perhaps all the troubles of the day would just float away or down the drain or whatever.

It wasn't until Anna sank into the sudsy, fragrant hot water that she realized her cell phone was still off and tucked away in her purse, which was still where she'd dumped it on her bed. Oh, well, let Edmond wonder. It might do him some good. In the meantime, Anna planned to lose herself in bubbles and a good book. Heavenly.

When Anna finally emerged from the tub, slightly prunelike but much more pleasant, she was surprised to see that it was nearly seven. She went straight for her bag, turned on her cell phone, and checked for messages.

"Hey, Anna," came Edmond's voice. "Some of us headed over to Blue Moon after work. Why don't you come and join us? There's a jazz group here tonight, and they're supposed to play some really wicked Coltrane. Call me."

That was it. Just one message. And he hadn't even phoned until

5:37. Did that mean he'd headed over there directly after work without even checking on her? Or perhaps he'd worked late, assumed she'd gone home, and was being a little less thoughtful than usual.

Anna tied her bathrobe securely around her and sat down on her bed to ponder her position. She could respond to his invitation by getting dressed and driving herself over to Blue Moon. She could easily make it by eight thirty. And the music did sound worthwhile. But, really, is that how she wanted to be treated? She preferred that Edmond take the role of the gentleman. Call it old-fashioned, but she appreciated being treated like a lady. Really, what was wrong with that?

Something else occurred to Anna. What if Lucy was there? What if right this minute she was sitting next to Edmond, looking at him with those big blue eyes, flipping her fluffy blonde hair over her shoulder and treating him like he ruled the world. Really, did Anna want to compete with that? And why should she?

No, Anna decided, if Edmond wanted to spend time with her, he should make the effort to come get her. And perhaps even apologize for, or at least explain, the scene in the break room. Then she would go out with him. Maybe.

Just in case, Anna got dressed. Rather, she got dressed up. She put on her short black skirt, and since it was still kind of rainy and cool out, she put on her black tights and tall black boots. Edmond loved this look on her. She topped this off with the cranberry cashmere sweater set that Edmond had given to her on her birthday in February. Perfect.

Then she went downstairs to see if there were any leftovers she could munch on while she waited for Edmond to call or come by.

"Looks like *someone's* going out tonight." Kendall rinsed a dish at the sink and nodded approval at Anna's outfit. "Hot."

"Thank you." Anna opened the refrigerator.

"So you patched things up with Edmond?"

Anna took out a piece of leftover chicken and just smiled.

"I can't imagine ever fighting with Killiki." Kendall laughed as she put her bowl into the dishwasher. "Of course, I know we will eventually. But it's always the making-up part that makes the fight worthwhile, right?" She winked at Anna.

Anna nodded as she chewed a bite of cold chicken.

"Hey, I found some bridesmaid dresses that look pretty cool," Kendall said as she reached for one of her magazines. "Megan and Lelani haven't seen them yet, but I'd like your opinion."

Anna blinked at the photo. "Black?"

"Actually, they're navy. But I think they look kind of sophisticated. And you might even be able to wear the dress again. You know, to a formal party or something."

Anna laughed. "If I had a buck for every time someone told me that."

"You've been in a lot of weddings?"

"There's a closet full of ugly dresses at my mom's house to prove it. I honestly don't know why she hangs onto the things, but I suspect it's because she hopes someday will be payback time."

"So you think this dress is ugly?" Kendall looked hurt now.

"No, actually, it's not bad. But are you sure about navy? I mean, you're getting married in June. Don't you want something a little more summery?" Anna flipped through the magazine, hoping to find something that seemed more fitting. "Like how about these dresses? They even look a bit like your gown."

"Those are nice. What do you think about the color choices?"

"That aqua is nice. It kind of reminds me of the Maui ocean."

"Oh, you're right!" Kendall leaned over to peer at the color swatch.

"My bridesmaids would be like the Maui ocean and I would be the …"
Kendall laughed. "The big humpbacked whale!"

Anna shook her head. "You'll look stunning in that dress, Kendall.
Seriously, even if your stomach gets as big as a basketball, you'll still
look gorgeous."

"You think?"

Anna nodded and took another bite.

"Well, thank you. I'm going to go online and find out how long
it would take to get these dresses. My plan is to get some of the major
decisions made before Mommy Dearest takes over. That way there'll be
less to argue about."

This reminded Anna of her own mother and her concerns over
making their travel plans. "Is Lelani around?" she asked as Kendall
headed up the stairs.

"She and Gil and Emma went to a movie, but I think Megan's still
here."

Anna finished her chicken and then hung around downstairs with
her cell phone handy. But Edmond didn't call. By five past eight she
was feeling pathetic and lonely. So she went to her room and passed
the time by reading her book, which she finally finished around eleven.
Then, feeling more than a little worried, she got ready for bed. She tried
to convince herself Edmond's silence was no big deal. After all, there
were no rules written in stone that said she and Edmond had to spend
every single Friday night together. But deep down inside, she knew
something was wrong. It was hard to describe the feeling, but it was
kind of like her life was tilting sideways and she was about to fall off.

Eight

Lelani

Lelani waited until noon to call her mother, when it would be nine in the morning in Maui. Late enough that her mother would be up, but not so late that she would be out shopping or lunching or whatever it was she did to spend her time and money on a Saturday.

"Showdown at high noon," Kendall had teased as she whisked Emma away for a sunny walk through the neighborhood so Lelani could speak without distractions. Lelani dialed her old home phone number and waited as the phone rang. She didn't recognize the voice of the woman who politely answered, "Aloha. Porter residence, how may I help you?"

"Aloha. I'd like to speak to Mrs. Porter, please."

"May I ask who is calling?"

Lelani wanted to ask who had answered but knew that would sound rude. "This is Lelani Porter."

"The *daughter?*" The politeness was replaced with coldness.

"Yes. Lana Porter is my mother."

"I'm sorry, but Mrs. Porter does not wish to speak to *you.*"

Lelani took a quick breath. "Then may I speak to my father, please?"

There was a long pause.

"I don't know who you are," Lelani said gently to whomever was on

81

the other end, "and I don't know what my mother has told you, but my father and I are on speaking terms, and I know that he would want to speak to me. But if he's not there, I'll simply call him at work and—"

"Please, just a moment."

"Thank you." Lelani closed her eyes and silently prayed for God's help. She knew this wasn't going to be easy, but she wanted to do all she could to handle it correctly. No regrets. She waited a long time, and after a while, Lelani wondered if she'd been forgotten altogether. Or perhaps she was being ignored. She glanced at her bedside clock. Eleven minutes had passed.

"Hello, Lelani," her mother said in a frosty voice. "I hope this is important."

"Did I interrupt something?"

No response.

"I'm sorry to bother you, Mother, but I wanted to let you know that I'm getting married and—"

"I am aware of this."

"Yes, but I wanted to—"

"I assumed you had already gotten married. You were so obsessed with the need to provide Kala with the perfect little home."

Lelani swallowed hard. "We call her Emma, Mother."

No response.

"Anyway, Gil thought perhaps it would be nice to have our wedding in Maui so that you and Dad could—"

"What? Pay for it? Do you honestly think you can do what you did to me and then come waltzing back here and expect me to pay for your wedding and—"

"No, this is not about money. I only wanted to ask—"

"All you do is take and take and take, Lelani. You give us nothing in return except grief and heartache, and then you take and take and take some more. How is it possible we raised such a selfish child? Oh, yes, I remember, by *giving you everything.* You had everything a girl could possibly want, Lelani. And yet it was never enough for you. And now you're calling to demand more."

"I'm not calling to demand anything." Lelani struggled to keep her voice calm. "I was only calling to see if you and Dad would want to come to my wedding."

Her mother laughed. "Yes, I'm sure that's all you're calling for."

"It's true. Gil thought that it might help our relationship with you to bring the wedding to Maui and—"

"And you have absolutely no intention of letting your parents pay for your wedding, correct?"

"Absolutely."

"So what kind of wedding are you planning?"

"Something simple. On the beach."

"A barefoot-on-the-beach wedding?" Her voice seeped with cynicism.

"Isn't that how you and Dad got married?"

She laughed harshly. "Yes, because we were poor."

"And so are we."

"So you are telling me you are poor and yet you can afford to travel here for your wedding?"

Lelani let out a long sigh.

"And how is it that you are so poor when your father is sending you good money for tuition and expenses and—"

"Because the money he sends goes directly to my education," Lelani said. "Not to a wedding. I still work at my job."

"Oh, yes, at the cosmetic counter."

Lelani looked over to Emma's crib. "You haven't even asked about Emma, Mother. Don't you want to know how she's doing?"

"Do you honestly think that I would expect you to tell me the truth, Lelani? Of course, you would say she is thriving and growing and deliriously happy to be living with her biological mother and a bunch of other strangers. And why not?"

"Okay, Mother, I want to ask you one more time: Would it help our relationship if Gil and I brought our wedding to Maui? Would you feel honored or loved by this gesture?"

"This *gesture*?" She laughed again. "If you ask me, it's too little too late. No *gesture* is going to heal the heartache you've caused me. And no *gesture* is going to make me forgive you. To me you are dead, Lelani. I feel sorry for our little Kala—sorry that I couldn't save her from you."

Tears burned Lelani's eyes, and it took every ounce of self-control not to say something terrible and hang up. "I'm sorry you've become so bitter, Mother. I know it must make you terribly unhappy."

"You're what makes me terribly unhappy, Lelani. And for that reason I ask you not to call here again. If you must speak to your father, please, call him at work. I have instructed the servants to protect me from your calls. It's not good for my health."

"Unforgiveness is not good for your health either, Mother."

A loud click told Lelani that this conversation was over.

With shaking hands, she folded her cell phone and took a long, deep breath. Tears were flowing freely now, but she didn't really care. In a way it was a relief to cry. And it was a relief to know exactly where her mother stood. Did that make the truth less painful? Probably not. At least she knew that the wedding was not going to take place in Maui. And she knew that she had given it her best shot. When she was calmer, she would call her dad and inform him of her plans to be married on the mainland. More than anything, she wished that he would come for the wedding, and that he would walk her down the aisle, but she knew that Lana Porter had more control over this decision than Lelani did.

Lelani slipped on a cardigan and went out to see if she could spot Kendall and Emma anywhere nearby. She might as well let Kendall off of babysitting duty, since she knew that Kendall had more garage sales to scope out today. Although Kendall did most of her garage-sale shopping on the opening day, she still liked to go looking on Saturdays too. Of course, Lelani hadn't noticed that there was a garage sale going on just down Bloomberg Place, and it was no surprise to find Kendall and Emma in the midst of things.

"Look at these baby clothes," Kendall exclaimed when Lelani joined them. "They're in perfect condition, and a lot of them are babyGap and OshKosh and all sorts of cool labels."

Lelani looked down to see Emma grinning up beneath a small stack of clothes. "Are you getting buried by Auntie Kendall?" she asked.

"Those are for Emma," said Kendall with enthusiasm. "Look at those pink Ralph Lauren warm-ups. They look like they've never been worn."

The woman hosting the sale came over to them. "These are things my granddaughter has outgrown. My daughter-in-law was just going to toss them, and I decided to add them to my garage sale." She held up a buttery yellow quilt for Kendall to examine. "This is part of the crib set I was telling you about. The rest of it's inside, but trust me, it's all in perfect condition."

Kendall grabbed it eagerly. "I want it."

As Kendall and the woman continued to chatter about baby things, Lelani picked up the garments layered on Emma's stroller and, to her surprise, discovered that they were all quite nice and would work for Emma.

"I didn't bring my purse," she told Kendall. "But these are all good choices."

Kendall reached for the pile. "Here, I'll take the clothes. You take Emma and we'll settle it later, okay?"

"Thanks." Lelani reached for the stroller.

Kendall frowned. "It didn't go so great with your mom, huh?"

Lelani just shook her head.

"I didn't think it would," Kendall said.

"Well, at least I tried."

Kendall grinned. "Hey, that means we'll get to come to your wedding still."

She nodded with renewed enthusiasm. "Yes! That's the upside."

"Better call Gil's mom. Anna said she's freaking over the travel plans to Maui."

"And now she won't have to." Lelani waved as she wheeled Emma's stroller to the sidewalk. Really, Lelani thought she should be glad that it had turned out this way. Sure, not everyone was happy. But Lelani doubted that even God himself could make Lana Porter completely happy. Perhaps in time, but not today. The good news was that everyone else would be a lot happier about this. Except that they'd lost one precious week of planning. Lelani would do all she could to make up for that. Besides, hadn't she said from the beginning that she wanted a simple wedding? Maybe this would help her to actually get it.

Back at the house, she called Gil's mother as she fed Emma lunch, quickly relaying the news.

"Fantastic!" gushed Mrs. Mendez. "It is what I had hoped and prayed for from the very beginning. You have made me very happy, Lelani!"

Lelani smiled as she spooned a sloppy bite of applesauce into Emma's wide-open mouth. "I'm so glad to hear that."

"But I am sorry if this means your mother is not happy."

"My mother is an unhappy woman."

"So I have heard."

"Gil was right to encourage me to try to include her. But she is so bitter." Lelani's voice broke. "I just don't think I'll ever have much of a relationship with her."

"Well, you have us now, *mi'ja*. We are your family."

Lelani nodded. "I really appreciate that."

"Speaking of family, how is my little Emma?"

"Right now she's sitting here eating her lunch."

"Well, I'm not doing much this afternoon. We thought we were having company for dinner, but something came up. So if you have any wedding planning to do—now that you're not going to Maui—I would be happy to watch our girl."

"Let me check with Megan first. She was helping with the wedding plans and she hasn't even heard the news yet. Then I'll call you right back."

Lelani finished feeding Emma, then set out to find Megan. The two women hadn't had a real conversation together in a couple of days, and Lelani was feeling a bit guilty.

She found Megan on the phone and wearing a grim expression. Lelani just waved and mouthed "Later," then went to her own room. She changed Emma's diaper, then sat her down on the floor. Lelani had carefully baby-proofed her bedroom so that it was almost as safe as a playpen, but more fun for Emma to go exploring in. Then Lelani sat on the floor, phoned Gil, and told him the news.

"I already heard," he said with a chuckle in his voice.

"Your mom?"

"She was elated and couldn't wait to tell everyone."

"I'm not surprised. And I'm glad that I made someone happy today."

"I heard it didn't go too well with your mom."

"That's an understatement." She filled him in a bit, taking care not to allow too much emotion into her voice. She felt that Emma was sensitive to that sort of thing.

"I'm sorry," he told her. "I guess it wasn't such a good idea. I just hoped that it might make a difference. Or heal something."

"And I appreciate that. But my mother, well, you know how she can be."

"I do, but the good news is now all our friends and my family can come. If Mama has her way, this wedding is going to be enormous. So you and Anna might want to give her a limit on guests. I already told her that we'd have to charge her extra for her guest list. I was joking, but she told me that was fine. Anyway, I told her to work it out with you. Sorry to have to cut this short, but I have some business to take care of right now."

"Of course. I just wanted to make sure you knew and that you were okay with not getting married in Maui."

"I'm happy if you're happy. You are happy, right?"

"Absolutely."

Yes, she was almost absolutely happy. Of course, the thorn in this bed of roses was still her mother. But that was nothing new. If her mother had to be a thorn, at least she was a whole ocean away. Not all girls were that fortunate.

Nine

Megan

"That's great news, Megan," Marcus told her.

"Yeah, I'd almost given up hope on getting the job. But the principal finally called me yesterday afternoon. I tried to call you, but when you didn't answer, I decided not to leave a message." She kicked off her shoes and switched her cell phone to her other ear.

"Sorry, I was at a meeting."

She wanted to ask what kind of meeting but knew that might sound obsessive. "Anyway, I'm totally jazzed about it. I already gave Cynthia my notice."

"Was she sad to lose you?"

"Actually, she was a little bummed."

"How about Vera?"

"I haven't told her yet. But I'm looking forward to it."

"Unless she decides to make your life miserable—I mean more so than usual—until you leave."

"Well, that's part of the good news. The teacher I'm replacing is due to have her baby in the next couple of weeks. After I explained the situation to Cynthia, she gave me the green light to leave whenever I need to."

"Cool."

"Yeah. Cynthia is really nice. If Vera weren't there, I might not have looked for another job."

"But you want to be a teacher."

"I know. But I guess change is hard for me."

"Even with Vera gnashing her teeth at you?"

"I'm embarrassed to say it, but yes." Megan sighed. "I guess I'm kind of a stick-in-the-mud at heart. Pathetic, huh?"

"Then you might not be too pleased to hear my news." His voice sounded cautious and sent a chill down her spine.

"What?"

"Well, it shouldn't be a total surprise to you, but Greg Mercer and I just got approved to go to Zambia."

"Meaning?"

"Meaning once we get our shots and pack our bags, the church is behind us—we're good to go."

"Don't you need a visa for Zambia?"

"That's the good news. If you go as a tourist, which we plan to do, you don't need one. Since this is a scouting trip, it's more like we're tourists anyway."

"Oh."

"Don't sound too excited."

"I am excited," she said quickly. "Really, that's fantastic, Marcus."

"But?"

"But it seems like it happened so quickly."

"Sometimes God works quickly."

"So will you quit the investment firm?"

"They're letting me take a year off. It's in my contract."

"Do you think you'll really go back?"

"Who knows? But I don't see any reason to burn bridges."

"No, of course not. In fact, Cynthia assured me that if the teaching thing doesn't work out, I can probably come back. Unless they've already filled the position."

"Why wouldn't it work?"

"I don't know. I'm only hired to the end of the year. There's no promise of a job in the fall."

"But if they like you …"

"The other teacher might decide to return. They say she's not sure. It's her first baby and she's pretty nervous."

"So maybe you'll have her job in the fall."

"Yeah." Megan wondered where Marcus would be in the fall. Probably Zambia. "Maybe."

"Anyway, I got a ton of stuff to take care of. Greg and I are heading over to REI to pick up some things we think we might need over there. We want to be prepared to camp and get by if we need to."

"Camping in Zambia?" She shook her head. "Sounds a little rough."

"It will be."

"Is it safe?"

He laughed. "You know what they say, Megan. In fact, haven't you said it to me before?"

"What?"

"The safest place you can be is in God's will."

"Oh, yeah. Right."

"Don't you believe that?"

"Of course. It's just hard to imagine you and Greg camping in Zambia."

"Did you know Victoria Falls is in Zambia?"

"Not actually."

"Most people think it's in Zimbabwe, but it's really in Zambia."

"I'll try to remember that if I'm ever teaching geography, which isn't likely, since I'll be teaching art."

"And you're going to be great at it too, Megan. I can just imagine you with a class full of kids."

"Yes, I seem to recall you saying how you would've liked having me as your teacher."

He laughed. "Yeah, but I might not have learned much."

"Anyway, I really am happy for you," she said with a lump in her throat. "It's amazing that this is all happening, almost just like you wanted."

"Yeah, we think it feels miraculous. Sorry to have to go, but I think Greg's at my door. Church tonight?"

"Uh, sure." And then they said good-bye, and that was the end of their conversation. As Megan hung up, she wondered if he was saying, "Church tonight?" as in, "I'll pick you up as usual?" Or was he saying, "Church tonight?" as in, "See you there?"

"Hey," said Lelani as she quietly pushed open the partially closed door. "Sorry to intrude, but it sounded like you were off the phone."

Megan nodded. "Yeah, no problem."

"Are you okay?" Lelani asked her.

Megan's mouth twisted into a pathetic half smile, and she shrugged.

"What's wrong?" Lelani sat down on the bed next to her.

"Marcus is going to Zambia."

Lelani nodded. "Yeah, you mentioned that was a possibility. But I thought you meant this summer."

"That's what I thought too. But it turns out that he and a guy from church will be going sooner than that."

"What about his sister's wedding?"

Megan shrugged. "I have no idea. But since it's nearly two months out, maybe he plans to be back by then. I forgot to ask."

"Speaking of weddings ..." Lelani had a sparkle in her eye. "I have some news."

"Did you and Gil elope last night?"

Lelani chuckled. "No, but that's not a bad idea."

"What?"

Lelani quickly told her that the Maui wedding was a thing of the past, and Gil and Lelani wanted to return to Plan A. They hoped to get married the second weekend of June somewhere in the Portland vicinity. "Do you still want to help me, or are you sick of this whole thing by now?"

"Of course I want to help. Do you know how disappointed I was when you changed your mind?"

"No, were you?"

"Well, I didn't want to make you feel bad, but I had been having fun dreaming up all kinds of cool stuff for your wedding. I mean it's kind of like interior design, only lots more fun."

"Great." Lelani looked relieved. "I'm sorry about losing a week. I guess we just needed to go that route to figure things out."

"So was it your mom? I mean, the one who put the kibosh on the Maui wedding?"

Lelani nodded. "But I really don't want to talk about that."

"I understand completely. I don't particularly want to talk about Marcus going to Zambia either."

"So you're not all that thrilled about it?"

Megan shrugged. "I am, and I'm not."

"Meaning, let's not talk about it?"

"I do have some other news." Megan told Lelani about the teaching job.

"That's fantastic!" Lelani gave her a high five. "Congratulations!"

"So …" Megan considered these new developments. "Between your wedding and my new job, I won't even have time to worry about Marcus off in Zambia getting sick or shot or whatever."

Lelani looked slightly shocked. "Do you really think he'll be in danger?"

Megan shook her head. "No, not really. Like he just reminded me, there's no safer place to be than in God's will."

"And he believes going to Zambia is God's will?"

"He does."

"Well, go, Marcus!"

"Yep. Go, Marcus." Megan grabbed the notebook that she'd been using for Lelani's wedding plans. "I think we need to get going too. Should we call an emergency wedding meeting?"

Lelani nodded. "Yes. I haven't even told Anna yet. And she's in charge of invitations."

"Great, you go tell her, and I'll make some quick phone calls about locations."

"Do you want to meet up in the dining room"—Lelani glanced at Megan's clock—"like at three?"

"Sounds like a plan."

And so, for the next hour, Megan called every possible location, and although it seemed mostly hopeless, she found a couple of hotels that were available. Not the greatest hotels, but better than nothing. She listed them along with the other possibilities including Gil's parents' home, which had been offered numerous times, and Kendall's house, which might not work now that Kendall was getting married the same day. Finally, Megan wrote down *Abernathy House*. But first she called her mom.

"I know this is a lot to ask," Megan said straight off. "But I think your house would be a beautiful place for a wedding."

"You and Marcus are getting married?" The utter joy in her mother's voice was undeniable.

"No, not at all!" Megan said. "I was asking for Lelani and Gil."

"They're not going to Maui for their wedding?"

Megan explained the change in plans. "And at this point its hard to find anything nice for the second of June. I've always thought our house would be a pretty location."

There was a quiet pause.

"It's a lot to ask, Mom. I mean I'll totally understand if you don't—"

"No, that's not a problem at all, Megan. In fact, the garden is looking better than ever this year, and if the weather cooperates, I think it would be a beautiful spot for an outdoor wedding. Of course, the reception could be inside or out. We're not talking about a large wedding, are we?"

"Lelani wants to keep it small and simple. And the reception will be at Gil's parents' restaurant, so having some kind of sit-down dinner is not a part of the deal."

"That's probably wise."

"So you'd really consider it, Mom?"

"Why not? I should tell you that I've already spoken to a realtor, and once I finish some improvements, which will make a wedding all that much nicer, I plan to go through with listing the house. In all likelihood, this will be the only wedding this house will see. At least while I'm still here. That is, unless you and Marcus suddenly decide that it's time to—"

"Actually, Marcus is practically on his way to Zambia now." The words were barely out of her mouth and she was crying.

"Oh, Meggie, it'll be okay. You know how Marcus feels about you."

"That's just it." She sniffed. "I don't really know. I mean I thought I did. But he's been so distracted with this mission stuff, I almost feel like I don't know him at all."

"But it's wonderful that Marcus wants to help others. Isn't that what you want too?"

"Yes, but I don't like being left behind while he goes off to do it."

"But you've got your teaching job, Megan. You were so excited about that."

"I am."

"And now you're helping Lelani with her wedding. You'll be a busy girl."

"I know." Megan reached for a tissue to blot her tears. "I'm just being silly. It's probably PMS, Mom. Anyway, don't worry about it. And thanks for being willing to let us use the house. I'm not even sure that Lelani will go for it, but if we get desperate—not meaning you're a last resort. But you know."

"Yes, I know. Feel free to bring Lelani over here, and traipse around as much as you like. I plan to do some updates in the bathrooms and repaint. Helen, my realtor, is telling me that I should upgrade the appliances and get granite countertops and a few other things. But I'm not so sure."

"I think the realtor's got it right, Mom. That house is so beautiful, but it is a little bit stuck in the eighties. If you want top dollar, especially in that neighborhood, you'll need to raise the bar a little."

"You sound just like a realtor." She chuckled. "Or a designer."

"Or a daughter who cares about you."

"Yes, that's it. If there's anything I can do to help for the wedding, Megan, like with flowers or decorations, well, you know me. I love that sort of thing."

Megan thought her mom's participation might make up for the fact that the wedding wasn't Megan's, but she knew that her mom wasn't trying to rush her to the altar.

"Thanks," Megan told her. "I'll definitely keep that in mind."

"Don't forget we have that family reunion the week before. I hope that doesn't put a kink in your plans."

"Hopefully, we'll have everything nailed by then. Remember, Lelani said *simple*."

"Simple is lovely, Megan, but it's not always easy."

"Right." Megan knew that was true. "Well, hopefully we'll have both—simple and easy." She told her mom good-bye, then went out to the dining room, where her three roommates were poring over bridal magazines and Web sites.

"Look at these bridesmaid dresses," Kendall said eagerly. And just like that, the four of them were arguing over color, style, and shoes.

"Hold it," Megan said with her hands in the air. "Let's put the dress issue aside until we get a couple of other things nailed down, okay?"

They quieted and gave her their attention.

"For starters, we need to pick a location. And then we need to agree on the number of guests." Megan glanced at Anna. "Right?"

Anna just nodded.

Megan took them through her short list of locations, and when she ended on her house, Lelani's eyes lit up. "Seriously?" she said with hope. "I love that house. Would your mother really let us use it for our wedding?"

"Absolutely. I just talked to her, and she said the garden is starting to look gorgeous."

"I've never even seen the garden," Lelani admitted, "but that house is beautiful."

"You've only been there once," Megan pointed out. "Are you sure?"

"I've never been there at all," said Kendall.

"Me neither," added Anna.

"Field trip," said Megan with enthusiasm.

"Let me call Gil's mom," Lelani said. "She offered to watch Emma for me."

"I thought she had company for dinner," Anna said.

"No, we talked earlier," Lelani said as she dialed her phone. "It was cancelled."

Anna looked disappointed but didn't say anything.

"If we nail the location," Megan told Anna, "you should be able to get to work on the invitations next week, right?"

Anna just nodded.

"Are you okay?" Megan asked her.

Anna shrugged.

"Man trouble," Kendall said in a hushed tone.

Anna frowned at Kendall.

"Sorry." Kendall held up her hands innocently. "But it's true."

"If it makes you feel any better," Megan told Anna, "me, too."

Anna looked confused. "What?"

"Man trouble."

"Did you and Marcus break up?" Anna asked.

"Not exactly. But he's going to Zambia, and I'm feeling a little left out."

Kendall put a hand on Megan's shoulder. "I guess we all get our tastes of heartache along the way, don't we?"

Megan forced a smile. Even though it was true, she didn't really appreciate the comment. She knew Kendall had been through "man trouble" before, but hadn't it been her own doing?

"Okay, let's go," said Lelani as she hung up the phone. "I'll go get Emma up from her nap and we can be on our way."

Lelani went with Kendall, since Emma's car seat was already in her car, and Anna drove Megan.

"So what's going on with you and Edmond?" Megan asked Anna, mostly because she didn't want Anna to ask her anything else about Marcus.

"I think he's found another girl," Anna said sadly.

"You think?" Megan frowned. "You don't actually know?"

"I haven't spoken to him since yesterday. But I saw him with this Lucy chick, and she was totally into him, and I just have a very bad feeling."

"Oh."

"Edmond and I usually go out on Friday and he never even called. Well, I guess he called, but he left a pretty lame message. Kind of this backhanded invitation, like, 'Come on by Blue Moon to hear some good music.' Not exactly like he was asking me out, you know what I mean?"

Megan nodded. "Actually, I know exactly what you mean." Then she told Anna how aloof Marcus sounded about church tonight. "Usually, he asks me if I want to go. At least I think he does. Or maybe we just agree. And maybe it's not exactly like a date."

"More like he's taking you for granted?" offered Anna.

"Yes, that's one way to describe it."

"Same with Edmond. It's like I've become nothing more than a habit. And then some pretty airhead comes along, and she gives him the big-eyed, you're-so-wonderful-Edmond crud, and he just eats it up."

"In my case it's not another woman, but another country."

Anna glanced curiously at her. "That is a little different."

"Even so, it's like he's more interested in Zambia than me. Zambia might as well be another woman."

Anna chuckled. "Actually, Zambia is an interesting name for a woman. You're sure he's talking about a country, right?"

Megan giggled. "Yes. I'm pretty sure he's talking about a country. Just the same, I think I'll be too busy helping with Lelani's wedding to go to church with him tonight," she said. "That is, if he even invited me to go with him, and that remains to be seen."

Anna nodded in agreement. "There's no sense in chasing a guy. If he's interested, he's interested, right?"

"Absolutely."

Anna thumped her steering wheel. "Hey, this is the first time you and I have had this much in common."

"It figures it would be *man trouble*," joked Megan.

"Yes, *man trouble*."

Megan laughed as Anna turned onto the winding street that would take them up the hill to the Abernathy house. She was trying to act like this was no big deal, like it was simply a little blip in her dating life, but the truth was, she felt a deep and lonely pang inside herself. She wondered how she could manage to get along with Marcus while he was clear over on the other side of the globe, and who knew for how long? *Man trouble, indeed!*

Kendall

"I thought I had Emma today." Kendall watched as Lelani zipped Emma into the pink Ralph Lauren warm-up jacket.

"No, this is an *abuela* day." Lelani picked up Emma. "Tell Auntie Kendall bye-bye."

Emma folded her hand into a tiny wave and said, "Bah-bah."

Kendall put her face close to Emma's. "Bye-bye, Princess Emma. I'll miss you."

Lelani laughed as they headed for the door. "You should enjoy any down time you get from now on, Kendall. In less than four months you'll be doing this 24-7."

"I know." Kendall watched sadly out the front window as the two of them left. Because it was sunny, she had planned to take Emma to the park. And now she wondered what she would do with her morning. Going back to bed was tempting, but since she'd already gone to the trouble of showering and dressing, it seemed a waste of time. Kendall thought hard. What did she used to do when she had time on her hands? Oh, yeah, shopping. But that was forbidden now. She had sworn to her Shopoholics Anonymous friends and, more importantly, to Killiki, that she would no longer shop for recreation. The SA group limited her to grocery or discount stores, neither of which were much fun. Consequently, they were not very tempting. And that, Kendall knew, was a good thing.

Of course, she could always check out her eBay bids. She was developing quite a little e-business these days, selling and buying and actually making a sweet little profit. Not enough to clean up all her bad shopping debt, but she was certainly making a dent. And thanks to Megan's budget plan, which Kendall tried to adhere to, the creditors were no longer hounding her for payments.

Or, she could do her homework for the marriage-counseling sessions that she and Killiki were doing online. Killiki's pastor had recommended it, and it was actually pretty fun, plus she got to see Killiki via webcam technology. The only problem was that Kendall did not enjoy homework. She never had liked homework, which was perhaps one of the reasons she dropped out of college. So she might as well put it off until Thursday, since their counseling session was that evening. That way it would be fresh in her mind.

Kendall wandered through her vacated house and wondered what to do with this unexpected free time. There was always cleaning, but then there would *always* be cleaning. She could put in a Pilates DVD, but that involved sweat, and she'd already showered.

It was such a sunny day, she had the urge to get outside. But walking by herself, well, that just didn't sound fun. At times like this she missed her little dog Tinkerbell. And she missed Emma. Finally, she decided to just get in her car and see where it took her. To her surprise, it took her to see Nana.

As usual, it took Nana a few minutes to realize who Kendall was. Whether it was early Alzheimer's or just plain dementia, Nana was definitely losing some brain cells.

"Kendall," Nana said for the third time. "Where have you been?"

"Living at your house." Kendall smiled.

"I have a house?"

Kendall thought for a moment. The last time they went down this avenue, Nana had begged to come home. "You used to have a house, Nana. But now you live here, remember?"

"Yes, here." Nana frowned at her small room. "Someone moved my TV last night."

Kendall looked at the TV in the small entertainment cabinet, which was built into the wall. "Oh?"

"They're always moving things around here," Nana continued. "And then they eat my food. They come at night, you know, when I'm asleep. They think I don't know what they're doing, but I do."

"Hey, Nana," said Kendall. "Want to go for a ride? It's sunny out, and we could get ice cream."

Nana was already out of her recliner and reaching for her old blue sweater and purse, a cream-colored Gucci from the sixties. Kendall hooked the purse handle over one arm as she helped Nana get into the sweater. Kendall knew the purse held little more than an old compact and lipstick and handkerchief. But the residents weren't allowed to keep money in their rooms, because it usually got lost or stolen.

"Ready?" Kendall asked.

"I was born ready." Nana chuckled as she hobbled toward the door.

"Do you think you need your cane?" Kendall reached for it.

"No, that's for old ladies."

"Mind if I use it?"

Nana laughed. "If you want to look like a fool, go right ahead."

They slowly made their way through the building. Nana called out to her friends, bragging about how she and Kendall were going out for a good time and too bad the rest of them couldn't come. Finally they got to the reception area, and Kendall signed her out.

"Shall we make a run for it?" Nana asked as she stood in front of the double doors.

"Yeah," Kendall told her. "Let's break outta here."

Nana pretended to run but actually shuffled through the automatic doors. Kendall, holding the cane in one hand and Nana's elbow in the other, stayed close by.

"There's my car," Kendall nodded toward the Mercedes.

"A convertible?" Nana sounded pleased. "Let's put the top down."

"Good idea!" Kendall helped Nana into the car, reaching into the glove box in hope of finding a scarf. "Hey, look at this," she said as she produced a red and black one and handed it to Nana.

Nana examined the silk. "Hermès," she said quietly.

Kendall peered at the writing. "You're right, Nana, it *is* Hermès. Man, you are good."

Nana chuckled. "Some things one never forgets." Then she struggled to put the scarf on her head. "Although I seem to have forgotten this. Can you help me?"

Kendall carefully wrapped the scarf around Nana's head, carrying the ends around the back to secure it smoothly. "Very nice."

Nana patted the scarf and smiled. "Thank you, I am *très* chic, no?"

"*Oui! Très* chic, madam." Kendall laughed as she reached over to release the top, then pushed the button to lower the roof. "How's that?"

Nana leaned back and smiled. "*Très bien.*"

"You lived in France for a while, didn't you?" asked Kendall as she slowly drove through the parking lot. That was all it took to open Nana's memory bank to when she and her husband lived in Paris during the fifties. It was like she became someone else as she spoke of the Champs-Élysées and the Arc de Triomphe and the Louvre as if they were all old friends. She described drinking espresso and red wine at cafés, where they would smoke cigarettes and talk for hours. It all sounded terribly romantic and reminded Kendall of some of the old classic films set there. Nana let out a long sigh.

"I have an idea," said Kendall as she drove along the river toward a small artsy town just outside of Portland. "Let's pretend we're in Paris today."

Nana clapped her hands. "Oh, yes, I like this idea."

Kendall managed to snag a parking spot right on the main street, then helped Nana out of the car. "I think we should start with pastry and espresso, don't you?"

Nana nodded, then patted her scarf. "Should I leave this on?"

Kendall studied the bright silk scarf and the slightly ratty cardigan and old Gucci bag. "You look marvelous, dahling."

Nana smiled and held her head high. "We shall proceed."

Fortunately, one of the cafés had outdoor seating and an open table. They sat and ordered espressos and a croissant and éclair, which they shared. Occasionally Nana lapsed into French and Kendall wished that she'd taken more than just one year of the language in high school.

"*C'est si bon,*" Nana said as she smacked her lips after polishing off the last of the chocolate éclair.

"*C'est si bon,*" Kendall imitated her.

"Now we will shop," Nana announced as she reached for her purse.

Suddenly Kendall felt seriously worried. Shopping was taboo to her. And yet she knew Nana used to be quite the shopper, which might be part of the explanation for why Kendall was the way she was. It had to be genetic. But she also knew Nana had no cash. And Kendall's cash was limited, plus she had promised not to do any recreational shopping. She did not plan to break this promise.

"I know: We will *window* shop," Kendall said firmly. "But first let me pay the bill here."

Before long, they were window shopping and actually having fun. Yes, at times it was rather tempting. Like when Kendall saw a spectacular Kate Spade bag that was basketlike and would be perfect for a honeymoon. But she controlled herself and wondered if she might find something similar (but much, much cheaper) on eBay. When Nana made an attempt to purchase a pair of size-six red patent-leather high-heeled pumps (such a bargain at only $69, although Nana wore size eight), Kendall clandestinely hinted to the salesgirl that they were "just looking."

"Sorbet!" Nana announced as they were leaving the shoe shop.

Kendall took a moment to remember that was like ice cream. "But should we have lunch first, Nana?"

Nana shook her head and solemnly said, "Sorbet."

Kendall patted her rounded tummy. "I don't know, Nana. I think the baby needs something a little healthier first."

Nana turned and stared at Kendall with a confused expression. "What baby?"

"Remember, Nana, I told you the last time I visited that I'm pregnant."

Nana blinked in surprise. "You're having a baby?"

Kendall nodded.

"Are you married?"

Kendall made an uncomfortable smile. "I'm engaged, Nana. We're getting married in June. And you're coming to the wedding, right?"

Nana grinned. "A June wedding. Lovely. Will the baby be there?"

Kendall patted her tummy again. "In here and under my wedding gown."

Nana chuckled now. "A pregnant bride. Now I've seen everything."

"So, if you don't mind, I'd like to get some lunch before sorbet."

"My treat," said Nana. Kendall didn't question her as they crossed the street to a small deli. To Nana's delight, the soup du jour was French onion, and they both ordered a bowl. Then they walked a bit more, and Nana seemed glad that Kendall had brought along the cane. Finally, Kendall could tell the old woman was wearing down.

"I know, let's drive down the Champs-Élysées," said Kendall as they got near the car.

"*Oui, oui!*" cried Nana. Soon they were driving along the river again. Kendall knew it didn't really look like the Champs-Élysées, but Nana did enjoy what was left of the flowering trees, although she also looked very sleepy.

"I think we should go home now," Kendall said gently.

Nana sat up straighter. "Sorbet first."

"Oh, yeah, right." Kendall tried to think of a swanky little ice-cream store along the way but could only come up with Dairy Queen. Still, she reminded herself, this was Nana and they were using their imaginations today. So she went ahead and pulled into the DQ.

"Vanilla sorbet or chocolate?" She asked with her best French accent.

"Vanilla, *si'l vous plaît.*"

"I'll be right back," Kendall said as she hopped out of the car to order their ice cream. She kept an eye on Nana as she stood in line. It looked like she was taking a little catnap. Kendall hoped she hadn't worn her out. Nana's life was so boring most of the time, not that she probably noticed. Still, it was fun to take her out and hear her stories of such a glamorous life. So sad to think she might forget everything someday. Or maybe she would remember it all somewhere deep inside of her. Who knew?

"Here you go, Nana." Kendall handed her the small dish. "Vanilla sorbet."

Nana dipped her plastic utensil into her DQ ice cream as if it were a silver spoon and a crystal cup, and as she tasted the cool treat, she might've been savoring some of the finest Parisian sorbet. "*Délicieux*," she proclaimed.

Kendall licked her cone and Nana daintily ate from her cup as Kendall slowly drove back to the nursing home, giving Nana enough time to finish every last drop. Then Kendall pulled up right in front of the entrance, helped Nana out, handed her the cane, then walked her inside.

"My granddaughter and I have just been to Paris," Nana announced loudly as Kendall signed her back in. "We had espresso and pastries and French onion soup, and the most *délicieux* sorbet imaginable."

Her friends were looking at her with expressions ranging from envy to interest to totally blank stares, but Nana continued to tell them about the red shoes and how they rode in a convertible. She patted her head. "And this is Hermès," she said proudly.

"You keep it until next time," Kendall told her, planting a kiss firmly on the wrinkled old cheek.

"And my granddaughter is going to have a baby," Nana continued narrating to whoever wanted to listen. "She's not married yet, but she will be in June." She peered at Kendall. "Is that correct?"

Kendall nodded. "Yes, you got that right. Now, I better go."

As Kendall walked away, Nana continued to regale her friends with stories of all the fascinating things they'd done in Paris, but lines between fact and fiction seemed to be getting more blurry. Perhaps that was simply how Nana's mind worked. Kendall supposed that she could relate to it on some levels.

Kendall felt totally happy as she drove home. She actually felt as if she had truly been to Paris. Perhaps she had, at least when it came to hearing Nana's memories. Really, she should have a Nana Day more often. Maybe next time they could go to Rome. Or maybe even Maui!

Eleven

Anna

Anna had managed to avoid Edmond throughout the weekend. Or so she told herself. The truth was, she thought perhaps he was avoiding her. That did not set well with Anna. Consequently, she dressed very carefully before going to work on Monday. After several false starts that left her bedroom looking like a mini rummage sale, Anna decided on the charcoal-gray pinstripe suit. She thought it made her look taller and thinner, not to mention very professional. Not wanting to be too professional, she paired this with her tall black boots and a silky white blouse that was cut just right—not so low as to be skanky, but not too prim either. She took time with her hair and makeup as well.

If she was going to break up with Edmond, and that was a distinct possibility, Anna was going to do it in style. She was going to walk away with her head held high, and she was going to maintain a sense of dignity that would demand respect from her coworkers. *See,* she thought as she unplugged her oversized curling iron that she'd been using to straighten her hair, *this is what comes from dating people in the workplace.* From now on she would know better!

"Wow, Anna," said Kendall as they met at the top of the stairway. "You look awesome. Is that like your power suit?"

Anna gave her a cool smile. "Something like that."

"I heard people are supposed to dress for the job they want, not the job they have," Kendall continued as they went down. "You look good enough to own the company." She chuckled. "I guess if you married Edmond, you sort of would."

"Edmond doesn't own Erlinger Books," Anna said sharply.

"Well, his family does. And I assume that—"

"People shouldn't make assumptions."

Kendall gave Anna a cautious look now. "Everything okay with you and Edmond? I mean I realize he kind of stood you up on—"

"He didn't stand me up," she said in a forced friendly tone, "we just decided to do some things separately."

"Oh?" Kendall was clearly curious but probably afraid Anna was going to snap her head off again.

"Sorry to sound so grumpy," Anna said with a smile. "It's just that I have a busy day ahead of me and I'm trying to—"

"No, that's okay," Kendall said quickly. "You know me and my big mouth, and then I go and put my big old foot in it. You'd think I'd learn to shut up sometimes."

Anna put a hand on Kendall's shoulder. "I actually like knowing that you say what you mean, Kendall."

"Really?"

"Yes. It's kind of refreshing. Especially when so many people can be insincere. So don't mind me."

Kendall brightened as Anna picked up her purse and headed for the door. "Well, have a great day, Anna. And you really do look spectacular."

"Thanks." Anna took a deep breath and stepped outside to what looked to be a fairly nice day. At least it was starting out that way. She paused for a moment, trying to decide whether to walk or drive. Normally, she would walk on a pleasant day like this. But she might need her car for a quick getaway. She was driving. And since she had plenty of time, she would stop for a perfect cup of coffee too. Then she would walk in, sleek black briefcase in one hand, Starbucks in the other, and act as if she owned the world. Yes, it would be an act—but it would be a good one.

"Anna," said Edmond when she was barely in the building. "How are you?"

She smiled brightly at him as she walked down the hallway toward her desk. "I'm great, Edmond. How are you?"

He looked slightly stumped. "Uh, fine."

Her smile got even bigger as she set down her briefcase. "Oh, good. Did you have a nice weekend?"

"Uh, yeah, I guess. Did you get my messages?"

She took a slow sip of her coffee, pausing to savor the flavor before she pressed her lips together as if trying to remember something. "Oh, yes, I think I got one or two of them. You know I was so busy, I sort of forgot about voice mail. I'm sorry." She looked directly at him, giving him her best innocent expression. "Was I supposed to call you back?"

"Well, yeah, I thought so, but maybe I didn't make myself—"

"I'm sorry. It's just been a busy weekend. Lelani and Gil have decided to have their wedding here after all. We were sort of scrambling to get things together, and there was just a lot going on."

He blinked, then adjusted his dark-framed glasses, frowning like he wasn't sure what to say next.

How about I'm sorry, she was thinking, but she simply smiled and took another sip.

"I thought you were going to join us at Blue Moon on Friday," he continued stupidly. "The music was really great and a lot of us were—"

"Hey, Edmond," said Lucy in a sugary-sweet voice as she walked up from behind him. She wore a very short denim skirt, dark hose, and a top that was way too tight. Didn't she know what *business attire* meant? Maybe someone should give her an employee handbook.

"Hello, Lucy," he said a bit stiffly.

"How's it going?" Then Lucy actually reached up and began rubbing Edmond's shoulders like she thought she was his personal masseuse. "Is that stiff neck of yours feeling any better to—"

"If you'll excuse me," Anna said quickly, "I really have work to do." She turned her back to them and set down her coffee, snapped open her briefcase, turned on her computer, and hoped that they would get the hint and take their massage elsewhere! To further her subtle message, she picked up her phone and called a copy editor, leaving a convoluted message about something on the copyright page that she wanted to revise before the day was over. So what if it wasn't real. She could explain that later. She'd simply claim she'd gotten her wires crossed.

She hung up and looked cautiously over her shoulder. They were gone, and now Anna was fuming. Not that she planned for anyone to know she was fuming. No way. Anna had learned long ago to keep her emotions in check—at least in certain situations, like school or work or public places. She did not like being stereotyped as a hothead Latina who couldn't control her temper. She left that to her mother. But Anna knew that if she were with her mother right now and if they were alone, Anna would cut loose and throw a regular hissy fit. She felt confident her mother would jump right in too. Maybe later.

"Hi, Anna," said Chelsea. "How's it going?"

Anna forced a smile. "Okay. How are you doing?"

Chelsea shrugged. "It's a Monday, what can I say? But at least Felicia's coming in late today. That's a nice perk."

"Well, I'm sure you have lots to—"

"Hey, we missed you at Blue Moon on Friday. Edmond said you were coming, but you never showed."

Anna just shrugged. "I was busy."

Chelsea nodded then stepped closer, lowering her voice. "Are you and Edmond still a couple?"

Anna narrowed her eyes. "What makes you think we ever were a couple?"

Chelsea waved her hand. "Oh, everyone *knows* you guys are a couple."

"Everyone?"

"Sure." Chelsea nodded. "I mean at least you *were* a couple. Are you still?"

"Why are you asking me this?" Anna scowled at her. "I don't see how it has anything to do with the workplace."

Chelsea made a nonchalant face. "I just thought you'd want to know."

"Know what?" Anna folded her arms across her front and waited.

"That Lucy is putting the move on Edmond."

Anna feigned a light little laugh. "Tell me something I don't know."

Now Chelsea looked surprised. "You know about that?"

"Sure."

"And you don't mind?"

Anna made what she hoped was a patient smile. "Edmond is a grown man, Chelsea. It's not as if I control him. And if some silly girl wants to throw herself at him, it's not as if I can control her either, now, can I?"

Chelsea just shook her head.

Anna glanced back at her desk. "And now I have work to do."

"I just thought you should know," Chelsea said in a slightly defensive tone. "I mean, since I work for Edmond's aunt and I kind of replaced him, it seemed like I had a responsibility to tell you."

Anna wanted to scream. Instead she took in a deep breath. "And I appreciate that, Chelsea. Thank you."

Chelsea nodded in a satisfied way. "Okay then. See ya around the watercooler." She laughed like this was funny, then headed on her merry way.

Anna sat down and began to go through her e-mail. Naturally, her concentration was shot now, but she at least sorted out the junk and dumped it. Then she went through the snail mail in her in basket. She took her time opening and sorting things. Usually, this was a job she hated, and she wished she had an assistant to do it. Today it was a relief, a welcome distraction.

After a while, Anna got herself firmly into work mode, pushing nagging thoughts of Edmond and Lucy into a far corner in her mind. She'd deal with it later. How she would deal with it, she wasn't sure. But she felt that a breakup was in her future. Of course, she knew this had as much to do with her pride as anything. She did not want Edmond to be the one to break up with her. No, she would beat him to the punch. At least she hoped so.

At noon, Anna knew that she had to get out of that place. And she had to get somewhere private—and quickly. As Anna got in her car and drove, she felt like a time bomb that was ticking fast. As if on autopilot, she drove to her parents' house. She had no idea if anyone was home, but that's where she was headed.

To her relief, her mom answered the door, even though Anna already had her key ready and was about to let herself in.

"Hello, *mi'ja*," her mom said happily. "To what do I owe this pleasure?" Emma came crawling in right behind her. "My two favorite girls both at the—"

"Oh, I didn't know Emma was here." Anna backed out of the door.

"Why should that matter?"

"Because, well, because, I should just—"

"Anna Maria Mendez …" She stopped herself, lowering the tone of her voice as she picked up Emma. "Tia Anna is here, Emma. Don't you want to invite her in?"

Emma grinned.

"But I just—"

"Come in, Tia Anna," her mother said in a childish voice. "We are about to have lunch, aren't we Emma? Leftovers as usual, but good leftovers all the same."

"I'm not hungry," Anna said as she followed her mom and Emma into the kitchen.

"Here," her mom handed Emma to her. "Put her in the high chair and we'll see who's not hungry."

Anna slid Emma into the high chair, then fumbled to get the seat strap secured as Emma squirmed, banging her hands on the tray with impatience and saying, "Da-da-da-da," over and over.

"Is she saying 'da-da' as in *daddy*?" asked Anna.

"No, that's just her favorite sound today." She set some tamales cut into small pieces on the food tray, then turned to Anna. "Tell me, *mi'ja*, what is wrong?"

Anna started to cry.

"*Mi'ja*?" Her mother took her in her arms and held her tight. "Talk to me. What is wrong? Did you lose your job?"

Anna peeled herself away from her mother, grabbed a paper towel to blot her tears, then shook her head. "My boyfriend."

"Your boyfriend?"

"I think I lost my boyfriend."

Her mother frowned. "You think you did?"

And so Anna sat down and told her the whole story, including the part where she had begun to fantasize that Edmond was the one and that there might be a wedding in her future. "I think I'm destined to be an old maid." She blew her nose on the paper towel and tossed it toward the trash, missing the can completely.

Her mother handed her a dishtowel. "Here, wipe your eyes, *mi'ja.* You are not destined to be an old maid. You're only twenty-six. You have lots of time. Besides, we'll be so busy with your brother's wedding, no one will have time to worry about your marital status. Your day will come, *mi'ja.*"

Anna felt blindsided by this casual acceptance of the romantic ruins of her life.

"Some people make too much of weddings and marriage. There really is no rush, Anna. Good grief, once you're married, you'll be married for a very long time. Why start anything too soon?"

Anna blinked and wondered who had kidnapped her mother and replaced her with this woman. "Are you saying you don't care whether or not I get married?"

She set a plate of tamales in front of Anna, then paused. "Of course, I care, Anna. I'm just saying what's the rush?"

Anna nodded and picked up her fork. Maybe she was hungry after all. She ate her tamales and listened as her mother talked to both her and Emma, telling them about how much a woman's life changes when she's suddenly in charge of a household. "You know what they say about women's work," she said to Emma. "It's never over. It just goes on and on and on forever and ever and ever."

Emma smiled up at her as if that was good news.

"Thanks for the tamales and sympathy," Anna told her mom. "I better get ready to head back to work or I'll be late." Then she hurried to the powder room to fix her face, check her hair, and attempt to bolster her spirits for the remainder of her day.

When she came out, her mother hugged her again. Then she held Anna at arm's length and looked directly into her eyes. "That *Edmond*," she said sternly. "I thought he was such a nice young man, and there he goes and does something like this." She released Anna, then shook her forefinger in her face. "Tell that Edmond, for me, that he is a lowdown dirty rat and not welcome at my table."

Anna kind of smiled. "I'll be sure to tell him that, Mama."

"I am not kidding."

Anna nodded and reached for her purse.

"And, *mi'ja*," she called as Anna walked to the door. "That suit is nice, but it makes you look old."

Anna just shook her head as she let herself out. Her mother probably would've preferred that Anna wear flashy tropical colors and ruffles. Oh, well, what her mother didn't know about fashion, she made up for in cuisine. Funny how something as simple as leftover tamales could be so comforting, but Anna thought that maybe, just maybe, she'd make it through this day.

Twelve

Lelani

"Thank you so much, Mrs. Mendez." Lelani hooked the handle of the diaper bag over her shoulder, then reached for Emma.

"You know you're not supposed to call me Mrs. Mendez." Gil's mother frowned and shook her finger at Lelani.

"I'm sorry." Lelani made an apologetic smile. "It's just I was taught to respect my—"

"I'm going to be your mother-in-law, no?"

Lelani nodded.

"Please, just call me Mama."

She nodded again but didn't admit that calling her Mama wouldn't come easily. For some reason she had no problem with "*abuela*" when it came to Emma, but calling her Mama would take some time and effort.

"Come on, Lelani, just try it. Mama."

"Mama." Lelani felt like she was about three years old. "Thank you for watching Emma … Mama."

"See, how hard was that?"

"I really do appreciate you having Emma. You're so good with her."

"I love babies."

Lelani pushed a strand of dark hair away from Emma's forehead. "I should probably cut her bangs, to keep them out of her eyes."

"Would you like help with that?" Gil's mother looked hopeful. "I used to cut Anna's and Gil's hair when they were young."

"Really?"

And just like that, the older woman was digging through a drawer and quickly produced scissors. "You put Emma in the high chair and give her something to keep her hands busy, and when she's not looking, I'll just snip away."

"Okay." Lelani did as she was told and within seconds, Emma's straggly wisps of hair were neatly snipped into rather short bangs. Lelani stared at her daughter with a mixed sense of horror and humor. "She looks so different."

"I didn't mean to cut them quite that short."

"Oh, they'll grow." Lelani patted Emma's head. "You look so much older now, like you're almost ready to head off to school."

"Goodness no!" exclaimed Mrs. Mendez.

"But it does change her face, doesn't it?" Lelani continued to stare at her daughter. "And it makes her eyes seem bigger."

Gil's mother leaned over and peered into Emma's eyes. "I know this sounds strange, but when I look into those big brown eyes, I can honestly believe that she really is Gil's son." She laughed uncomfortably. "Not that I would love her any more if she was." Now she looked intently at Lelani. "Besides, I know there will be more babies."

Lelani didn't know what to say. The truth was, she and Gil had never discussed the possibility of more children. Oh, Lelani knew that they would probably have more eventually. But right now it seemed like something far off in the distant future, and she assumed Gil felt the same way.

"There will be more babies, no?" Gil's mother was still peering at her.

"It's hard to think about more babies when Emma isn't even one yet," Lelani hedged.

"Isn't her birthday coming up soon?"

"Yes, next Tuesday as a matter of fact."

"Oh, we must have a party for her."

"Yes, I was just thinking that I need to get—"

"Oh, please, please, please, *mi'ja*. Let me give the party for my adorable granddaughter."

"But I planned to—"

"You have so *much* to do, Lelani. The wedding, your job, your classes. Please, just allow me to do this one little thing, I beg you."

"But I—"

"No buts." Mrs. Mendez smiled victoriously. "It's settled. We will have the party here. Tuesday evening." Her brow creased. "Let's make it dinner too and—"

"I'd like to help in some—"

"You just bring the partygirl. Leave the rest to me."

"But I—"

Mrs. Mendez shook her finger again. "I said no buts."

Lelani didn't know what to say. And so she just nodded.

"Six o'clock on Tuesday then?"

"Six sounds fine."

"We wouldn't want it to be too late, now would we?" Gil's mother patted Emma's chubby cheeks and grinned. "You be sure to wear your best party dress." Then she turned to Lelani. "Does she have a party dress?"

"She will," Lelani said quickly, in case Mrs. Mendez planned to take over in that department, too. "Now, I really should go. Gil and I have plans to go look at the place where we may be having the wedding."

"Oh, my!" She clapped her hands. "You found a place. Excellent."

"Yes." Lelani smiled. "I think it's perfect, but I want Gil to see—"

"I would love to see it too."

"And you will," Lelani promised.

"Today?" she asked hopefully.

"Well, let's wait until Gil sees it. Just in case it doesn't work out." Lelani was making her way to the door now.

"Can you give me a clue?"

"A clue?"

"Where it is. Is it a church? A hotel? How about the Rose Garden? I've heard they have lovely weddings—"

"Lovely weddings that are booked about a year in advance."

"Oh, well, we wouldn't want to wait a year."

"I'm sure Gil will fill you in on the location as soon—"

"But now I'm dying of curiosity, Lelani. Not just one little clue?"

Emma was starting to wiggle, and if Lelani didn't hurry, she'd probably fuss to get back down. "It's Megan's house," she said as she reached for the doorknob.

"Megan's house?" Lelani might as well have said they were having the wedding in some dark back alley.

"I mean Megan's mother's house. It's actually very beautiful and—"

"But if you're only going to have it at a house, why not have it here?" Gil's mother waved her hand as if she were Vanna White about to produce a vowel.

"Your home is lovely too, Mrs.—I mean Mama. But you'll have your hands full with the reception. I still can't believe how generous of you it is to host the reception. I was just telling a friend about your offer, and she thought I was very lucky to have such wonderful parents-in-law." Lelani gave her a bright smile. "And now I really must go. Thank you again, *Mama*!"

Lelani burst out of the door and practically ran to Kendall's car, quickly buckling Emma into the car seat. It was so generous of Kendall to let Lelani borrow her car. That would've given Lelani a good excuse for hurrying, because surely Kendall needed her car by now.

As Lelani drove to Bloomberg Place, she tried not to obsess over Gil's mother's helpfulness. Oh, she knew others might call it interference, but she also knew that Mrs. Mendez meant well. How was she going to get used to calling her Mama?

✂

"I insist," Megan said for the second time. "You two go over to Mom's house and just make yourselves at home. My mom said it was perfectly fine and she won't be back from her meeting until after nine. So you can watch the sunset and everything."

"You're positive." Lelani frowned.

"Absolutely."

"And you really want to keep Emma too?"

"I hardly ever get to take care of Emma," Megan said as she handed Lelani the house key.

"But what about putting her to bed?"

Megan seemed to consider this. "Well, if I have any problem, I can ask Kendall. She seems to have this whole baby thing down."

Lelani nodded. "She does."

Megan looked out the kitchen window. "And it looks like your groom has arrived."

Lelani bent down and, wiping some food from Emma's cheek,

kissed her baby's head. "You be a good girl and finish eating that squash for Auntie Megan, okay?"

Emma banged her cup on the tray, saying, "Mama—Mama—Mama," with a big goopy smile.

"At least someone has no problem with that word," she said.

Megan frowned. "Huh?"

"Later." Lelani kissed Megan's cheek too. "Thanks again."

"Don't feel pressured," Megan said as Lelani was leaving. "If you don't want to use our house, it won't hurt my feelings."

"Thanks and you said that already," Lelani called back. She opened the door just as Gil was coming up the walk. "Looks like it's just you and me."

"What about Emma and—"

She explained as they got into the pickup. "Megan just thought it would be easier for us to make a decision. Less distraction. And she assured me that her feelings won't be hurt if you don't like it."

He nodded, but his expression was hard to read.

"Is anything wrong?"

He kind of shrugged as he started the engine.

"Gil?"

"Oh, it's just that my mother has gotten it into her head that if we're only going to have the wedding at a friend's house, we should have it at her house."

"She told you that?"

"I'm sure she called me before you pulled out of her driveway."

Lelani chuckled. "Your mother is a real go-getter."

"Tell me about it."

"It's not that I don't like your parents' house, Gil. But I don't think they need to host both the wedding and the reception."

"That just shows that you don't really know my mother yet."

Lelani didn't know how to respond to that. The truth was, she felt she was getting to know Gil's mother a whole lot more than she wanted to. Not that she would admit it.

"She's a stubborn woman," Gil said.

"So am I."

Gil chuckled. "Maybe so, but you're a lot softer kind of stubborn."

"Was that an insult?"

He looked at her innocently. "Not at all. It was a compliment."

"Okay."

"A soft kind of stubborn is a good thing. But if you were stubborn, well, like someone who will go unnamed, I'd probably be running in the opposite direction."

Lelani wanted to say that Gil's mother made her want to run in the opposite direction too. But that would be rude. Besides, he seemed to be pretty aware.

"Did your mother tell you that she's going to host Emma's birthday party next week?"

Gil didn't say anything.

"I couldn't really tell her no. I mean I tried to, but as you mentioned she's a bit stubborn."

"How are you doing with that? I know you wanted to give Emma a birthday party too."

"I did."

"I can tell Mom to back off if you—"

"No, no, don't do that."

"But Emma is your daughter, Lelani. And if you want to give her a party, you should be able to—"

"It's okay, Gil. Really. It actually makes sense. Your mother is right.

I have a lot going on right now. Planning the wedding, work, classes …
I should welcome her generosity."

"But—"

"No buts!"

He chuckled. "Hey, you're starting to sound like my mother."

"I suppose she might rub off on me."

"Well, don't let her rub too much onto you. You know why Anna
has such a hot temper now, don't you?"

"What do you mean?"

"She's grown up fighting to get her way against our mother."

"But Anna hardly ever loses her temper."

"She's gotten better about that. But you should've heard her as a
teenager. She and Mom sounded like World War III sometimes. They
actually threw things."

"They threw things?"

"Well, not all the time. But occasionally." He laughed. "Like I
remember the time Anna pitched Mom's cookie jar."

"Anna threw a cookie jar?"

"Yes. It was a special piece of pottery that had been in Mom's family for years, valuable too. But Anna threw the whole thing, cookies and
all, right onto the tile floor. It actually cracked some tiles."

"Your mom must've been furious."

"As I recall they both ended up in tears and hugging. Mostly I felt
bad for the cookies. They were chocolate chip."

"So are you saying that if I get into a fight with your mother, I
should reach for the nearest cookie jar to make things better?"

Gil threw back his head and laughed.

Soon they were walking around Megan's mother's house. Lelani
explained all the things that Mrs. Abernathy had promised would be

improved. Not that she was trying to talk him into it exactly, but she wanted him to get the complete picture.

"This garden is awesome," Gil told her as they sat out on a bench and soaked it all in. He pointed to a low spot in the yard. "If we set up the altar, or whatever you call it where couples say their vows, down there, and if we had chairs arranged in rows back in here, it would be kind of like stadium seating."

Lelani considered this. "And since that's the west side, if there was any kind of sunset going on, it might end up being really pretty."

"Or else our guests would be blinded by the light."

"Unless it was raining." Lelani frowned at the clouds gathering to the west.

"I wonder how many guests we could have inside."

"Megan and her mom thought we could get about seventy in there if they put the furnishings in storage."

"They're willing to do that?"

"Well, since Megan's mom is selling and moving, she said she plans to remove a lot of things anyway."

"And they really don't mind if we have it here?"

Lelani studied his face, trying to determine what he was thinking. Instead she decided to kiss him. A few minutes later, after they stopped kissing, she asked him how he really felt.

"I feel like the luckiest guy on the planet, and I'm thinking, who needs a wedding? Let's just catch the next flight to Vegas and—"

She laughed. "That's not what I mean, Gil. I mean how do you feel about this for our wedding location?"

"How do you feel about it?"

"I think it's romantic."

He nodded.

"And affordable." She grinned. "But really that's not why I like it."

"The truth is …" He looked around the yard and then back to the house. "It's perfect."

"Really, you think it's perfect."

He nodded. "In fact, I wish I could afford to buy this house for you, Lelani."

She laughed hard now. "Maybe someday."

"Yeah, it's a little out of our budget for now. But speaking of living quarters, I've been wondering about my townhouse and whether we should—"

"I love your townhouse, Gil."

"Seriously?"

"Yes. It's a great location, both for your work and my school. And it's not too big and not too small. In fact, it's just right."

He grinned, then pulled her toward him again. "Just like you. Just right."

So it was settled. The wedding would be at Megan's childhood home. Now if Gil's mother could just accept that.

Thirteen

Megan

"Hey, I missed you at church this weekend," Marcus said after Megan answered her phone.

"Oh, yeah." Megan struggled to hang onto the phone as she carried Emma to the bathroom, having decided that the easiest way to clean Emma for bed would involve a bath.

"Everything okay?"

"Yeah, everything's fine, Marcus. But right now I've got a messy baby in need of a bath and since I'm not exactly an expert, I'm going to have to hang up."

"Yeah, sure, okay. I was just checking."

"Thanks." And before she could say good-bye, the phone slipped from her grip but closed itself upon landing, which in essence meant she'd hung up. She'd have to explain later.

"Okay, Emma, you are a mess of squash, chicken and noodles, and applesauce, and it smells like your diaper is not in great shape either." She stood Emma at the edge of the bath and wondered how to proceed. "Let's start by filling your tub," she said as she turned the water onto warm and began filling the yellow plastic insert. "And we'll throw in a few duckies. Then we'll get you stripped down."

Easier said than done, Megan decided after she'd managed to spill some of the diaper's contents onto the bathroom rug, which she then shoved out of the way. She tried using toilet paper to clean up the messiest part of Emma's bottom, but that wasn't working too well either.

The bathroom door cracked open and Kendall stuck her head in. "Need any help in here?"

"Do I ever!"

"Looks like a disaster area," Kendall said as she came into the already crowded bathroom. She rolled up the rug and tossed it out the door, then handed Megan a box of baby wipes. "These work much better than toilet paper." She flushed the toilet and rolled up and disposed of the smelly diaper, then sat down on the toilet lid and continued to walk Megan through bath time.

"See that rubber ducky with the blue bottom?"

"Blue bottom?" Megan frowned at Kendall.

Kendall picked up a duck and showed Megan. "This tells you if the water's too hot."

"Is it?"

Kendall stuck her hand in as Megan was peeling off Emma's undershirt. "It's barely even warm."

"Oh, well, I filled it up a while ago."

"Let me take the chill off." Kendall ran the water, and Emma was ready to get in. "The ducky with the blue bottom says the temperature is perfect," she announced.

"Ba-ba-ba!" cried Emma.

"Is that a lamb imitation?" asked Megan as she set Emma in the tub.

"She's saying *bath*," Kendall told her.

"Oh, yeah, right."

Kendall explained how to shampoo Emma's hair. She found the baby washcloths and hooded baby towel and actually made herself very useful.

"Thanks for your help," Megan told Kendall as she toweled off a squeaky clean Emma. "I know I couldn't have done it without you."

"Well, thank you, Megan." Kendall beamed. "Coming from you, that's quite a compliment."

"Huh?"

"You're always so capable about everything."

"Me?" Megan lifted Emma and carried her to Lelani's room to finish getting her ready for bed.

"You know how to decorate houses, how to budget money, you're a pretty good cook, and now you're about to start teaching school."

Megan considered this as Kendall handed her a diaper.

"You pretty much have it all together."

Megan couldn't find the tapes on the diaper.

"Well, almost together." Kendall laughed. "That diaper is upside down."

"Oh, right."

Before long, the diaper was right-side up, Emma had on her footed pajamas and was ready for bed. But as soon as Megan laid her in the crib, she began to cry. And she didn't want her pacifier. Megan was clueless. Where was Kendall?

Megan went out to search for her and found her in the kitchen removing a baby bottle from the microwave. "I assume that's for Emma?" Megan asked.

Kendall chuckled. "Yeah, I prefer my milk in a glass."

"So is that why she's fussy?"

"Emma always has a bottle before bed." Kendall checked the temperature on her wrist.

"You really are good at this, aren't you?"

"I'm learning." Kendall held the bottle out for Megan.

"Uh, Kendall, do you want to put her to bed?"

"Don't you?"

"Well, Marcus called and I was taking care of Emma and I sort of hung up on him. He's getting ready to head off to Zambia before long and I think I need to talk—"

"Say no more." Kendall reached for Emma.

"I owe you."

But Kendall was already waltzing Emma away. Megan had to locate her phone. When she finally found it, she saw that she had several messages, all from the same unfamiliar number. She quickly dialed her voice mail and was surprised to hear Mrs. McCall speaking. "Megan, it's urgent that you call me back. Heather just went into labor, and it looks like we'll need you to take over her class tomorrow. Is that going to work for you? Please, call me."

So Megan called and assured Mrs. McCall she would be there.

"Oh, I'm so glad. I was going to just call someone on the regular sub list, but it would be so much better if you stepped in. You know how students can be when there's a sub."

"Yes," Megan said, although she had no idea. "I understand."

"So we'll see you tomorrow. School starts at eight, but teachers come at seven thirty. If you come a bit earlier we'll make sure you get a full tour of the school. And you'll need to do some paperwork too. Thanks!"

Megan could hardly believe it. She was officially starting her new teaching job tomorrow. First she called Cynthia and left a message about the situation. Then she studied her closet. She so wanted to make a good first impression. But what would impress middle-school students? Kendall and Lelani were the fashion experts, but she could tell that Kendall was still putting Emma down. And Lelani wasn't back yet.

She played with several outfits and was about to give up when she heard Lelani speaking quietly to Kendall. "She's asleep?" Lelani was asking.

Megan came out into the hallway. "Kendall helped out," she admitted sheepishly. "I honestly couldn't have done it without her." Then she told them about starting her new job in the morning. "But I need help."

"Help?" Lelani frowned.

"With my wardrobe. What do you guys think I should wear? I mean, I want to make a good first impression."

Soon the three of them were in Megan's room, going over her clothes.

"You want something artsy," Lelani said.

"But something cool." Kendall picked up a sweater and shook her head. "Not so cool."

"And something that suggests authority," Megan added.

Finally, they all three agreed on an outfit. Megan tried it on just to be certain. "You're sure this old broomstick skirt isn't out of style?" Megan frowned at her image in the mirror.

"Not when you pair it with that denim jacket," Lelani assured her.

"And that scarf adds a nice punch," Kendall told her.

Megan looked down at her boots. "But what if it's sunny and hot tomorrow?"

"I'm predicting rain," Lelani told her. "Oh, by the way, Gil loves your house."

Megan felt a rush of happiness. "Really, he said that?"

"He said he wished he could afford to buy it."

Megan frowned now. "Yeah, me too."

"Anyway, we both feel that it's perfect for the wedding." Lelani sighed. "The hard part now will be to convince Gil's mother."

"She needs to be convinced?" asked Megan.

"I think she's a bit jealous. She thinks if we're having the wedding in a house, why not have it at her house?"

Megan nodded. "I guess that's a good question."

"Have you seen her house?"

"No, but I've heard Anna describe it. It sounds like it's pretty big with an in-ground pool and a large basement and—"

"And it's decorated in, well"—Lelani lowered her voice—"a somewhat gaudy style. Mrs. Mendez loves color and she uses it liberally."

"That's true," Kendall admitted. "I only saw it briefly when I dropped off Tinkerbell before we left for Maui. And it's a little ... well, imagine *My Big Fat Greek Wedding* with a Hispanic flare."

"I wouldn't go that far," Lelani told them. "But it's not exactly my taste. Or Gil's or Anna's, either."

"It might work," Megan said, "if someone wanted to have a south-of-the-border wedding. That could actually be kind of fun."

"Fun for someone else," Lelani said. "Maybe Anna. Anyway, you'll both get a chance to see the house up close and personal next Tuesday, since Mrs. Mendez will be hosting Emma's first birthday party."

"But you wanted to do that," Megan pointed out.

"Don't remind me."

"You were going to do it all in pink," Kendall said sadly. "Didn't you already get some paper plates and things?"

"I'll offer them to Gil's mother, but I'm sure she'll do whatever she likes."

"Tell her that Emma needs to have a *pink* party," Kendall demanded. "She's going to be the princess in pink and she—"

"I'll try, but I won't be holding my breath."

Megan put her hand on Lelani's shoulder. "I realize you'll need to pick your battles with that woman, but don't let her walk all over you either."

"That's right," Kendall agreed. "You need to draw some lines early on. In my marriage-counseling class, they call it boundaries. And that reminds me: I should probably go call Killiki."

"Thanks again for helping with Emma," Megan told her as she left.

"This will be a big change for you," Lelani said to Megan. "Are you excited?"

"I actually am." Megan picked up a discarded belt and rolled it into a donut, then put it back into a basket.

"Because I know how you can be resistant to change."

Megan nodded. "Yes. But this feels like a good change."

"Well, it's getting late and I have classes tomorrow."

"You and me both."

"If I don't see you in the morning, good luck. And sleep well."

As Megan put away her clothes and got ready for bed, she thought that sleep might not come easily. She was too excited. It was nearly eleven before she realized she hadn't called Marcus back. She shot him a quick e-mail, telling him about starting her new job and saying that she'd call him tomorrow. What she'd say when she called him wasn't perfectly clear. She didn't want to make him regret his interest in serving God in Zambia. And she didn't want to make him feel guilty for making her feel slightly abandoned.

Pretty much all she could do when she thought about Marcus these days was to pray. So, once again, she prayed for God's will in his life. And if that meant Marcus might be in Zambia for a while, or forever, Megan knew she'd have to accept it.

With God's help, she could.

Fourteen

Kendall

After a restless night of too many trips to the bathroom, followed by a horrifying nightmare in which Kendall misplaced her infant only to find the poor naked baby sitting in a pile of broken glass and choking on french fries, Kendall decided to sleep in. It wasn't her day to have Emma, and a few extra hours of shut-eye would be most welcome.

But shortly after making this decision, she woke to the sound of someone—a man—yelling on the stairs, calling out, "Anybody home?"

Kendall sat up in bed, rubbed her eyes, and realized the voice sounded faintly familiar.

"Kendall?" he called again. "You up here?"

Kendall jumped out of bed, opened the door, and saw her dad, all six foot five of him, standing at the top of the stairs wearing a silly grin and a pair of hideous plaid golfing shorts. And there, right behind him, was her mom!

"About time you got up, lazy girl," called her mom.

"Look at you, Kennie," Dad said as he hugged her. "Fat and sassy."

"She's not fat, she's pregnant," Mom said as she pushed her way past to hug Kendall.

"How did you get in?" Kendall asked.

"Remember, I used to live here," Dad told her.

"I know."

"And I always keep a spare key handy."

"But we changed the locks," she pointed out.

He chuckled. "Doesn't do much good when you forget to lock the front door."

"Oh."

"Come on, Kennie," Dad said, "get dressed and moving. Don't you know we're burning daylight here?"

"Where are we going?"

He shrugged. "I don't know."

Her mom was already heading downstairs, telling Kendall to hurry up and join them for coffee.

"Let me get dressed first," she called as she hurried back to her room. It would've been nice if they'd given her some warning instead of just popping in like this. Even so, she couldn't help but be a little excited to see them. Of course, she knew what this meant: So long to any sense of control over her own wedding. She huffed and puffed as she tugged on sweats and slippers and hurried downstairs to see what her parents were up to. But when she got there, they appeared to be gone.

She looked out the front window to see that their humongous motor home with tow car attached was parked right in front of the house. Her dad was setting up a camp chair right on the parking strip next to the sidewalk, as if he planned to stay awhile. "Come and join us for a cup of joe, Kennie," he said when Kendall emerged from the house. "Mom's just making some now."

Kendall heard the whir of the coffee grinder and decided to peek inside. She'd only seen this recreational vehicle once, and then only the exterior.

"Hello?" she called as she entered the luxurious home on wheels.

"Wow," she said as she looked around at the leather furniture, gorgeous wood cabinets, granite countertops, stainless appliances, and enormous flat-screen TV. "Pretty swanky."

"Oh, this is nothing," Mom told her. "You should see it with the slide-outs opened. It's actually quite roomy."

"No wonder you guys never come home." She thought about this. "Actually, this is your home, isn't it?"

"It is for now."

Kendall watched her mom turn on the sleek stainless coffeemaker. "Will it always be home?"

Her mother's brow creased. "I don't know. Maybe."

"Oh."

"Do you want the grand tour?" Her mom had a remote control and was pushing buttons. Things began to move.

"Are we about to lift off?" Kendall asked as she grabbed the back of a leather recliner.

Her mom pointed to the wall that was moving. "I'm just showing you what it's like when it's opened up."

"Wow!" Kendall looked at the space, which had more than doubled into a great room with a full-sized kitchen, comfortable dining area, roomy sitting area, a wet bar, and enough floor space to have a small dance. "This is great. I could practically have my wedding in here."

Mom laughed. "Hardly."

"If it was a small wedding."

"Come on back and I'll give you the ten-cent tour."

Kendall followed as her mom showed her a laundry closet with a stacked washer and dryer, a powder room, and a bathroom with more granite, oiled bronze accessories, and full-sized porcelain fixtures. "And this is the master suite." Her mom pushed open a set of french doors to reveal a king-size bed, a sitting area with yet another plasma TV, and two rather spacious closets, complete with organizers.

"And back here is the master bath." Mom opened the door to a bathroom that was actually bigger than the one that Kendall and Anna shared.

"You even have a tub," Kendall ran her hand over the granite countertop and nodded. "I think I could live here too."

"Not with us, you couldn't." Mom closed the bathroom door.

"I mean live here as in this is sweet. I can see why you call it home."

Her mom smiled now. "Yes, home sweet home."

"Where's that coffee?" called Dad from outside.

"Coming," Mom called back. "Here, you take the cups and I'll meet you … on the terrace."

In the short time that Kendall had been in the motor home, her dad had managed to put out an awning, set up several chairs and a small table, and had the exterior TV tuned into a golf network.

"Here," Mom called from inside. "Someone come get this."

Kendall set the mugs on the table and went back to see that her mom not only had coffee, but a basket of muffins too.

"Yum!" Kendall grinned as she reached for them.

"I didn't actually bake them."

"I'm not complaining."

"And that's not all." Her mom disappeared back into the RV.

"This is great," Kendall said as she set the coffeepot and muffins on the little table. "Like a little party."

"It is a celebration," Mom said as she emerged with a bottle of champagne, a carton of orange juice, and three champagne glasses.

"Cool." Kendall sat down in a chair. "What're you celebrating?"

"You!" Dad popped the cork and laughed.

"Me?"

Mom nodded as she filled a champagne glass halfway with orange juice, waited for Dad to top it off with bubbly, then handed it to Kendall.

"I'll have a virgin mimosa," Kendall said as she set it on the table. "For the baby, you know."

Mom nodded. "Yes, of course, good choice."

Soon they were all toasting. "To Kendall and her baby and upcoming marriage."

"Wow," Kendall said for about the fifth time. "This is kind of overwhelming. But nice."

"Well, Dad and I talked, and we decided it was time to give you a show of confidence."

Dad held up his mimosa to make another toast. "And here's to you, Kennie. You have just set an all-time record."

"A record?" She looked at both of them curiously. "For what?"

"It's been almost six months since you've asked either of us for money."

"Really?"

"Do you know how happy that makes us?" Her dad's blue eyes lit up.

"How happy?"

"So happy that your mother wants us to pay for your entire wedding. You can have whatever you want, baby doll."

"I've already started making lists," her mother said eagerly. "And I've done some online shopping, and I contacted the cake lady. Remember the cake for Kim's wedding?"

"You mean the wedding that wasn't?"

"Well, the cake was going to be spectacular. It was royal icing. You know, the kind that's hard and looks so pretty."

Kendall imagined a cake made of stone. "If it's hard, does it taste good?"

Her mom frowned. "Who actually eats wedding cake anyway?"

"I do." She took another muffin.

"Yes, dear, and you might want to rethink that second muffin. They're loaded with fat, you know. That is unless you want to look like a beluga bride."

Dad laughed. "Beluga bride marries Maui man."

Kendall replaced the muffin and frowned.

"Now." Mom stood and brushed crumbs off her sleek white jeans. "You go and get dressed in something respectable and we'll go shopping."

Kendall felt a surge of hope, which was quickly replaced with a dash of reality. "I'm not supposed to shop."

"Of course you're supposed to shop," Mom told her.

"No. I'm in a recovery program."

Dad laughed. "A recovery program for shopping."

And so Kendall told them about SA and, despite their snickers and chuckles, she declared that she had to stick with the program. "I promised Killiki and my housemates too."

"But you won't be spending your own money, Kendall." Mom poured herself another mimosa. "Don't you see that's different?"

"I don't know." Kendall folded her hands over her rounded tummy and thought.

"Isn't there a hotline or someone you can call, Kennie?" Her dad held out his cell phone for her. "After all, we are talking about your wedding."

"Yes!" She turned and headed for the house. "I'll call the hotline."

It took her a couple of minutes to dig out the number, but it wasn't long before a real live woman was on the other end. Kendall quickly described her dilemma.

"That's a tricky one," the woman told her. "On one hand, your father is right. It's your parents' money, so it's not like you're really putting yourself into debt. On the other hand, all that shopping could be a trigger."

"A trigger?"

"You know, that one little thing that causes a person to go off the deep end. You could have such a great time shopping with your parents' money that you suddenly think it's okay to go out and shop with your own. Or worse, with plastic."

"I don't even have credit cards anymore."

"Yes, good for you."

"So what do I do?"

"Okay, here's what I recommend: Go ahead and shop with your mother. But only for wedding things. And keep track of what you're purchasing in a notebook."

"Write it all down?"

"Yes. That's an accountability thing."

"Okay."

"And then when the shopping's done, do not go near a mall. Period."

"Right."

"And feel free to call if you get tempted."

"Okay. Thanks!" Kendall hung up, then called Killiki and told him of the recent development.

"That's pretty cool that your parents want to help you, Kendall. I feel bad that I'm not around for you right now."

"I understand. But we talk every day."

"Yeah, but I wish we weren't so far apart."

"Me too."

"So, anyway, it's great that your parents feel so supportive now. That's a big change, don't you think?"

"Yeah, I was kind of blown away at first."

"At first?"

"Well, then my mom started getting kind of bossy. But I expected that."

"As far as the shopping thing, I have to agree with that hotline person. If you're not spending your own money and you realize it's a one-time thing, and if you take all that seriously, well, it seems like it would be okay. If it helps, you can be accountable to me every day. I'll ask you if you went shopping or anything."

"You'd do that for me?"

"Of course, sweetheart. I love you."

"I love you too." For the next few minutes they argued about who loved whom more. Finally, reluctantly, they said aloha, which meant both hello and good-bye and was, Kendall thought, a gentler way to end a conversation. Then she cleaned up and got dressed and went out to tell her parents the good news.

When she got outside, she saw that one of the neighbors, a thirty-something woman who had just moved in next door, was talking to her dad.

"But how long do you plan to park it there?" she was asking.

"As long as I want," he shot back. "This is free country, you know."

"But there are regulations about things like this."

"You mean CC&Rs?" Dad narrowed his eyes and, despite the crazy shorts and bright orange ball cap, looked a lot like the corporate attorney he used to be.

"Yes," she said eagerly. "Codes, covenants, and restrictions."

He laughed. "Not in this neighborhood."

"But there are city laws."

"Sure. You can't park a vehicle for over twenty-four hours on the street. But if I just take it for a spin around the neighborhood, a new twenty-four-hour period begins."

"Well, what about those things sticking out into the street?" she pointed to one of the slide-outs.

"We'll pull them in on that side." He looked up at the front yard. "Or better yet, we might just park the RV on the lawn and let it all hang out."

"Dad!" Kendall was getting worried.

He laughed. "I'm just joking with her."

"Oh?" Kendall kind of smiled at the neighbor.

"Well, I don't think it's very funny."

"And I don't think it's very neighborly to come over here without even introducing yourself and get on our case for merely visiting our daughter."

"I just wanted to make sure you knew—"

"The rules?" he shot back at her.

"Uh, my name's Kendall Weis." Kendall stuck out her hand. "And this is my dad, Michael Weis. He's a retired attorney and he sort of knows the law, if you know what I mean."

"Not only that, but I grew up in this house and I know this neighborhood, and if I want to park my motor home here for the next year, I'd like to see you try and stop me."

The woman backed off.

"What's the problem out here?" Mom asked as she emerged from the RV.

"This *friendly* neighbor came over to complain about our motor home trashing up the nice neighborhood." Dad glared at the woman.

"This is my mom, Bev Weis," Kendall said. "You still haven't given us your name."

"Toni." She stepped back again.

Mom frowned. "You don't like our motor home parked out here?"

"I just thought it might be against, uh, the rules or something." Toni was clearly outnumbered.

"It's not as if we were moving in," Mom said hotly. "We only planned to stay a few hours—"

"A few weeks," Dad snapped. "What's it to you?"

"Come on, you guys," Kendall said cheerfully. "Let's not blow this all out of proportion. I mean, Toni is my neighbor, and you have to admit it's kind of shocking to look out your front window and see this giant motor home." She turned to Toni now. "But you should see it inside. It's got granite and stainless and plasma TVs and—"

"And it cost a whole lot more than your house," Dad finished for her. "And it's staying here until I say it's not. *Capisce?*"

"Dad!"

"What? I have my rights and I know it."

Kendall made a weak smile, then shrugged as Toni turned away with a disgusted expression and stomped back toward her house.

"That went well." Kendall shook her head.

"All right then. Let's go and shop until we drop." Mom slung the strap of her sleek Coach bag over her shoulder as she linked arms with Kendall. "Your car gassed up and ready?"

"Oh, yeah."

"Let the good times roll," Dad called as they headed toward the garage. And Kendall knew that the fun had just begun.

Fifteen

Anna

"So is it true?" Chelsea seemed to have cornered Anna in the restroom. "Did you and Edmond really break up?"

Anna just shrugged and continued washing her hands.

"That's what everyone is saying. And Lucy is acting like she plans to take full advantage of the situation."

Anna shrugged again as she reached for a paper towel.

"I thought we were friends, Anna."

Anna thought that with friends like Chelsea … Well, Chelsea was probably one level higher than Lucy anyway. "We are friends," Anna said calmly. "Business friends."

"So are you going to just let Lucy walk away with your man?"

"Who said he was my man?"

"Even Felicia mentioned it."

Anna was surprised. "Felicia said something about Edmond and me?"

"Well, she is Edmond's aunt. Maybe she actually cares about him."

Anna wanted to laugh. But she also wanted to cry. "What did she say?"

"I heard her talking to Rick. You know, Edmond's uncle."

Anna rolled her eyes. "Yes, I know that. He's also my boss."

"Right. Anyway, they were talking quietly and Felicia said that Edmond hadn't been himself lately, and she thought it was because of you."

"Because of me?" Anna wanted to hit something. Or someone.

Chelsea nodded. "Felicia sounded like you had hurt Edmond somehow. She said it was just like the other time."

Anna considered this.

"What happened the other time?"

Anna threw the wad of paper towel into the waste bin and just sighed. "Really, Chelsea, you should focus more on your work and less on people's personal problems."

"But what about when people's personal problems come into the workplace?"

Anna walked to the door now. This was actually a good question, but one that Anna had no intention of answering. "See you later, Chelsea."

"Don't say I didn't warn you."

Anna didn't respond to that. Not outwardly. Inwardly, she was seething. Fortunately the workday was almost over. Only one more day of the work week left. She wondered how she'd made it through four days without saying more than a few words to Edmond. But he seemed to be avoiding her as well. Really, perhaps the best thing was to deal with this maturely, like two grownups—just lay the cards on the table and get it over with.

In fact, that was what she planned to do. She picked up the phone and called Edmond's cell, leaving him a message that she wanted to speak to him after work. "It's urgent," she said, then immediately wished she hadn't. Urgent? Why was it suddenly urgent after nearly a week of this silly standoff?

But what if Chelsea was right? What if Edmond really was blue about the whole thing? Of course, if that was the case, why hadn't he come to her by now? Shouldn't he have apologized?

At five o'clock, Edmond had still not returned her call. Of course, she knew he usually kept his cell phone off during work hours. Felicia had trained him well in that regard. She straightened her desk, refilled the paper tray on her printer, organized her pens, and even refilled her stapler until it was a few minutes past five. Then she stood up, gathered her things and, telling herself she was off the clock now, headed straight for Edmond's office. Without even knocking on the door, she burst in.

To her stunned and speechless amazement, Lucy was in Edmond's office too. And it almost seemed as if she had Edmond pinned against his desk. Anna blinked and looked again. By this time Edmond had somehow managed to slither away to the other side of the desk, where his cheeks were quickly reddening. "Anna!" he sort of gasped.

She simply turned and walked out, firmly closing the door behind her. She wanted to scream and swear and throw things and basically just go into hysterics. Instead she took the stairs, counting each one as she stepped until she was finally outside and getting into her car. Once she was inside her car and pulling away from the building, she let out a bloodcurdling scream that actually hurt her ears. And then she began to cry. She was crying so hard that she had to pull over until she could focus her eyes again.

Then, instead of going home where they would feel appropriately sorry for her, she drove to a place she seldom visited. Well, besides Christmas and Easter. She drove to church, parked her car, and went inside the sanctuary, where she sat for a while. Finally, she went to confession, where she told Father Thomas that she had sinned by wanting to murder someone.

"Actually two people," she corrected herself. "I wanted to kill them both equally." He pressed her to explain her situation further, and she filled him in on all the details. He told her what to do as penance, which actually seemed rather minor for something as serious as murder. "Are you sure?" she asked him.

"Sure?"

"That it's enough. I mean I truly did want to kill them. I imagined them both dead."

"Do you still want to kill them?" he asked quietly.

She thought a moment. "No."

"Go and sin no more."

She nodded and stood, thinking that was a lot easier said than done.

As soon as she got to her car, she called Edmond's cell phone, hoping that it would go straight to voice mail. Of course, it did not.

"Anna," he said eagerly. "We do need to talk. And you're right, it's urgent."

"Yes," she said with surprising calmness. "That's why I called."

"Oh, good." He sounded relieved.

"It's obvious that our relationship isn't working, Edmond. And instead of getting all crazy and saying or doing anything terribly stupid, let's just admit that it's not working and call it a day. Okay?"

"But, Anna, I need to—"

"I know you're sorry, Edmond, and I'm sorry too. And I'm basically kind of exhausted right now. So let's not drag this out. I forgive you. You forgive me. Let's act like none of this even happened. Thank you." And then she hung up and turned off her phone. Like peeling off an old Band-Aid, breakups were probably best done quickly.

✄

Anna was curious to see a big hulking motor home parked in front of their house. And yet she was still in semishock, so nothing could surprise her too much. She parked her car in the driveway, then walked past the "campground" and into the house. She wanted to go straight to her room, where she could sit and stare at the wall and hope for the pain to subside, but Lelani was talking to her.

"Anna, you've got to talk to your mom about the guest list. She just keeps adding to it, and I've made it clear that we can only have eighty guests max. It means we all have to cut back. But it also means the wedding will be more intimate and—"

"Yes, yes," Anna said woodenly, "eighty guests. Got it."

"Are you okay?"

Anna forced a smile. "Of course, I'm fine. Just tired."

"Did you see Kendall's parents' motor home out there?"

"How could I not see it?"

"You should see the inside. Mr. Weis just gave Emma and me the grand tour. It's really something."

"I can only imagine."

"Are you sure you're okay?"

Anna nodded. "Like I said, just tired."

Lelani put a hand on her shoulder. "You do seem tired. I hope I'm not putting too much on you to help with the invitations. Am I?"

"No, I want to do it."

"Oh, yeah, I almost forgot. In case you haven't heard, Emma's birthday party has been moved from here to your parents' house."

"Are you okay with that?"

Lelani shrugged. "It's probably a good thing. So much to do. And your mother seems to thrive on being busy."

"Yes. She's a regular Energizer Bunny."

"I don't know how she does it."

"The same way your mother does it."

"Huh?"

"A little four-letter word."

Lelani looked puzzled.

"H-E-L-P. She hires help. You should see her little black book. She has someone for every imaginable task—from accountants to window washers and everything in between."

Lelani laughed like she thought Anna was joking.

"My mother's talent is organizing, and then she takes over." Anna smiled sweetly.

"Anna, you do seem tired. Why don't you go have a rest?"

"That's what I plan to do." But Anna knew that she would have another good cry first. Hopefully she would cry herself to sleep. Then perhaps she could cry herself into such a state that she would lose her voice and call in sick in the morning.

Sixteen

Lelani

"Oh, we won't need any of that," Gil's mother waved her hand as Lelani tried to give her a bag of party things she'd gotten for Emma a few weeks ago. "You shouldn't have wasted your money. I have it all taken care of." The older woman sank down into her green velvet recliner and sighed in a satisfied way.

"But I already had these things," Lelani explained.

"Save them for her next birthday."

"Where's Emma?"

"Napping."

Lelani frowned at her watch. "Still napping at this time of day?"

"Yes, I held her off as long as I could and just put her down a few minutes ago."

"But now I'll need to wake her."

Gil's mother smiled slyly. "That's the beauty of it. Emma will continue her nap. You can run on home and enjoy a nice little break. And when you and Gil come back for the party, Emma will be awake and ready for her big night. Don't you see? Now hurry along, there's much to do."

As she drove home, Lelani knew she should be grateful for this unexpected "break," but instead she felt irritated. She had looked forward to spending a little time with her daughter, dressing her up special, taking some photos, and finally returning to the Mendez house. All that had been taken from her. Still, she reminded herself, Gil's mother meant well. And no doubt there would be times when Lelani would truly appreciate this kind of generosity. Just not today!

"Where's the birthday girl?" Kendall asked when Lelani came into the house carrying her bag of unwanted party supplies.

"Abuela Mendez is keeping her."

"Keeping her?" Kendall frowned. "That woman is starting to seriously worry me."

"Just keeping her until the party. She thought I needed a little break."

"Seems like she would have plenty to do putting the party together."

"Seems that way. But she has help. In fact, I saw a Parties to Go van driving toward their house. I wouldn't be surprised if she'd hired that to be done as well." Lelani pulled out a package of pale pink crepe paper and looked longingly at it. "Guess this will have to wait for next year."

"Unless you want to have two parties," Kendall suggested eagerly.

"Two weddings, two birthday parties … are we starting to see a pattern here?"

Kendall laughed. "I see your point. Speaking of weddings, my parents just left."

"I noticed their RV was gone. Is your dad taking it for another spin around the block?"

"No, they decided to relocate to an RV park about fifteen minutes from here. They needed to empty their tanks, whatever that means."

"Well, I'm sure the neighbors won't miss them." Lelani looked out the window and chuckled. "Last night I imagined Toni standing out there in the middle of the street, screaming *Move that bus!*"

"Hello," called Megan as she came into the house.

"You're home early," observed Lelani.

"That's because I didn't have to ride the metro. Marcus picked me up."

"How is old Marcus?" asked Kendall. "We haven't seen his face around here in ages."

"Marcus is fine." Megan set her oversized bag on one of the dining room chairs. "He's had his shots, got his ticket, and is on his way home to pack his bags."

"When does he leave?" asked Lelani.

"Tonight."

"Tonight?" Lelani looked shocked. "How are you doing with that, Megan?"

She made a half smile. "I just hope he'll be safe."

"We should all be praying for him," Kendall said. "For his travel and health and everything."

"I know he'll appreciate that."

"Are you really okay?" Lelani gently asked her again.

Megan kind of shrugged. "It's hard."

"I can imagine," said Kendall. "I mean, Maui seems like a long ways away, but Zambia. I don't even know where that is."

"In Africa," Megan said dryly.

"I know *that*."

"Sorry." Megan sighed. "It's been a rough day, and saying good-bye to Marcus didn't make it any better."

"But won't you see him off at the airport too?" Kendall asked.

"I wanted to, but he said no. It's a really late flight." Megan looked like she was on the verge of tears.

Lelani put her hand on Megan's shoulder. "I'll understand if you don't feel like coming to Emma's party to—"

"No way," Megan said. "That's the one thing I am looking forward to after a day like this."

"So, what are the Madison Middle School monsters up to these days?" asked Kendall.

Megan rolled her eyes. "You know, I've been there a week now. I'd think they'd get over themselves, but it's like they're still testing me. Today in third period, Levi and Jackson used a photo from a porn magazine as their inspiration for their charcoal drawing."

"Eeuw." Kendall made a face. "Was it any good?"

"Their proportions were off, but the shading wasn't bad." Megan shook her head. "I confiscated the evidence and sent them both to the office."

"Well, at least it wasn't a drug deal this time." Lelani shuddered. "It's hard to believe middle school kids are so ... so ..."

"Rotten," Kendall supplied.

"No, I was thinking *sophisticated*, but that's not right. I just don't remember kids being like that when I was in junior high. Oh, there was drinking and skipping classes to surf and things like that. But no hard drugs or porn or kids having sex right there on school property." She frowned at Megan. "As a parent I'm starting to feel pretty worried. What will it be like when Emma is in middle school?"

"There are a lot of good kids too," Megan said. "And Emma will be one of those. Speaking of our little princess, where is she?"

Lelani explained and then excused herself. "I might as well enjoy my little break, right?"

"Especially since it's getting littler by the minute."

"Why didn't you just bring Emma home?" Gil asked Lelani as they were driving over to his parents' home.

"She was napping." Lelani looked at the pale pink party dress laid out on the seat between them. She'd gotten it on sale at Macy's not long after they'd returned from Maui. It was the quintessential little-girl dress, and she couldn't wait to see Emma in it. Plus, she had white tights with a ruffled bottom and the sweetest little pink Mary Janes, as well as a pair of pale pink satin bows for Emma's hair.

"Uh-oh, looks like we're approaching a traffic jam."

Lelani looked up to see a long string of red taillights ahead. "Can you take an exit and another route?"

"We just passed an exit. The next one, I'm guessing, is probably about where the traffic jam begins. Probably a wreck up there."

Lelani knew it was useless to be impatient, but she really wanted to get to the party early enough to get Emma ready. "How long do you think it'll be?"

"Who knows." He had his Blackberry out and was already dialing. "Hey, Dad," he said cheerfully. "Tell Mom we might be late. Traffic jam on the 205." He made an apologetic smile to Lelani. "Hard to say. But we'll be there when we get there." He chuckled, then hung up.

"Sorry, Lelani," he said as he reached for her hand. "I know you wanted to be there early."

"It's not your fault."

"If I could arrange for a helicopter to pick you up, I would."

She smiled and squeezed his fingers. "I know you would."

"So how goes the wedding planning?"

"Well, Anna has sent the invitations."

"How did Mom respond to the cuts in the guest list?"

"I honestly don't know. I left that in Anna's capable hands."

"Speaking of Anna, is something up with her?"

"I'm not sure. She's been really quiet lately. She says she's swamped at work, that it's always like this at this time of year. Some big publishing show in New York that everyone has to get ready for. Anyway, she hasn't been around much. I'm just thankful she had time to get those invitations done."

"And you're still certain that I don't need to wear a tux?"

"That's what Megan is saying."

"Because as much as I hate them, I'm totally willing to put on a monkey suit for you, Lelani."

"Thanks, but this isn't going to be a formal wedding."

He leaned over and kissed her. "Have I told you that I'm the luckiest guy on the planet?"

"Not lately."

He kissed her again. "Well, it's true. I'm marrying the most wonderful woman. Not only is she beautiful and intelligent, but she's sensible too. And she has the most adorable little girl. Quite the package deal."

"Well, thank you." She kissed him back. And so, as they waited for traffic to move, they took advantage of the time and were eventually surprised to hear the sound of a horn informing them that it was time to move.

Within minutes they were parking in front of his parents' house. Not exactly in front, since there was already more than a dozen cars filling the driveway and lining the street.

"How many people did your mother invite?" Lelani asked as Gil helped her out of the car.

He shook his head. "It seems she invited, well, just everyone."

The party seemed to be in full whirl when they entered the house. Relatives mingled everywhere, along with streamers and balloons and party favors and hats, all in a brightly colored fiesta theme: screaming shades of tangerine, lime, electric blue, and magenta.

"And here's our birthday girl now," Gil's mom was announcing as a young woman (not someone Lelani knew) led Emma into the great room. Emma looked a little frightened as she held this woman's hand and toddled into the center of the crowd. She wore a bright magenta dress with so many ruffles that she looked like a hot-pink Michelin baby. Her legs were bare, and her feet were clad with white ruffled anklets and shiny black patent-leather shoes. Her chin was quivering, like she was about to start crying.

"Isn't she gorgeous?" cried Gil's mother as Lelani handed Gil the pale-pink dress, then pressed her way through the crowd and scooped up Emma just as she was starting to cry.

"Happy birthday, sweetie," Lelani said calmly. "Want to come outside with Mommy?"

"Mama-Mama-Mama!" Emma's face erupted into a relieved smile and she clung tightly to Lelani.

"I'm taking the birthday girl out for some fresh air," Lelani said as she pushed her way toward the patio. Gil was next to her, sliding open the door so she and Emma could escape. And then it was just the three of them out by the pool.

"I'm surprised your mom took the cover off the pool," Lelani said as they sat down on patio chairs. "She usually leaves it locked up when Emma is here."

"She likes having it opened up for parties," he said with a grim expression. "But I'm a little surprised too."

"It's not that I'm afraid exactly," Lelani admitted. "I know that Emma can sort of swim, with assistance. But if she were alone and wandered in."

"I'll speak to Mom about it." He put a hand on her shoulder. "Are you okay?"

Lelani forced a smile for Emma's sake. "Yes. I'm fine. And look at you, Emma girl, you are looking like one little hot tamale in your big ruffled dress."

Emma grinned and began to babble.

"What's wrong?" asked Gil's mother as she came out to join them.

"I think Emma was a little overwhelmed," Lelani said. "I didn't want her to have a meltdown in front of all your friends."

"She seems perfectly fine to me." Mrs. Mendez held out her hands to Emma. "Want to come with Abuela?"

But Emma didn't reciprocate.

"You go back inside, Mom," Gil told her. "We'll be along shortly."

Other guests were starting to trickle outside too.

"Everything looks very festive," Lelani told her.

"And you see that I remembered you wanted Emma to wear pink?" she said hopefully.

"I see that." Lelani nodded.

"There's lots of food," she continued. "And we have the piñata and birthday cake and presents and—"

"Yes, yes," Gil said a bit impatiently. "I'm sure you have a lot to do, Mom. Just let Emma chill for a while, okay?"

"But you will bring her back inside," she pleaded, "so everyone can see her?"

"Of course," Lelani assured her.

"It looks like the party's coming out here anyway," Gil said.

"Hey, there's Auntie Megan and Auntie Kendall," Lelani told Emma. And soon they were joined by a more familiar set of faces.

"Happy birthday, Emma," Megan told her.

Kendall planted a kiss on Emma's head. "Happy birthday, princess." She tweaked a ruffle. "Let me know if you need a new fashion consultant," she said quietly, and they all laughed. Emma clapped her hands and laughed too.

"Where's Auntie Anna?" asked Lelani.

"In the kitchen," Megan said.

"Someone should tell her to come out here and see her niece," Gil said.

"We already did," Kendall told him. "But she's in a stubborn mood."

"Is Edmond with her?" Lelani asked.

"No," Megan said. "Besides you and Gil, we're all dateless tonight."

"Don't remind me," Kendall told her. "I've been seriously missing Killiki today. I tried to talk my parents into flying them and me over to Maui just so they could meet him. They were actually thinking about it."

"Seriously?" Lelani wanted to suggest that perhaps they could stay at her parents' guest house but knew it wasn't a good idea.

"Yeah. But then my dad went online to price tickets. So much for that idea."

"You should tell your mom that you'd settle for less of a wedding in exchange for a Maui trip," suggested Megan.

"Too late for that." Kendall sighed. "She's already booked this winery that her friend owns."

"A winery?" Megan frowned. "You're getting married at a winery?"

"It's actually a gorgeous location. But not cheap." Kendall shook her head. "Nothing about this wedding is going to be cheap."

"Except your dress," Lelani reminded her.

"Even that's turned into a battleground."

"Why? That dress is absolutely perfect," Megan told her.

Gil laughed and reached out for Emma now. "Come on, Emma, why don't you and I escape all this wedding talk."

But Emma just sat there looking at him.

"Come on, Emma," Lelani urged. "Don't you want to go with Daddy?" They had begun calling Gil "Daddy" shortly after the engagement. It just seemed less confusing that way.

"Want to come dance with Daddy?" Gil asked sweetly.

"Da-da."

"She said Da-da," Gil exclaimed.

"Da-da!" she shouted again. And then Emma stuck her hands out and went to him. They all laughed and clapped, and Gil danced her around the pool as she said "Da-da," over and over.

Eventually they went inside, mixed a bit with the guests, and Lelani got to meet the mystery woman who'd escorted Emma into the party (a second-cousin named Molly—or was it Sally?) as well as a lot of other relatives whose names Lelani would never be able to keep straight. Then they filled brightly colored plates with food and reconvened by the pool, where, to Lelani's relief, Anna joined them.

"So they let you off KP," Megan teased.

"I don't mind helping," Anna told them. "Sometimes it's easier than mingling."

Lelani nodded. "I understand."

"Happy birthday, Emma," Anna told her. "You're quite the party girl, you know."

"Time for the piñata," Mrs. Mendez was calling out.

"Oh, great." Gil groaned. "Time to beat and murder the poor piñata again."

Anna grimaced. "Remember the time Elisa almost put out Danielle's eye with the stick?"

Gil laughed. "It seemed like someone was always getting hurt."

"It sounds brutal." Lelani clung to Emma. "I'm not sure I want—"

"Bring out the birthday girl," someone was calling now.

Gil reached down for Emma. "Don't worry, I'll protect you."

Fortunately, they didn't blindfold Emma. Gil held her up while she swung the stick, and someone had rigged the piñata to release the goodies before it was beaten senseless. Finally, after the breaking of the piñata, the eating of the cake, and the unwrapping of a small mountain of gifts (with the help of some young cousins), Lelani could tell that Emma was getting close to that place of melting down.

"We should be going," she told Gil's mother. "But thanks for everything. It really was a wonderful party."

Mrs. Mendez smiled. "Oh, I'm so glad you liked it." Then she turned to the others. "Everyone say good night to the birthday girl." Lots of birthday wishes and good-byes were shouted out.

"Thank you all for coming," Lelani called back.

"And we'll party again," Gil's mom called out, "just one month from now at the big wedding!" This was followed by more cheers and congratulations. Gil called out good-bye, opened the front door, and led the trio into the cool fresh air.

"Did I just hear your mother inviting everyone in there to the wedding?"

Gil shrugged. "It sure sounded like it."

"What will we do?"

"Let Anna and Mom sort it out."

"Poor Auntie Anna," Lelani said to Emma.

He nodded as he opened the door to the truck. "Poor Auntie Anna."

Seventeen

Megan

"Okay, class," Megan said loudly, "that was very amusing, but let's get back to our projects." She'd just sent Jackson to the office—the third time this week—after catching him smoking in the ceramics room. He vehemently denied it and had hidden the cigarette somewhere, but she could smell the smoke, both on him and in the room. It was a wonder the smoke alarm hadn't gone off. The class was all excited now and seemed unable to settle down and focus on their work. Megan wondered if she'd ever manage to control these kids. How did anyone do it?

Finally the day ended and Megan went down to the teachers' room to get a bottle of water. Still feeling somewhat out of place (and slightly like an imposter, since she felt she hardly deserved the title of teacher), she tended to avoid the teachers' room. After all, wasn't that where the "real" teachers hung out?

"Hey, Miss Abernathy," said one of the guy teachers, "how goes it down in the artsy corner of the campus?"

She tried to remember his name but came up blank. "For starters, you can call me Megan. Half of my class does anyway."

"Join the club," said a woman in the corner grading papers. Megan thought her name was Becky and that she taught French or Spanish or maybe both. "If you want respect, get a job at Starbucks."

163

Megan laughed. "That's occurred to me. I hear they have a great health plan."

"I'm Harris." He stuck out his hand and shook hers. "I don't think we've actually met. I teach eighth-grade English, and if you think art is hard, you should try that."

"Do they actually learn anything?" she asked.

He chuckled. "Hard to tell. But I just keep on trying."

"How long have you been teaching?" He didn't seem that old and also was rather attractive. Not that she was looking. She certainly wasn't looking!

"This is my third year, but it feels more like thirty."

"Does it get easier?"

He grinned. "Do you want the truth?"

"No." She shook her head. "I probably can't handle the truth."

"At least you got here on the tail end," Becky said. "By this time of year, we're counting the days until school's out."

"What is it now?" Harris asked.

"Nineteen, can you believe it?"

"Nineteen," Harris said dreamily. "It almost seems doable."

"Well, I'm outta here," Becky said as she shoved her papers into a bag. "Happy weekend, you guys."

"You too," Megan called. She turned to Harris. "Nineteen days might sound doable to you, but I'm still measuring my days by hours and minutes."

He nodded. "I know how that goes."

"So, do you have any tips?" she asked hopefully. "Any secret ways to maintain, make that *restore*, order?"

"First of all, you can't control them."

She nodded. "I'm sort of getting that. But if you can't control them, how do you get them to do what you want?"

"It helps if you make them think they want to do it too."

She considered this.

"I know that Heather used to run her classroom rather loosely."

"Loosely?"

"Yes. Art was one place where kids could sort of let their hair down, if you know what I mean. Probably one of the reasons she's got some of the rowdy kids in there."

"But how did she control—okay, not control. How did she keep it from being total chaos?"

"She played music. Seems like she was into bluegrass."

"Bluegrass?"

"Not the real twangy kind of bluegrass, but some of the newer stuff. Folk music too. She said it brought out the creativity in them."

"Okay." Megan was making mental notes. "Anything else?"

"Sometimes she brought them donuts."

"Donuts?" Megan shook her head. "Meaning I have to bribe them to like me?"

He grinned. "You do what it takes."

"Okay, food and music. I got that. Anything else?"

"Mostly I think you just need to relax. I think these kids are really reflective, whether they know it or not. If the teacher is uptight, they get uptight, only their kind of uptight is to act out. You need to get comfortable with them, Megan. Just be yourself and I'm sure they'll lighten up."

"That's actually sounds like really good advice."

"The proof of the pudding is in the eating."

She laughed. "Haven't heard that one in a while."

He looked slightly embarrassed. "I'm a sucker for colloquialisms. I even collect them in a little black book."

"I guess there are worse hobbies." She was making her way to the door now.

"Speaking of hobbies," he said as he followed her out into the hallway. "I assume that you're single since you go by *Miss* and I don't see a ring."

"You're right, I'm single, but I do have a boyfriend." She said this quickly, then partially regretted it, since it was probably an overstatement. She had *thought* she had a boyfriend, but saying good-bye to Marcus this week hadn't exactly *felt* like it. Oh, sure, they had kissed, but it was brief and not anything like the farewell kiss she had hoped for. In fact, she wondered if Marcus had been sending her a not-so-subtle message.

"Ah, yes, the boyfriend." Harris smiled. "I should've known."

"He just left for Zambia," she said a little sadly.

"Zambia?" Harris's brow creased. "What's he doing there?"

"Good question. I think he plans to dig wells or something."

"How long will he be gone?"

"I'm not really sure."

"But you're sure he's your boyfriend?" Harris looked hopeful.

Megan shrugged. "I guess I'm not positive." Suddenly she felt on the verge of tears. "I'm sorry, Harris," she told him, "but I guess I'm still feeling a little blue. And it's been a hard week."

He put a hand on her shoulder. "I'm the one who should be sorry, Megan. I sometimes come on a little too strong. And I totally respect that you have a boyfriend. If you need any more teacher advice, though, please feel free to ask."

"Thanks." She nodded and swallowed against the hard lump that was growing in her throat. "I appreciate that. A lot. And now I have a ceramics room that needs attention." She turned and walked away, but she could feel his eyes on her as she moved down the hall. While this unexpected masculine attention felt nice, she wished it was Marcus watching her instead. And she wished that Marcus would call or e-mail or send a letter or something! He had told her before he left that communication would be sparse at best and not to expect much. But still!

⋙⋘

With exactly four weeks until wedding weekend, things at Bloomberg Place were hopping. Megan actually welcomed this distraction. It allowed her to block out the trauma of teaching kids who didn't seem to want to learn, as well as the sadness of missing Marcus. She didn't really expect him to call, but she had hoped he would. If for no other reason than to simply say he'd made it there safely. But she told herself, "No news is good news," and left it at that.

"I just do not understand why you want to wear a *discount* wedding dress," Kendall's mom was saying for the umpteenth time. All four housemates and Mrs. Weis sat around the dining room table working on a project that she had insisted they all needed to help with—hot-gluing ribbon and lace around small flowerpots. They'd fill these with foam and moss and miniature rosehip topiaries, then use them "not only to grace every table, but to be party favors as well," she had told them with enthusiasm. Megan wondered why Mrs. Weis hadn't picked something simpler, like fresh flowers in clear vases anchored with pebbles and small shells, which is what she was planning to do for Lelani's wedding dinner. So she wasn't about to suggest it now.

"Have you actually seen Kendall's dress?" Lelani asked in a slightly impatient tone.

"Of course I've seen it."

"And you don't think it's lovely?"

"Lelani helped me pick it out," Kendall said hopefully.

"You mentioned that already, Kendall." Mrs. Weis frowned at Lelani now. "I realize you're both getting married on the very same day, which I must admit seems a bit odd to me, but I hope that there isn't any competition going on between you." She chuckled. "I raised four daughters, I know how it can be between girls."

Lelani looked stricken.

"There is no competition between Lelani and Kendall," Megan said. "It's not like that all."

"Not at all," Kendall said firmly.

"That's right." Lelani set down her pot with a thud. "I really think the dress we picked for Kendall is beautiful."

"Have you seen the dress *on* Kendall?" demanded Megan.

"Well, no—"

"Kendall," commanded Megan, "Go and put it on."

"Yes!" Kendall stood. "Great idea."

"I'll help you," offered Lelani, who looked close to tears.

It was very quiet at the dining room table. Only Megan, Anna, and Mrs. Weis were working, but the silence was so thick that Megan finally felt the need to say something. She cleared her throat.

"Just so you know, Mrs. Weis," she began carefully, "Lelani probably doesn't have a single competitive bone in her body."

Anna nodded. "That's right."

"Oh, nonsense." Mrs. Weis waved a hand dismissively. "All us girls are a little competitive sometimes, especially when it comes to weddings and dresses and—"

"I'll admit I can be competitive," Megan said, "and I'll admit I can be territorial and protective occasionally. But Lelani definitely is not."

"And," continued Anna, "Lelani is one of the sweetest people I know."

Megan wanted to add, "Unlike Kendall," except the truth was, that had changed. That was the old Kendall. They were seeing a new side of Kendall these days. Mrs. Weis might do well to follow her daughter's example.

"Here comes the bride! Big, fat, and wide!" Kendall sang loudly as she came down the stairs.

They all got up and went out to see. She not only wore the gown, but Lelani had put her hair up and placed a pretty sparkling tiara sort of thing in her hair. And Kendall was glowing.

"Wow!" Anna nodded. "You look fantastic."

Megan actually whistled.

"Well ..." Mrs. Weis studied her daughter as she came down the last few steps. "I suppose that will be okay."

"I'd say it's a lot more than okay," Megan tossed back.

"I think the most important thing is that I *like* it," Kendall proclaimed. "After all, it is *my* wedding." She laughed. "Well, mine and Killiki's. I wish I could get his opinion on the dress."

"He's going to love it," Lelani assured her.

"Fine, fine, Kendall. Now go upstairs and take it off before you get it dirty," her mother told her. But as soon as Mrs. Weis turned around, Kendall did a little happy dance and gave them all two thumbs-up, mouthing, "Thanks!"

With a small sense of satisfaction, Megan picked up the glue gun and attacked the next pot. "How many of these are we doing?" she asked.

"About a hundred."

Anna and Megan exchanged glances but said nothing.

"Oh, and before I forget, you girls need to go to Jean Pierre's Atelier by the end of next week for your fittings."

Megan controlled herself from saying, "Oo-la-la."

"What color did you finally decide on?" Anna asked with what seemed like only polite interest.

"Fuchsia," she told them, "but not a loud fuchsia."

"Now there's a color everyone looks good in," said Megan as she patted her strawberry-blonde hair. Fortunately Mrs. Weis didn't detect the irony in her voice.

"Yes, Kendall's sisters are all summers, so they are cool palettes. And I'm sure that Lelani and Anna are both winters, also cool." She frowned at Megan now. "Although I suppose you're a warm palette."

Megan knew enough about colors to know what she was talking about. "I'll just be sure to wear some fuchsia-toned lipstick and blush."

"Yes, that might help."

Of course, Megan had no intention of wearing fuchsia-colored makeup. She'd look like a clown.

"Hey, what about Marcus's sister's wedding?" Anna said. "Are you still going to that?"

Megan considered this. "Well, I did receive an invitation, although I'd planned to go with Marcus."

"Will he back in time for the wedding?"

"I'm not sure. But I thought he was going to be in it, at least to usher or something."

"Oh, ushers are easily replaced," Mrs. Weis told them. "Goodness, I remember Katie's wedding. The attendants to both the bride and groom kept changing their minds. It's a wonder we were able to get them lined up at all when the day finally came."

"I can just imagine," Megan said, trying to hold in her sarcasm.

"How many attendants in Kendall's wedding?" Anna gave Megan a warning look, like she'd better start minding her manners.

"Six," Mrs. Weis proclaimed. "Kendall's three sisters—Kate, Kristin, and Kim—plus you three makes six. So we have a perfect seven with Kendall."

"That is, if my sisters agree to be in it," Kendall said as she and Lelani rejoined them.

"Of course they'll agree. Weren't you in all their weddings?"

"Sort of." Kendall's brow creased. "I was like six when Kim got married, so I had to be a flower girl. Then I was only thirteen at Kate's wedding, so I was a junior bridesmaid. And when Kristen almost got married I was finally going to be a real bridesmaid, but the whole thing was called off."

"Yes, well, anyway, I'm sure your sisters will participate in yours."

"And they'll be like the oldest bridesmaids ever." Kendall laughed.

"And Kendall's brothers, Kevin and Eric, will fill in for some of the groomsmen." Mrs. Weis looked at Kendall now. "Did you and Killiki figure out the rest yet? We need to get those tuxes ordered, pronto!"

"Yeah, who are your groomsmen?" Megan asked.

"Killiki is bringing his buddy Aaron to be his best man. And Gil agreed to participate too." Kendall looked hopefully at Anna now. "Do you think Edmond would be—"

"I think he might have his hands full with that bar mitzvah. He told his dad he'd help with some of the preparations."

"Oh, right." Kendall looked at Megan now. "And I suppose you can't really say for Marcus."

"Not really."

"Well, I'm sure we can dig up a couple more guys," Kendall said lightly.

"Oh, yes, of course," her mother said, "just go out and dig them up."

"Gil and I have lots of cousins," Anna offered, "and some of them are pretty experienced at weddings."

"Are they as good looking as Gil?" asked Mrs. Weis.

"Oh, Mom." Kendall just shook her head and Anna made a funny face and Lelani started laughing.

"Maybe Anna can have them send portfolios with all their vital statistics and headshots," Megan teased. When Mrs. Weis wasn't looking, she winked at Kendall. Getting to know Kendall's mom explained a whole lot. Or as her teacher-friend Harris might say, "The apple doesn't fall far from the tree." But at least Kendall had started to grow up.

Eighteen

Kendall

"I want to pull my hair out and scream," Kendall told Killiki after they finished their online counseling session and were talking in private.

"Oh, but you were great tonight, Kendall. You did all your homework and everything."

"Not because of that." Kendall leaned back onto her bed and sighed. "That was the best part of my day."

"Then why do you want to pull your hair out? And it's such pretty hair."

"My mother."

"Oh, that."

"Yes. That. She is driving me crazy with her wedding madness. And she's driving everyone else crazy too."

"That's too bad. But you know what they say: What doesn't kill us makes us stronger, right?"

"But right now I feel like killing my mother."

"Oh, Kendall, that's not good."

"I know."

"We need to respect our parents."

"What exactly does that mean? Am I supposed to respect her when she's hurting my friends' feelings? Or when she's making the flower lady feel bad? Or when she's acting like a spoiled brat because she can't have the exact pair of shoes that she's certain would be perfect with my dress, when I really don't care that much?"

"Tell her you'll go barefoot."

"I cannot wait for you meet to my mother." Kendall laughed. "I'm actually kind of thankful that you won't get here until the wedding. She might make you want to run for your life."

"She must be a good woman to have made a daughter like you."

Kendall closed her eyes. "Oh, Killiki, I really don't deserve you. When I think of all the stupid mistakes I've made in my life … when I think about how shallow I've been, and sometimes still am! Like you should've seen me flipping out when my mom said I couldn't wear flowers in my hair."

"She said no flowers in your hair?" Killiki sounded seriously disappointed.

"She said it was tacky and something a hippie from the sixties would do. So we got into it right there in the flower store, and I actually threw a temper tantrum. I said I would have flowers in my hair and no one would stop me, and if she didn't like it, she could just go get in her motor home and drive it over the edge of a cliff."

"You said that?"

"Yeah, I'm not proud of it. But the flower lady kind of liked it. She agreed that I should wear flowers in my hair."

"So did your mother come around?"

"I'm not sure. I think we're still at a standoff. I decided not to discuss it anymore, but I'll order the flowers on the sly and when the time comes, I'll get my way."

"I think you'll look beautiful with flowers in your hair. Or even without. I just wish your wedding preparations weren't such an unhappy thing."

"It wouldn't be if my mother would back off."

"It makes me wish we'd just gone with a simple ceremony over here, but I really want to meet your family. By the way, did your dad tell you we talked yesterday?"

"You did?"

"He seems like a nice guy."

"He actually is. But he refuses to participate or take sides in any of these wedding conflicts."

"Smart man."

"I guess."

"So maybe you should give yourself a break, Kendall. Why not take a day or two off from all this wedding planning? Really, how can there be so much to do for just one day?"

"I think my mom lies awake at night plotting new and improved ways to complicate this wedding so much that no one will enjoy it."

"I'll enjoy it."

"I hope so."

"But, seriously, Kendall, give it a break. If you were here, I'd say go hang at the beach and just relax. Float in the water and feel your baby swimming."

"It's been moving a lot lately. My OB doc asked if I wanted to know what gender it was when she did the ultrasound this week and I said absolutely not."

"What do you want it to be?"

"Like I keep saying, just healthy."

"I think a little girl like you would be nice."

"How about a little boy like you?"

He laughed. "Well, it would be a real miracle if he looked like me."

"Well, next time around then."

"For sure."

"But maybe I'll take your advice and take a break tomorrow. I've been wanting another Nana Day."

"Yes," he said eagerly. "You had so much fun when you and Nana went to Paris. Why not do it again?"

"Only this time we'll go to Rome." Kendall thought. "Or Maui."

"Wherever you go, make sure you call and tell me all about it."

"Okay then. If I want to get up early enough to get out of here before Mom blows in, I'll need to get some sleep."

"Yes, it must be late there."

"I love you, Killiki." She smiled at the photo on her bedside table. It was of the two of them, taken on the day she left Maui. She still had on her cast, but she looked utterly happy. They both did.

"I love you too, my sweet mermaid princess. Sleep well."

"You too."

⋲●⋌

Unfortunately, Kendall slept a little too well. It was nearly nine when she woke up and hurried to get dressed. She actually took a couple minutes to pen her mom a quick note, which she planned to leave on the dining room table. Really, how could her mother fault her for going to visit Nana? Not that her mom was terribly close to her mother-in-law, but she should appreciate that Kendall was.

She was just about to put the note on the table when her mother burst into the house. "Good morning," she sang out.

"Uh, hi, Mom." Kendall put the note behind her back.

"What's that?" her mom asked curiously. "A surprise?"

Kendall sheepishly held out the note. "I was leaving it for you."

Her mother snatched the note and read it. "Oh, is that all? I thought maybe you and Killiki had decided to bail on your wedding."

"No, of course not."

"Your father said he sounds like a very nice young man."

"He is."

"I wish he could come over here sooner than just three days before the wedding."

"He's got work."

"How busy can a plumber be in Maui?"

"As busy as anywhere. Besides, he already bought his ticket."

"He could change it." Her mom crumpled up the note now. "You won't be needing this."

"So you don't mind then?" Kendall reached for her bag.

"I do mind. You're not going anywhere, Kendall."

"But I—"

"We have a whole list of things to do today."

"A list?"

Mom reached into her purse and pulled out an actual list and handed it to Kendall.

1. Wedding veil

2. Shoes

3. Decide on cake flavor

4. Order embossed napkins in pink or fuchsia or both?

5. Decide on menu—chicken or beef to go with fish?

6. Order rental tableware—something sleek and elegant

7. Decide/order tablecloths in pink or fuchsia or both?

8. Orchids—we need orchids!

"This won't take long," Kendall said pointing to the list. "Item one, *no*. Item two, don't care. Item three, vanilla. Item four, both. Item five, chicken. Item six, whatever. Item seven, both. Item eight?" She looked at her mom. "Why do we need orchids when we already settled on our flowers?"

"Because I just realized your wedding colors are like orchids, and orchids will be the perfect flower because they are tropical." She smiled triumphantly. "You know, like Maui!"

Kendall brightened. "Oh, yes, that does make sense."

"But it also means we need to go back to the florist and change our order."

Kendall remembered the look on the petite Asian woman's face. She knew she would not be pleased to see them back again so soon. "Why don't we let that cool for a day or so?"

"Because orchids must be ordered in advance."

"Then you take care of it while I go visit Nana."

"You are not going to visit your grandmother, Kendall. Not when you have so much to do and to decide."

"I just told you my decisions, Mom, and now I'm going to see Nana. She's not getting any younger, you know."

"Oh, that reminds me, we'll need to find her something to wear to the wedding too."

"That's what I'll do today," declared Kendall. "I'll take Nana dress shopping. She'll love it. We can get her some shoes and—"

"No, if anyone is taking her shopping, it will be me. Besides, you're not supposed to shop by yourself, remember?"

"I would be with Nana."

"Fine, but you can do that later. Next week even."

"I want to do it today!" Kendall felt a tantrum coming on.

"Don't act like a child."

"I am the child." Kendall stomped her foot. "I want to go see Nana and you cannot stop me. I already answered everything on your dumb list anyway."

"My dumb list?" Her mother was getting angry.

"Sorry, Mom. It's not really dumb. I'm just tired of wedding stuff. And really, didn't I answer all the questions? I can write it down if you—"

"But I left one thing off that list and it's very important and it must be done today, Kendall."

Kendall did not believe her. "What?" she asked with narrowed eyes.

"It's something we both completely forgot. Hopefully it's not too late, although Anna told me she's already sent the invitations, but she can probably do an e-mail."

"E-mail for what?"

"In our rush, we completely forgot to register you for china and silver and linens and all—"

"I don't want china and silver and—"

"Of course you do."

Kendall considered this. "Okay, I guess I really do. But do we have to do that today?"

"It's less than four weeks to your wedding? Do you understand what that means?"

"That Killiki and I will be married and on our way to Maui." Kendall sighed. "Four weeks feels like forever."

"*Kendall!*" Mom bopped her on the head.

"What's that for?"

"Welcome to reality." Her mother jingled her keys. "Now let's go."

"I can't believe you're not going to let me see Nana today." Kendall made a pout. "I'm going to tell Daddy."

"You can't. He's golfing all day and I'm sure his phone is off."

Kendall reluctantly followed her mom without speaking out to the little SUV they dragged along behind their motor home.

"You should be thanking me, Kendall." Mom said as she drove toward the city. "We come all this way, go to all this effort, not to mention expense. And I manage to throw you together what promises to be a very nice wedding and all I get from you is grief. I don't know how I managed to raise such ungrateful children."

"I'm sorry, Mom." Kendall felt guilty now. "I know you're going to a lot of work. But the truth is, I never wanted a great big fancy wedding. I would've been fine with—"

"You would've been fine getting hitched barefoot and pregnant," Mom snapped. "I know. How do you think that makes me feel? It's bad enough that you got pregnant out of wedlock. But my friends told me I was old-fashioned to hold that against you. They said that's what all the girls are doing these days, and that there's no shame in it. And I'm trying to be understanding, but do you think it'll be easy for me to see my big pregnant daughter waddling down the aisle, Kendall? With all my friends there, acting all PC yet chuckling among themselves at my expense? Have you any idea how I feel?"

"I do now." Kendall slumped down in the passenger seat. "I'm sorry that I'm such an embarrassment to you, Mom."

Her mom sat up straighter, holding her chin firm. "Well, I probably shouldn't have said all that, Kendall. But I'm just trying to be honest with you. All this wedding planning comes with some hidden costs. It's not easy on your father either. Oh, he may joke and act like everything's peachy, but trust me, he's embarrassed too."

Kendall turned eagerly to her mom. "Do you want to call the wedding off?"

"Of course not. Why would we do that?"

"To avoid further embarrassment?"

"Look, Kendall, if you would just try to cooperate with me for this wedding, that might help us all to avoid further embarrassment. The key to smoothing these things over is to put on a good show. And that is exactly what we intend to do."

"A good show."

"Speaking of a good show, have you done that paternity test yet?"

"No. It puts the baby at risk."

"Nonsense. People do it all the time."

"Maybe in movies and TV, but Lelani said—"

"What does Lelani know?"

"She's a med student and she knows a lot. She said that ..." Kendall struggled to remember. "The procedure is invasive and puts the baby at risk of a miscarriage. Do you want me to have the test, then miscarry the baby?"

"Of course not."

"Why are you so concerned about a paternity test anyway?"

"Well ..."

"Why, Mom?"

"I might've let it slip out that the father of the baby is a celebrity."

"No way!" Kendall sat up straight. "Why would you do that?"

Her mom didn't answer.

"Mom?"

"I don't know, Kendall. Maybe it made me feel better about the situation."

"Why?"

"Well, think about it. Your baby's father is a movie star."

"My baby's father is a plumber," Kendall snapped.

"Killiki is the baby's father? But you said that—"

"Killiki is going to be the baby's *real* father. His biological father is something totally different."

"Yes, I know, but Matthew Harmon is the baby's father? Right?"

Kendall turned away and stared out the passenger side window.

"He is, isn't he?"

"What difference does it make?"

"It makes a lot of difference, Kendall."

"I don't see why."

They were both silent as her mom exited the freeway. Kendall wished she'd stood up to her mom and visited Nana. Killiki had told her to take a break today. More than ever, she needed it. Well, tomorrow was her day to watch Emma. That in itself would be a break. Then tomorrow night, she would set her alarm clock to go off early, and she would get dressed and leave the house before her mother had a chance to corner her again. And then she would have a Nana Day. This time they would go to Maui. Kendall would scout out all the Hawaiian shops and restaurants, and maybe she'd even buy them both leis to wear.

Knowing that she had an escape plan made it easier for Kendall to play the happy bride as she "helped" her mother to make boring decisions about what shade of pink the wedding napkins should be and whether raspberry filling between the vanilla cake layers would look appropriate. She survived the trek through the department stores and picked a plain china pattern that she wasn't even sure she liked, and silver that she doubted they would ever use, and linens in colors that seemed terribly boring.

"Neutral is the only way to go," her mother assured her when

Kendall wanted to put a set of tropical-looking sheets on the list as well. Just for fun.

It wasn't easy, but somehow (maybe because she was actually praying for strength), Kendall didn't argue with any of this. She knew that fighting against her mother would only prolong the agony. So she decided to smile and get it over with. Tomorrow would be a whole new day.

Nineteen

Anna

"Did you know that Lucy is telling everyone that she and Edmond are dating?" Chelsea had trapped Anna at her desk, where Anna was quietly minding her own business and eating a cup of soup during her lunch hour. Why Chelsea had decided to become Anna's best friend was a mystery. Despite Anna's cool response to Chelsea's friendliness, the girl was relentless. Perhaps Anna's best defense was to simply go along with it.

"I hadn't heard that," Anna admitted. "But then I don't spend much time in the break room either."

"I know. Everyone thinks you're a workaholic, Anna. You make the rest of us look bad." Chelsea laughed like that was supposed to be a joke. "Anyway, it's true. Lucy is acting like she and Edmond are a hot item and getting hotter all the time."

"And how does Edmond act?" Anna kept her voice even, hoping to sound nonchalant, although she was anything but.

"Edmond?" Chelsea's brow creased. "He's hard to read."

"How so?" Anna took another bite of soup.

"He's pretty quiet. And sometimes it seems like he's trying to avoid her."

"Really?" Anna felt her hopes rise.

"Other times, he acts like he's enjoying the attention. She really pours it on, you know."

"I know."

"And what about the way she dresses?" Chelsea continued. "Felicia even mentioned it the other day."

"She did?" Anna felt another twinge of hope. Perhaps Felicia would read Lucy the riot act or throw the employee handbook at her.

"Yeah, Felicia said the way Lucy dresses could change the Erlinger image."

"That's true."

"Felicia thinks Erlinger has gotten pretty stuffy and old-fashioned. She said that the cutting-edge market is younger, and that we need to do books that reflect that."

Now Anna was confused. "What does that have to do with Lucy?"

"Felicia said we should all start dressing more youthful. She even wants to bring in casual Friday so that employees can wear jeans to work." Chelsea grinned. "Cool, huh?"

Anna just shook her head. One of the things she'd always appreciated about Erlinger Publishing was that it had remained a traditional publishing company. Respectable and solid and dependable. Jeans on Friday? That seemed like a step down to Anna.

❧

Anna had been putting off this conversation with her mother. Oh, she had hinted, but her hints fell on deaf ears. But tonight, as soon as dinner was over, Anna was going to make herself clear. Crystal clear.

"Dinner was delicious," Anna told her mom as she helped to rinse plates and load the dishwasher.

"Thank you, *mi'ja*." Her mother poured herself another cup of decaf. She sat down at a stool next to the island and watched as Anna finished up.

"And that birthday party for Emma last week was great too."

"I hope Lelani appreciated it."

Anna nodded. "She did."

"Good. Sometimes it's hard to tell. She's a very sweet girl and so polite, but she keeps her feelings inside. Have you noticed?"

Anna closed the dishwasher, then stood and sighed. "Sometimes it's good to keep your feelings inside."

"Oh, no, *mi'ja*, that can make you sick. High blood pressure, heart attack, all sorts of bad things."

"But what if you let your feelings out and hurt other people as a result?"

"People forgive you."

"Right."

"Is something bothering you, *mi'ja*? Say, you never told me how things are with Edmond. I noticed he wasn't at the birthday party. Did you get over your little squabble yet?"

"It wasn't really a squabble, Mama. And everything is fine. That's not what's bothering me, okay?"

"So what is it then? Have I done something?"

"Sort of."

"What?" Her mother's dark eyes looked alarmed.

"Well, I've told you that you needed to limit your guest list for the wedding. I mean, I've told you about a dozen times. So has Lelani and Gil and—"

"Oh, that? That's nothing."

"It isn't nothing." Anna frowned at the double negative. She hated to use bad grammar. "It's something, and it matters."

"What matters?"

"That you keep inviting everyone."

"Not everyone, Anna. Just our family and friends."

"But it's too many."

"Nonsense. The more the merrier, right?"

"Wrong."

"Anna!"

"Sorry, but I've cut your list."

"You cut my list?"

"You wouldn't do it, Mama. Someone had to. And it turned out that someone was me. So if you want to get mad and express your feelings, go ahead. I can take it." Anna braced herself.

"You cut my list?" her mother asked again.

"Yes. I had to. Megan's mom's house can't possibly hold two hundred people. I had to make some decisions. I can give you the final list, or you can just be surprised. But the invitations are sent and that's all there is to it."

"How many people did you cut?"

"A lot." Anna put her hands on her hips. "Fortunately for you, Lelani's list was very small, so most of the guests are from our family and Gil's circle of friends."

Her mom was standing now, starting to pace, and shaking her head. "This is not good, Anna. Not good at all."

"This is the way it has to be, Mama. It's the way Gil and Lelani want it. And, don't forget, it's their wedding."

"Feelings will be hurt."

"And hopefully they will express themselves," Anna said a bit too loudly. "Let it all out in the open, right? So no one suffers a heart attack."

Her mother frowned. "That is not funny."

"Isn't that what you just told me?"

"This is different. You are talking about offending our relatives."

"I'm sorry. If they're offended, so be it."

Her mother started talking in Spanish. Never a good sign. Anna was tempted to sneak out when her back was turned but knew that was cowardly. Then she got an idea. "I know what you can do, Mama!"

"What, *mi'ja*? How can we stop this disaster?"

"You can send out your own set of invitations and invite everyone and anyone you want to the reception at the restaurant. Have as many as you want or as many as the building code allows. Why not?"

"I don't know. Inviting people to only the reception?"

"Lots of people do it like that. Sometimes people have very small private weddings followed by a huge reception."

"Do people bring gifts to a reception only?"

Anna shrugged. "Does it matter?"

"It matters to me."

"Why?"

"Because a reception is expensive. I expect them to bring a gift in exchange."

Anna had to laugh. "Seriously?"

"I am not joking with you, *mi'ja*."

"Well, I guess that's up to you."

"Fine then." She nodded firmly. "I will invite *everyone* to the wedding reception. No one will be left out."

"Good for you, Mama." Anna hugged her. "And now I have to go."

Anna felt relief as she drove home. Problem solved. Well, *one* problem solved. It actually felt like a very minor problem compared to her shattered love life. But how does one fix something like that? And if anyone was going to do the fixing, shouldn't it be Edmond? Yet the last she'd seen of Edmond, he was walking out to his car with Lucy.

Anna wanted to believe that Lucy was simply following him. Or stalking him. But since the two were actually having a conversation, that seemed unlikely. No, Anna told herself, it was time to get over Edmond. Just move on!

>●<

"Okay, we need to decide something," Anna told Megan. "Big shower or small shower?"

Megan pointed to the living room. "I'd say that dictates a small shower."

Anna nodded. "I have to agree."

"Is this going to rock your mother's boat?"

Anna shrugged. "If she doesn't like it, she can get one of the cousins to throw another shower—a gargantuan shower. There's no limit to how many bridal showers a person can have, right?"

"Right. And, as maid of honor, I have the right to throw any kind of shower I like, right?"

"Right."

"Then let's do this thing."

So they set to work making a guest list and addressing invitations, and since they were only including close friends and a few family members, it all fell into place quite nicely.

"Is Lelani sure these are all the friends she wants from work?" asked Megan as she held up the small list.

"That's what she told me."

"Then I think we're ready to go to the next step."

"Food?" Anna stuck another stamp on an envelope.

"I was thinking Hawaiian."

"Like what?" Anna frowned. "Want to roast a pig in the backyard?"

Megan laughed. "Not really. Let's keep it to desserts, but we can have things like pineapple, papaya, bananas, and coconut."

"Right." Anna made note of this.

"And my mom has some good shower games."

"Should the decorations be Hawaiian too?" asked Anna.

"Yes. Let's keep the whole thing Hawaiian. But don't tell Lelani."

"How about if I handle the food?" Anna suggested. "I'll ask Gil to have Vito, our best dessert cook at the restaurant, concoct us something tropical and decadent, okay?"

"Perfect. I'll handle the decorations and prizes for the games." Megan sealed an envelope and added it to the stack.

"And we'll work out the other details later?"

"Sounds like a plan." Anna attempted a smile as she stuck on another stamp.

"How are you doing, Anna?" Megan asked gently.

"I'm okay."

"I mean about Edmond. I know you're trying to hide it, but I can tell you're still pretty bummed."

Anna felt worried now. "You haven't told the others, have you?"

"No, not at all." Megan shook her head. "And Lelani is out with Gil, and tonight is Kendall's online counseling session, so we can talk freely."

"It's just that I'm trying to keep a low profile. Everyone is supposed to be happy with all the wedding stuff and the bridal showers—you do know that Kendall's sister is giving her a shower, right?"

"I just heard that today."

"Anyway, I don't want to look like I'm the poor brokenhearted girl bringing everyone down, you know what I mean?"

"I do know." Megan sighed. "I feel kind of like that too."

"No word from Marcus?"

Megan just shook her head.

"It must be hard to communicate from Zambia."

"But not impossible."

"It hasn't been that long yet."

"I know." Megan put the last envelope on the small stack. "Mostly I just want to know he's okay."

"He's probably having the time of his life."

Megan smiled sadly. "I hope so."

"We're quite the pair, aren't we? Our own little lonely-hearts club."

"Pity party of two."

Anna kind of laughed. "Pathetic, aren't we?"

"Yeah, but let's keep it to ourselves. My heart might be lonely, but I'm not wearing it on my sleeve."

"And my heart might be broken, but no one except you knows, okay?"

Megan held her hand up like a pledge. "Our secret."

"I especially don't want Gil to know I'm down. This is a special time for him, and I don't want to spoil it. My mom was a little suspicious last night, but she's so caught up in wedding plans that I'm sure she'll forget."

Megan put a rubber band around the envelopes. "I'll mail these tomorrow. Thanks for helping."

"I needed a distraction."

"Anytime you need to talk, Anna, I'm a good listener. I kind of know how you're feeling. Probably even more than I'm letting on."

"The same to you—I mean, if you want to talk."

"So are you going dateless to the weddings?"

Anna considered this. "I don't know. Being dateless at Gil's wedding and reception is kind of like painting a great big target on my back. I'm older than Gil, unmarried, not engaged, not even dating. That's asking for real trouble."

"Why not just ask someone to escort you?"

"That's easier said than done."

"There's a nice single guy teacher at my school. I could—"

"No thanks. I don't do blind dates."

"How about someone at your work?"

"I don't know. That could get messy."

Megan nodded. "Maybe it's not such a good idea to date guys from work."

"Tell me about it." Anna rolled her eyes. "But how about you? Will you go dateless to the weddings?"

"Oh, I don't have a problem with that." Then Megan frowned like she wasn't as confident as she sounded.

"You sure about that?"

"Something just hit me."

"What?"

"Gil and Lelani are getting married in the house my dad built. The house that I had always hoped to get married in … someday. The house that will probably be sold before summer ends …" Megan eyes glistened with tears. "Suddenly it feels like I'm not only losing my dad's house and my dream wedding, but Marcus too."

Just like that, they were both crying. Hugging and crying, and crying and hugging. Anna was thankful that no one was around to witness this little scene. Really, they needed to keep displays like this one to a minimum.

Twenty

Lelani

"I'm warning you guys," Kendall said as they were getting ready to leave the house. "This shower will probably be a little stressful."

"Stressful how?" Lelani asked as she picked up Emma and slung the strap of her diaper bag over one shoulder.

"Well, for starters, my sister Kate, our hostess, is still barely speaking to me. My sister Kristen thinks that it's crazy that my parents are, in her words, throwing away good money for my ridiculous wedding. And Kim thinks I'm a total fool for getting pregnant."

"Let the games begin," Megan said.

"We're dropping Emma off at my mom's first," Anna told them. "So we'll be a few minutes behind you."

"Lucky you." Kendall made a face as they went out the front door.

"It'll probably be just fine," Lelani assured her.

Megan nodded. "I'm sure your family will have on their party manners."

"Let's hope." Kendall waved as they went to their separate cars. "See you guys there."

"Poor Kendall," Lelani said to Anna as she buckled Emma into her car seat in back. "Hearing her talk about her family makes me thankful mine isn't around to help with my wedding."

"You still have my mother to deal with," Anna reminded her. "That's bad enough."

Lelani chuckled as she got into the passenger seat. "I think she holds back a bit since I'm not actually her daughter."

"Just wait until you're married."

Lelani considered this. Perhaps it was possible that Gil's mother could become more intrusive after the wedding, but it was hard to imagine.

"Sorry," Anna said, "it's not like I'm trying to frighten you off. The good news is that Gil will stand up for you. If anyone can hold back our mother, it's Gil. He's always had a way with her."

"I've noticed."

"Speaking of your mother-in-law to be, I should probably warn you."

"Warn me?"

"Don't say you heard it from me."

"What?"

"She's putting together a little bridal shower for you."

"But you and Megan were—"

"Yes, but you know how it goes. Mama thinks ours is too small."

"I was really looking forward to it."

"And it's still on for next Thursday."

"But two bridal showers?" Lelani frowned. "Is it really necessary?"

Anna chuckled. "My mother's shower will be a chance for all our female relatives to really check you out—with permission."

"Oh." Lelani was starting to feel like a bug under a magnifying glass.

"Anyway, just so you know, it's planned for next Saturday night, and Mom's pretending that she's just having you and Gil for dinner.

But she'll make Gil leave as soon as he gets there. Poor Gil doesn't even know what's up."

"All this attention …" Lelani sighed. "It's a little overwhelming."

"At least it will be over soon."

Lelani counted the days left on her fingers. "Just eighteen days until I'm Mrs. Gil Mendez."

"You're not going to hyphenate your name?"

Lelani firmly shook her head. "No. I'm old-fashioned that way."

"That will please my parents."

"And Gil will adopt Emma, and she'll be a Mendez too." Lelani glanced at Emma, who was chewing on the ear of her bunny. "Emma Lolana Mendez."

"Pretty. Is *Lolana* Hawaiian?"

Lelani nodded. "It means 'soar.' I guess I hoped it would give her wings."

"With you and Gil as parents, I bet she will soar."

Lelani reached over and squeezed Anna's hand on the gear-shift knob. "Having Auntie Anna and such caring grandparents will help a lot too."

Anna nodded, but her eyes were sad.

"You haven't seemed yourself lately, Anna. I know I keep bugging you about it, but is something wrong?"

Anna glanced her way and smiled. "No, I was just thinking."

"Thinking?"

"Thinking how lucky Gil and you are to have found each other. And Emma too. I mean, do you ever consider how easily you and Gil might not have met? What if you hadn't answered the ad for Kendall's house? Or what if I hadn't? Then we wouldn't have met. You wouldn't have met Gil. And none of this would be happening."

"That is interesting, isn't it? I remember regretting it at first. I mean renting a room from Kendall. But then I got to know you guys … and Gil. It was almost as if the whole thing was ordained, like God had a hand in bringing us together."

"Do you really believe that?"

"Which part?"

"That God had a hand in it? I mean, do you honestly believe that God has time to get that personally involved in our lives?"

"It's still something I'm working on, the concept that God cares about someone as insignificant as I am."

Anna chuckled as she pulled into her parents' driveway. "*Insignificant* is not a word that my brother would use for you. In fact, I wouldn't either."

Anna helped Lelani gather Emma's things from the car, and then they both went up to the house.

"Here she is," declared Mrs. Mendez as they all entered the house. "My little angel girl has arrived." She extended her arms, and Emma leaned toward her.

"Thank you again for having her," Lelani said as she handed Emma over. She always had mixed feelings during this exchange. On one hand she was hugely relieved that Emma was glad to visit here. On the other hand, Lelani wished she didn't have to leave her.

"Anna," her mother said in a conspiring way. "I need to talk to you."

Anna rolled her eyes at Lelani but followed her mother into the kitchen, where they talked in hushed tones.

"Hello, Lelani," said Mr. Mendez as he came in from downstairs. "How is my favorite daughter-in-law to be?"

"I'm doing well. Thank you. How are you?"

"I'm on my way to the restaurant to iron out some squabble with the help." He took a set of keys from the bowl by the front door. "Two waitresses in love with the same cook." He shook his head. "It could get messy."

"Good luck," she called as he hurried on his way.

Just then her phone rang. Hoping it was Gil calling to solidify their plans for this evening, she answered quickly.

"Lelani? Lelani Porter?"

A shock wave ran through her as she recognized the voice. But then she told herself, *No, it couldn't be.* "This is Lelani Porter," she said stiffly. "Who's calling?"

"It's Ben."

Her knees felt weak. Not in a good way, but more like she was going to be sick. She reached for a nearby chair, easing herself down.

"I'm sorry to catch you off guard like this."

"How did you get this number?" she asked icily.

"Your mother."

She leaned over, holding her phone with one hand and her head with the other.

"How are you doing, Lelani?"

She wanted to say something horrid and mean. She wanted to ask him how he dared to call her after all they'd been through. More than that, she wanted to hang up. Instead, she asked, "What do you want?"

"To talk to you. To see how you're doing, what you're doing. I've been thinking about you and—"

"This isn't a good time," she said.

"When would be—"

"I'm sorry, but I have to go." She snapped her phone closed just as Anna emerged from the kitchen.

"Are you okay?" Anna asked as she came over and stared at Lelani with wide eyes.

She just nodded.

"You look like you don't feel well."

"Are we ready to go?" Lelani hurried toward the kitchen area. Gil's mother was just putting Emma into the highchair.

"Emma was acting hungry," Mrs. Mendez said a bit sheepishly. "I thought I'd offer her some peaches."

"That's nice," Lelani said woodenly. "But we should probably go now."

She waved her hand at them. "Yes, by all means, you two girls get going."

Lelani still felt slightly sick when they got outside. Her head was hot and fuzzy and she honestly wondered if she was going to throw up.

"Lelani?" Anna asked as they both stood by the car. "Are you okay? Seriously, you don't look well."

Lelani placed both hands on the hood of the car and leaned forward, trying to breathe deeply, willing herself to relax. Anna stood by her, waiting.

"I'm sorry, Anna." Lelani took in another deep breath and felt tears running down her cheeks now. "I just need a minute, okay?"

"Okay."

Lelani took in several more calming breaths, then listened to the sound of the birds in the trees, felt the gentle, warm breeze blowing on her face, and finally turned to Anna. "I'm sorry. I must seem like a basket case."

"You seem very sick or upset or something."

"Let's get in the car and I'll tell you about it as you drive, okay?"

Anna nodded and soon they were both in the car. Lelani calmly told Anna about the phone call. "I don't know why I felt so blindsided by it. It's not as if Ben were dead, although in my mind, I think I convinced myself that he was."

"What did he want?" Anna's voice had an edge to it. Perhaps it was concern for Gil.

"I have no idea. But I told him it wasn't a good time to talk. I wish I'd just told him that no time was a good time and that I never want to hear from him again."

"Is that how you feel?"

Lelani saw that Anna was frowning. "Yes, of course. I have absolutely no interest in him."

"But he is Emma's father."

"Biologically."

"Yes, but—"

"Gil is Emma's father. Gil is the man I love. And if I never saw or heard of Ben again, I would be perfectly happy." Lelani's hands clenched into fists. "The truth is, I actually hate him. It doesn't feel good to hate anyone. But I feel hatred toward him, and I can't believe he called."

"How did he know how to reach you?"

Her fists grew tighter. "My mother."

"Do you think she contacted him?" Anna's dark eyes looked angry.

"But why?"

"Maybe to upset things right before your wedding?"

"She's a mean, miserable woman, but it's hard to imagine she'd go that far out of her way to stir things up for me over here."

"Stranger things have happened."

"I suppose." Lelani took in another slow, calming breath.

"So what are you going to do?"

"What do you mean? What can I do?"

"Suppose he wants to see you. Or maybe he wants to be involved in Emma's life. Or what if he wants to share custody?"

"Oh, Anna!" Lelani leaned her head back and groaned. "No, that can't be what he wants."

"But what if he did?"

"Then I would fight him."

"What if he is in cahoots with your mother, Lelani, to get Emma back to Hawaii?"

"Oh, I really don't think—"

"Yes, you're right. That's pretty far-fetched." Anna shook her head. "I'm always reading those suspense books, you know. Edmond has warned me that they can mess with my mind."

Even so, Anna's words put a real fear into Lelani's heart. What if Ben had been talking to Lelani's mother? Alana could be very convincing when she wanted something badly enough. What if she somehow made Ben believe that it was his responsibility to rescue Emma and bring her back to Hawaii? No, that was ridiculous and not even worth thinking about. And yet ...

"So what are you going to do?" Anna persisted. "You could go into call history and call him back and read him the riot act. Tell him to stay out of your life and—"

"I don't think it would be wise to anger him."

"Yes, you're probably right," Anna conceded.

"But it might not hurt to set him straight." Lelani reached for her phone. "I can tell him that I'm about to be married to the most wonderful man on the planet. I'll explain that Emma is thriving and that I'm going to finish med school and that I have found family and friends and a fulfilling life here in Oregon."

"Yes!" Anna nodded vigorously. "Do that."

"I will," Lelani declared. "But if you don't mind, I'll wait until we get to Kendall's sister's house."

"Sure. Whatever."

That's just what Lelani did. After Anna parked and went inside, Lelani remained in the car, searched for the number, and then hit redial.

"I'm glad you called back." Ben's voice was as calm as it had been when they were dating, back when he had smoothly concealed from her the fact that he was married. "So tell me how you *really* are, Lelani. I've missed you."

"I'm doing very well," she began in a formal tone. "I'm getting married in a couple of weeks, and I'll be finishing my medical degree, and my daughter is delightful. Life is good. Very, very good."

"Getting married?"

"Yes. A wonderful man who loves me and Emma and wants to   "

"Ah, but do you love him, Lelani?"

"Of course I love him. I wouldn't marry him if I didn't."

"But being a single mother ..." He sighed. "I always assumed that you'd given the baby up."

"You were wrong."

"Yes, on many levels."

"What is that supposed to mean?" she snapped at him.

"This isn't a conversation I want to have on the phone, Lelani."

"I'm sorry, but that's the only way we're going to have it."

"But can't I just see you? And the baby too?"

All kinds of alarms went off in Lelani. The last thing she needed was a face-to-face confrontation with this ghost from her past. What could he be thinking? How dare he even suggest it? She suddenly remembered the ocean that separated them. "You do know that I live on the mainland now, don't you?"

"Yes. Your mother mentioned Oregon."

"So, you see, a face-to-face—"

"That's why I called. I'm at a medical conference in Portland for the next few days and I had hoped—"

"I don't know why you're doing this, Ben. I really don't want any part of it. Don't you understand? You hurt me deeply and you are a part of my life that's over and gone, dead. Can't you get that?"

"So you refuse to see me?"

Lelani didn't know what to say.

"And you refuse to let me see my child?"

"I don't know, Ben. This is all so confusing and hard."

"I don't want to hurt you, Lelani. In fact, I mostly want to tell you I'm sorry."

She closed her eyes and clutched the phone tighter. Why this? Why now?

"But if you refuse to—"

"Let me think about this, Ben. I'll get back to you, okay?"

"Okay." He sounded hopeful.

"I want to talk to my fiancé and get his opinion."

There was silence now.

"Because I love him, Ben. I love Gil and I am going to marry him."

"So you said. But as I recall you said that you loved me once too."

"That was another lifetime ago."

"And I was married."

"And you lied to me."

"I know. I'm sorry."

"I really need to go now."

"Just one more thing, Lelani."

"What?"

"I'm not married now."

Lelani just shook her head. What difference did it make? What difference did he think it would make? Even if got down on his knees and crawled across broken glass to beg her to take him back, she would not. She got out of the car, then reached into the backseat for her purse and noticed Emma's bunny had fallen on the floor. As she retrieved the bunny, she realized something on a level that really hadn't ever hit her before: The man she'd just been talking to, the man she'd just told off in no uncertain terms, the man she had once loved and slept with, was also Emma's father.

But really, what difference should that make?

Twenty-one

Megan

Megan noticed Lelani had finally arrived, but she didn't come into the great room where Kendall's sister Kate had set up the bridal-shower festivities. Instead, she lurked around the edges of the party. Perhaps she couldn't see a place to sit, since the women were packed in there like sardines. Apparently Kendall's family had lots of friends. But after a while, Megan realized that Lelani looked seriously troubled. Megan got up and made her way across the noisy room to find out.

"Are you okay?" Megan asked quietly.

"Did Anna tell you?"

Megan shook her head. "What?"

Lelani grabbed Megan's arm and pulled her into the quiet foyer. "Ben, Emma's biological father, just called."

"Why?"

"He's in Portland and wants to see me."

"Oh." Megan didn't know what to say.

Lelani folded her arms tightly across her front with a scowl. "I don't want to see him, Megan. I don't!"

"What are you going to do?"

"I have no idea." Lelani looked close to tears.

Megan put a hand on her shoulder. "You know that if there's anything I can do to help, just—"

"Will you go with me to see him?" Lelani said urgently. "I think maybe I could do it if I had someone for moral support."

"Shouldn't Gil go with—"

"I thought of that already, but I'm not sure it's a good idea. Ben is older and he sort of tries to control situations and, trust me, he knows how to do it. In fact, I think I'm just realizing that he's very manipulative. I can't stand the thought of Ben doing or saying anything to hurt Gil or put him down."

"But Gil is such a great guy, I don't see how—"

"You don't know Ben. I've seen him cut other guys to shreds and then smile as if it were nothing."

Megan frowned. "This was the man you once loved?"

"I didn't see him like that in the beginning. In the beginning I was under his spell, mesmerized."

Megan nodded sadly.

"But I can't bear to see Ben do that to Gil."

"I can understand."

"But maybe you're right. Maybe I should at least ask Gil if he wants to come with me."

"Maybe." Megan wasn't so sure. What if this Ben character really was mean and evil and vile? He certainly sounded like a nasty person. And why was he so eager to see Lelani anyway?

"I just know that I can't see him alone, Megan."

"And I don't think you should."

"I'll talk to Gil, but I'd still like you to come with me, if you're willing."

"Sure, I'll go with you." But even as Megan said this, she wondered if it was such a good idea. "You figure things out with Gil and let me know what the plan is."

"But first we better go in there and participate in Kendall's shower." Lelani took a deep breath and made an attempt at a smile.

"Kendall's sisters really are something else," Megan said in a hushed tone. "I know she can use our support."

"Thanks for your willingness to help me with Ben," Lelani whispered. "You have no idea how much I appreciate it."

Megan nodded and wished she felt as confident as she was trying to appear, but the truth was, she was not looking forward to meeting this creep. She wished she'd been able to tell Lelani as much. And yet, she wondered how she would feel if the tables were turned and she needed Lelani's help. Besides, she reminded herself, she *was* Lelani's maid of honor. Perhaps her responsibilities included telling off old beaus and sending them packing.

Megan had not exaggerated about Kendall's older sisters. They made their jabs and took their pokes in a subtle, socially acceptable way, but always at Kendall's expense. At one point, as they were standing by the refreshment table, Kim jokingly reminded Kendall and everyone within hearing distance that Kendall had been "judged mentally unstable" just last fall. Megan had to step in.

"Kendall isn't that much different from a lot of girls our age," she told Kim and everyone listening, "except that unlike some people, Kendall does seem to be learning from her mistakes."

Kendall beamed at Megan. "Why, thank you!"

"And isn't that how life is supposed to be?" Megan continued. "You do what you think is best, you make some mistakes, you get up and shake yourself off, and hopefully you do better the next time."

"Hopefully," Kim said in a flat tone.

"Come on now, everyone," Mrs. Weis was calling. "Time for the toilet-paper wedding-gown contest. You're the bride for our team, Kendall."

"I better give you some extra rolls of TP," Kate said teasingly, "because that's going to be one super-sized wedding gown." Fortunately Kendall either didn't get this or simply had the good sense to take it in stride. But Megan was starting to piece together some of the reasons why Kendall was the way Kendall was—rather, the way she had been. Megan really did believe that Kendall was changing and growing. But she was surprised that Kendall's own family wasn't a little more understanding. Megan had grown up as an only child and often felt she'd missed out on a lot by not having siblings. Now she wasn't so sure.

✂

"Why should you have to go out to meet him?" Anna asked Lelani. They were back at Bloomberg Place, and Lelani was trying to decide how to handle this meeting with her ex.

"Good point," Megan agreed In relief. Really, the last thing she wanted to do tonight was to borrow Kendall's car and drive into the city for Lelani to meet Ben. "It seems unfair that you should be the one going to the trouble of driving over to his hotel and—"

"That's right," Kendall chimed in. "You should definitely *not* go to his hotel. That's like a setup, Lelani."

"Good grief, I wasn't going to his room," Lelani said defensively. "It's nothing like that!"

"We know," Megan assured her. "But Anna brought up a good point. If Ben wants to see you, make him come here. And then you'll have all of us to back you up."

"That way Gil wouldn't have to get off work," Anna pointed out. "Not that he isn't perfectly willing."

"And you can put Emma to bed." Megan rubbed her hand over Emma's sleek hair as Kendall held the baby and swayed.

"You guys are right," Lelani said. "I'll call him and tell him that's the only way I'll meet with him. If he doesn't like it, he can take a hike."

"Yeah!" Megan reached up and gave her a high five.

"I'm going to get Emma ready for bed," announced Kendall. "You can call Ben and set this thing up."

"If you want, we'll stay out of the way," offered Anna. "I have some work I need to do anyway."

"And I have a phone appointment," called Kendall as she carried Emma away.

Lelani tossed Megan a hopeful glance. "But you'll stick around, won't you?"

Megan just nodded. At least it should be easier doing this confrontation on their own turf. If things got out of hand, she could always signal Anna and Kendall to come out and help. Surely the four of them could take down this jerk if they needed to. Not that she really expected anything that dramatic, but who knew?

By quarter after eight, Emma was asleep, Kendall and Anna were in their rooms, and only Lelani and Megan were sitting in the living room. Megan had made them a pot of green tea, decaf, because she didn't think they needed any additional stimulants. Lelani was already on pins and needles and, although Megan was trying to keep a calm demeanor, she was feeling edgy too.

"Can we pray?" Lelani said.

Megan blinked in surprise. "Yes, of course. That's an excellent idea." So they grasped hands, bowed heads, and they both prayed and asked God to take control and bring some kind of good out of this meeting. "Amen," Megan said as they heard someone at the door.

"I'll get it." Lelani slowly stood and walked in a determined way to the door.

Megan just nodded nervously, then watched as Lelani opened the door. "Hello, Ben," she said in a chilly but polite tone.

"Lelani," he said warmly. Megan saw his hand extend from behind the door and take Lelani's, but she pulled it away.

"Come in," she said coolly. "My best friend, Megan, is here. I asked her to join us."

A tall man stepped into the room, then glanced in Megan's direction. His tanned face broke into a charming smile as he walked toward her and Lelani made a quick introduction.

"A pleasure to meet you, Megan." His chocolate-brown eyes glowed as he reached for her hand, giving it a solid, warm shake.

"And you too," Megan said woodenly. She tried not to stare, but this guy was handsome, head-turning handsome.

"Please, sit down," Lelani gestured to a chair. Then she went around and sat next to Megan, just as they had choreographed it.

Ben sat down, leaning back into the chair and crossing his legs at his ankles, the picture of comfort and ease. "This is a nice place you have, ladies."

"Thank you," Lelani said. "We're renting rooms here."

He nodded. "And the baby, Lelani? Is she here too?"

Megan felt Lelani stiffen. "Yes, Emma lives with me."

"And she is well?"

"Very."

He nodded again. "Good." Now he smiled directly at Lelani. "And you're looking well too. Much better than the last time I saw you."

"You mean when I was pregnant?"

He sat up straighter and looked slightly uneasy. "That's not what I meant, Lelani. I meant that the last time I saw you, you were … unhappy. Not yourself."

"You're right," she said. "I *was* unhappy. I was pregnant, I was dropping out of med school, and I had just found out that my boyfriend was
married and that he wanted me to get an abortion."

"Who wouldn't be unhappy?" asked Megan.

Ben leaned forward now, nodding with what seemed like empa-
thy. "I understand that completely now." He looked directly at Lelani.
"That's why I wanted to tell you how sorry I am."

"Apology accepted," Lelani said.

Megan saw the hurt register in his eyes as he pressed his lips
together.

"I'm sorry if I seem a bit abrupt," Lelani said, "but this has taken
me by surprise, Ben. I honestly never expected to see you again."

"Never?"

She shook her head. "In my mind, you were gone. Dead."

He frowned. "That's a bit harsh."

Lelani took a slow breath.

"I think it's a bit harsh that you treated Lelani the way you did,"
Megan said, "and I'm surprised that she was even willing to speak to
you today."

"But you haven't heard my side of this story, Megan." He looked at
her appealingly. "You seem like a sensible woman. I'm sure you would
want both sides of the story."

Megan glanced uncomfortably at Lelani, who was saying nothing.

"Or maybe I'm wrong. Maybe there's nothing I can say."

"I can't imagine there's anything you could possibly say that
would change my opinion of what you did to Lelani," Megan told
him. "I've shared a home with her since last September, and I've never
seen a more tortured person. Not only was she devastated over how
you treated her, but she was coerced to leave her baby with her parents.

She came over here sad and alone and broken, trying to piece a life together, struggling to get by. But now she's finally happy and has so much to look forward to and—"

"I'm fully aware that Lelani plans to get married," he said this more to Lelani than Megan. "But I question whether that's what she really wants."

"Don't speak as if I'm not here," she told him.

"I'm sorry." His brows arched slightly. "But I assumed that Megan was doing your talking."

"I'm only trying to support her."

He gave Megan a half smile. "Is that because she was afraid to be alone with me?"

Megan frowned. "I don't think she was afraid. More like uncomfortable."

"And why do you think that is, Megan?"

Megan was at a loss for words.

"Do you think it's possible that Lelani still loves me? That she was afraid that seeing me again could come between her and … what's his name again?"

"Gil." Lelani said sharply. "And, no, I am not afraid you could come between Gil and me."

He leaned toward Lelani, looking directly into her eyes, almost as if he thought he could hypnotize her. Megan couldn't take her eyes off of him. "I didn't only come to tell you how sorry I am, Lelani," he said gently, "but I came to tell you that I love you. I have always loved you. And I am finally free of my marriage."

"You ended your marriage for me?" Lelani's voice was skeptical.

"My marriage had been over for years, Lelani. But we both finally agreed to put it to rest. We divorced about six months ago."

"Six months ago?" Megan asked. "Why did it take you so long to—"

"I needed time to think things through. And I wasn't even sure how to reach Lelani."

"You found me easily enough when you were ready to."

"So I did," Ben told her. "And I came to you."

"You came to a medical conference," she said in flat tone.

"I came to see you."

"So you've seen me," she told him, "and you've apologized. I honestly don't think there's anything more to be said."

"Except that I love you, Lelani. I said it already, and I'm saying it again."

Lelani stood now. "Yes, I heard you, Ben. And I'm sorry, but I do not return these feelings."

Ben stood too, his eyes locked with Lelani's. "So you're throwing me out?"

"I'm not throwing you out." Lelani shrugged. "But I don't think there's anything more to say."

Megan stood too.

"What about the baby? Emma?" he asked.

"What about her?" Lelani just looked at him.

"She's my child too, Lelani."

Lelani bit her lip and looked at Megan.

"She's your child biologically, Ben," Megan said evenly. "But you haven't had anything to do with her during Lelani's pregnancy or the first year of Emma's life. You haven't been much of a father, have you?"

He didn't answer.

"Did you pay child support?"

"No, but Lelani didn't ask."

"So a mother must beg for a father to support his own child?" Megan frowned at him. "Is that how it works?"

Ben turned his attention back to Lelani. "Do you want me to send support for Emma?"

"All I want"—Lelani spoke slowly, deliberately—"is for you to walk out of my life, once and for all, and leave me alone."

"That's what you really want?" He still seemed unconvinced.

She looked straight into his eyes. "I'm sorry if I'm hurting you, Ben. But I have a feeling you'll get over it. The truth is, any love I had for you is dead now. Completely and totally dead. Can you understand that?"

He just nodded with sad, dark eyes.

"But I do have something to thank you for," Lelani's countenance softened. "Thanks to what I went through with you, I learned how to recognize what I wanted in a man. And I found that in Gil. My love for him is alive and thriving and real."

He sighed. "I understand."

"And I am also grateful to have Emma. She is the single most important person in my life and I never would've had her without you. So thank you."

"I think this is my cue to exit." He gave Megan another half smile, then turned to leave.

"Do you want to see Emma before you go, Ben?" Lelani offered gently.

He paused, then shook his head. "I don't think so."

"Okay." Lelani seemed relieved.

"I'll just let myself out."

After Ben was gone, Lelani collapsed into tears. Megan hugged her and assured her that she'd handled everything just fine, just fine. Then they said good night and went to their rooms. Megan tried not to listen as she got ready for bed, but Lelani's stressed voice carried right through the thin wall as she replayed the whole story to Gil on the phone. Then there was a long silence. As Megan got into bed, she assumed the call had ended. But then she heard Lelani's voice again. This time she sounded more like herself, calm and peaceful, and Megan suspected that Gil had said just the right things to smooth everything over.

Once again, Megan felt like Lelani and Gil really were a match made in heaven. At least she hoped so.

Twenty-two

Kendall

Monday morning, Kendall woke to the sound of her phone ringing. Naturally, it was her mother. "Hi, Mom," she said groggily.

"Sorry to wake you," her mom said cheerfully. "But they're having a big sale at Macy's and I thought you and I could—"

"Sorry, but I already have plans."

"You're babysitting Emma again?"

"No, not today."

"What then?"

"I have a date with Nana."

"Oh, well, that can wait."

"No, it can't, Mom." Kendall stood up and began pacing in her room. "I called her yesterday and promised that I was coming."

"But, Kendall, it's less than two weeks until—"

"Trust me, Mom, I know exactly how many days, hours, and minutes there are until the wedding. I also know that you and Kate deliberately didn't invite Nana to my shower last weekend."

"Who told you that?"

"Kristen. She said you were worried that Nana would make some kind of an embarrassing scene. Well, you know what, Mom? I would've liked it if Nana had made a scene. It would've been fun."

"Oh, Kendall!"

"I'm sorry I can't go shopping—" Kendall suddenly remembered something. "Hey, I'm not supposed to go shopping anyway!"

"Fine, fine. Do as you like."

"Thank you." Kendall said good-bye, hung up, and then got dressed. When she got downstairs, all three of her housemates were in the kitchen, and Megan was telling Anna about the visit from Ben.

"I want to hear the details too," Kendall said eagerly.

Lelani quietly sipped her coffee as Megan recapped how Ben had come and proclaimed his love for Lelani, and how Lelani had turned him down flat.

"You guys would've been proud of her," Megan said as she filled her to-go coffee cup. She nudged Lelani. "I mean, Ben is one smooth dude, and he was trying to say all the right stuff, and he actually kind of looks like Orlando Bloom—"

"Seriously?" Kendall was intrigued. "Orlando Bloom?"

Lelani just shrugged. "He's good-looking."

"So is Gil," Anna said.

Lelani laughed. "Yes! Absolutely! Gil is *way* better looking than Ben. And Gil's beauty is more than skin deep."

"Have you told Gil all about this yet?" Anna asked Lelani.

"Of course. I filled him in on every single detail." Lelani poured some cream in her coffee.

"Do you wish he'd been here last night?" Kendall asked curiously.

Lelani frowned. "I sort of did, but I think maybe it was better he wasn't." She grinned at Megan now. "And you should've heard Megan raking him over the coals."

"Good for you!" Anna patted Megan on the back.

"If I don't hurry, I'll miss the bus," Megan said as she grabbed up her bag.

"And I think I hear Emma now," Lelani said. "She slept in this morning, and Abuela will be here to pick her up soon."

"And I need to get ready for work," Anna added.

Then Kendall was alone in the kitchen. As usual, she took her prenatal vitamins, poured a glass of orange juice, popped some toast in the toaster, and opened up a container of yogurt. Before her pregnancy, she'd never been much for breakfast. But her OB doctor made it clear that babies get hungry before noon. As Kendall sat in the kitchen, she wondered what it would be like eating breakfast with Killiki in Maui. She'd only been to his house once, and while it was a bit on the small side and definitely in need of a woman's touch, the location was superb, and a spacious lanai looked out over the beach. Perfect for breakfast … or lunch … or a dinner at sunset. In just two weeks, she would be there with him.

As Kendall buttered her toast, she tried to wrap her head around how Lelani must've felt to suddenly have her baby's father standing in front of her and saying he loved her, and yet she had stood up to him and turned him away. Kendall wasn't sure if she could be that strong. That worried her.

"Here comes little Miss Sunshine," Lelani said as she lifted Emma into her high chair and buckled her in. "She woke up singing away."

"I hope my baby is as happy and good as Emma."

"Just think, Kendall," Lelani opened the fridge and took out the milk. "Your baby will be born in Maui. That alone should make her or him happy."

Kendall nodded eagerly. "I was just thinking about that. I mean, about living in Maui with Killiki. In two weeks we'll be there. Can you believe it?"

"Lucky girl." Lelani grinned as she filled Emma's pink sippy cup with milk, then placed it on her high-chair tray.

"So, you really told Ben off last night? And you aren't having any second thoughts?"

Lelani was opening a jar of applesauce, but her back was to Kendall.

"I'm not trying to be nosy," Kendall said. "But I am curious. I mean I was just imagining that it was me, and that Matthew suddenly showed up and said those things."

Lelani turned and stared at Kendall with wide eyes. "Would you leave Killiki for Matthew?"

"No, of course not. I love Killiki and he loves me. And we are a match made in heaven." Kendall sighed happily. "I just know that."

"And yet …?"

"I guess it's a little scary to think about. I mean, there was a time not that long ago when I thought I'd do anything to get Matthew Harmon."

"But you've changed."

"Yes. But still, wasn't it hard for you last night? I mean, seeing Ben face-to-face and hearing him say those things?" She studied Lelani's expression as she sat down in the chair next to Emma.

"It wasn't easy, that's for sure." Lelani spooned a bite into Emma's wide-open mouth. "But in a way, it felt like … closure."

"Like the end of a chapter."

"More like the end of a book. A very unhappy book."

"So you're sure that it's completely over between you and Ben?"

"Absolutely." Lelani nodded firmly.

"But what about Emma?" Kendall rubbed her own belly now. "Did Ben want to be a part of her life?"

Lelani kind of laughed. But it sounded sad. "No, I don't think so."

"So, he's really out of the picture?"

"He is for me. I guess I can't predict whether he'll ever want to be involved with Emma's life, or if she might someday want to know him, or how I would handle that if she did."

"Killiki says—actually I think it's in the Bible—that each day has enough problems for itself and we shouldn't go looking for more from the next day. Or something like that."

"Yes. I agree. No one can predict the future. For me and for Emma, the best thing I can imagine is being with Gil. Even though the wedding is in less than two weeks, it feels like a long ways away."

"I agree." Kendall stood. "Today I am having a Nana Day."

"Tell her hello for me."

"I'll do that. I think we'll go to Maui today." Kendall chuckled. She'd already told them about their France day.

"Then let me send a lei for her. It's not made of real flowers, of course, but it might be fun."

And so when Kendall went into Nana's room, she tried to ignore the smell and the general feeling of bleakness as she said, "Aloha!" Then she placed the purple lei around her grandmother's neck and kissed her on both cheeks.

"What is *this*?" Nana asked in a slightly cranky voice.

"It's a lei."

Nana's old fingers felt of it. "Not real flowers, are they?"

"No. But maybe we can find some today."

Nana peered up at Kendall. "Who are you anyway?"

Kendall just smiled. "I'm your granddaughter Kendall. And today we're going to Maui."

"Maui?" Nana's brow creased. "What's that?"

"An island in Hawaii." Kendall frowned down at Nana's pajamas. "But you're not dressed yet."

Nana just scowled and shook her frazzled looking head.

Kendall wasn't sure what to do now. Should she help Nana get dressed or call someone to help? She noticed a tube coming out from Nana's pajamas. She followed it to see that it was attached to bag half full of yellow liquid, but it took her a moment to realize it was a catheter. "Are you sick, Nana?" she asked.

"Sick and tired of this place," Nana grumped. "Can't you bust me out of here?"

"Well, I came to take you for an outing." Kendall frowned down at the bag.

"Good morning, Mrs. Weis," said a nurse's aid, who had just let herself into the room. "How are we feeling this morning?"

"*We* are feeling terrible."

"Alex said you need some help and I—"

"All I need is to get away from you people," snapped Nana. "My granddaughter is going to bust me out of here. Aren't you ... uh? What's your name again?"

Kendall sighed. "Kendall."

"And my name is Glenda," the nurse's aid said.

Nana snickered. "Glenda the Good Witch."

"If you can excuse us for a few minutes, I'll help your grandmother to get cleaned up and ready for the day."

"I ... uh ... I'll wait outside." So Kendall went out into the hall and waited. After a few minutes, she wandered down to the main desk and asked the receptionist about Nana. "It looks like she's got a catheter, and I had hoped to take her out for—"

"Oh, Mrs. Weis is restricted to the facility," the woman told her as she pointed to something in a notebook. "Looks like she's got a UTI."

"UTI?"

"Urinary tract infection. She's on antibiotics and isn't well enough to go out."

"Oh." Suddenly Kendall wanted to leave. She wanted out of this horrid place with its horrid smells. But she felt sorry for Nana. Kendall understood why her grandmother wanted out too.

"You can visit with her here," the woman said cheerfully. "I'm sure she would enjoy that just as much."

Kendall wasn't so sure, but she figured it was worth a try. When she went back to the room, Nana was wearing clothes. Her hair was combed (badly), and the bag was emptied. Glenda (the Good Witch) was over by the sink, apparently washing her hands or something.

"They told me that you can't go out today," Kendall told Nana as she sat down on the loveseat adjacent to Nana's recliner.

"What do you mean I can't go out?"

"That's right," Glenda told her. "You need to stay in residence until you're better, Mrs. Weis."

"I am better," Nana declared. "I'm clean and dressed and I'm ready to go." She pushed herself up from her chair, and Kendall didn't know whether to help or not. But as hard as Nana tried, she could not manage to stand. She was too weak.

"So, I'll just stay here with you," Kendall said pleasantly. "We can visit."

"I don't want to visit," Nana proclaimed. "I want out of this place. Now!"

"But they said—"

"I don't give a—"

"Now, now, Mrs. Weis," Glenda said as she brought over a plastic cup of water and another small paper cup with some pills in it. "No need to get upset."

"I'll get upset if I want to."

Glenda glanced at Kendall. "She had a rough day yesterday." She held out the cup with the pills to Nana. "Just take these, and you'll be getting better in no time."

"In time to go to … to some island?" Nana's brow wrinkled with confusion. "You said an island, didn't you?"

"Yes," Kendall assured her. "Maui."

"That sounds like fun," Glenda said cheerfully. "Now just take these pills so you can feel good enough to go to Maui with your grand-daughter." She chuckled. "I wish I could go too."

"You can't go. You have to stay here and take care of old people." Nana's hand trembled slightly as she tipped the cup of pills into her mouth, then reached for the water and gulped it down.

"Good for you, Mrs. Weis." Glenda took the cups and returned to the sink.

"Now I can go to … where was it?"

"Maui?"

"Yes." Nana nodded. "Now I can go to Maui."

"Not just yet," Glenda said as she gathered her things.

"When?" demanded Nana.

"When you're better." Glenda had her hand on the door, but she was looking at Kendall like she wanted to say something. Kendall got up and stood between Glenda and Nana.

"She'll be sleepy soon," Glenda said quietly.

"Why?"

"Because the doctor is keeping her sedated."

"Why?"

"Because of the UTI."

"But that shouldn't—"

"She gets agitated and tries to remove the catheter. Besides being messy, it's very painful and—"

"Okay," Kendall said. "I get it."

"Good-bye, Mrs. Weis."

Kendall closed the door behind Glenda, then turned to see that Nana still had an expectant look in her eyes. "Perfect!" Nana clapped her hands. "You got rid of Glenda the Good Witch and now you can break me out of here."

"But Nana—"

"Get my purse. And my sweater." Nana tried to push herself up again but couldn't.

Kendall didn't know what to do. So she got Nana's purse, which she set in her lap, and Nana's sweater, which she draped over her shoulders.

"I need a suitcase," Nana said.

Kendall made a pretense of looking around the room, taking her time and wondering how to deal with this. Mostly she didn't want to hurt Nana's feelings. "There doesn't seem to be a suitcase," she said finally.

Nana just nodded and sighed. Maybe the meds were working.

Kendall sat down on the loveseat again. "You'll get better, Nana. And then we'll go to Maui." Kendall started chatting at her, explaining that she was getting married and that they still needed to find Nana a dress for the wedding and that Kendall and Killiki would live in Maui and maybe Nana could come visit them in Maui for real.

Nana seemed to be relaxing.

"Do you want to lean back and put your feet up?" Kendall asked.

Nana just nodded, and Kendall helped her to adjust the recliner.

"I can't wait for you to meet Killiki," Kendall continued to ramble. "He's the one who helped me to realize how much I needed God in my life. Actually, we all need God. But Killiki made it seem so simple. You just tell God you're sorry for making a mess of things, and then you ask for Jesus to come into your heart, and you get a whole new fresh start."

"A fresh start," Nana mumbled as she closed her eyes.

"Yeah. And, let me tell you, I sure did need one. I don't think anyone is as good at making messes as I am. But Killiki loves me anyway. And he said that's how God feels too. You can be a complete mess and he still loves you."

Nana was starting to snore, and Kendall figured the sedatives had kicked in. She was disappointed that she couldn't take Nana out for their Maui trip but thought maybe it was for the best. Nana could rest up and get better, and perhaps by the end of the week, they could go shop for a dress.

But as Kendall drove home, she felt sorry for Nana and the way she seemed trapped in that nursing home. She remembered the desperate look in Nana's eyes as she begged Kendall to "bust" her out of there.

Kendall had an idea. Why couldn't they move Nana out of the nursing home and back to her own house? In two weeks, both Lelani and Kendall would be gone, and then Anna and Megan had until the end of the month to find another place. But what if Anna and Megan were willing to remain in the house? And what if their rent money could be used to hire some assistance to care for Nana?

She was so excited about her idea that she decided to call and leave messages for both Anna and Megan, saying that this could be a way for both of them to remain in the house. Megan could move her room upstairs, and the caregiver and Nana could occupy the bedrooms on the first floor. Really, wouldn't that make everyone happy?

Twenty-three

Anna

Anna didn't know what to think when she listened to Kendall's message about moving the elder Mrs. Weis back to Bloomberg Place. Her first response was to say, "No way." But the more she thought about it, the more it seemed to make sense. It wasn't as if Kendall was asking them to care for her grandmother, just to share the home with her and a full-time caregiver. This would alleviate Anna's need to move out, and so far she hadn't found anything that was both suitable and affordable. She most definitely did *not* want to move back home. It was bad enough to have lost Edmond, but to lose her independence as well? That was just more than she could bear.

Edmond had made small talk to her today. It was work related and Anna responded in a businesslike and professional manner. Decidedly grown-up. No small accomplishment, considering the fact that Lucy had been standing nearby. Lucy had been anxiously waiting for Edmond's attention. She reminded Anna of the little lapdog that Kendall once had, but Lucy wasn't even as cute as Tinkerbell.

"Rick wants to see you in his office," Lucy had announced as if the summons were a matter of national security. "It's urgent." Then, like the faithful puppy, Lucy trotted behind Edmond toward the elevators, and Anna even thought she saw her tail wagging.

"How long do interns usually stay?" Anna asked Chelsea as they ate together during their lunch hour. Today Anna had ventured to the break room. So far, to her relief, she had seen no sign of Edmond or Lucy. She tried not to imagine the two of them behind closed doors, pawing each other in Edmond's office.

"I'm not sure," Chelsea admitted. "But Lucy seems to be well liked."

Anna controlled herself from rolling her eyes.

"Felicia seems very fond of her." Chelsea frowned down at her half-eaten sandwich now. "In fact, I wouldn't be surprised if she was considering offering Lucy my job."

"Your job?" Anna was surprised.

"Everyone knows I make a mess of things." Chelsea just shook her head. "I'm sure I'll be getting my notice soon."

"Then you need to try harder," Anna said. "Unless you don't want your job."

"Of course I want it. But it seems like everything I do just goes wrong. And I'm pretty sure Felicia is fed up."

Anna studied Chelsea for a moment. Her stringy light-brown hair and poorly chosen outfit of rumpled tan cords and a wrinkled blue T-shirt (which actually had a stain near the neckline) hardly inspired confidence. In fact, Anna wondered how Chelsea had even managed to land the job in the first place.

"Do you mind if I ask what your qualifications are, Chelsea? I mean, for being Felicia's assistant."

Chelsea rattled off a rather impressive list of marketing jobs, as well as her training and her college GPA, and Anna just shook her head. "You could've fooled me," she said.

"Huh?"

"I'm sorry for being blunt," Anna said, "but the way you look, and the way you act sometimes, well, I just never would've guessed that you've had so much experience."

Chelsea looked perfectly dismal now. "I know."

"Then why don't you do something about it?"

Chelsea just shrugged. "What?"

"Change something."

Chelsea looked hopefully at Anna now. "How?"

Anna held up her hands. "You know, improve your appearance. Dress more professionally. Get your hair done. Show some confidence."

Chelsea got that hopeless expression again. "I don't know how."

"Oh, come on," Anna urged her. "You work in marketing. You know that the way we sell things is all about the packaging. But look at you, Chelsea. What are you selling?"

Chelsea just shook her head. "I've tried changing my appearance, but it never works, I always end up looking like a clown or a hooker or something. For me, frumpy works."

"Okay." Anna stood and brushed crumbs off of her neat navy skirt. "If that's working for you."

"Wait," Chelsea stood too, gathering up her uneaten sandwich.

Anna just stood there.

"Can you help me, Anna?"

Anna considered this. Really, the last thing she needed right now was another project. On the other hand, what if Felicia did decide to let Chelsea go and keep Lucy on as her replacement—permanently? Maybe it was a long shot, but maybe it was worth it.

"Here's the deal," she told Chelsea. "My hands are kind of full right now. I have two roommates getting married in less than two weeks, and I'm in both of their weddings. I have one bridal shower to help host. And I'm still trying to find a place to move into."

"Wow, you are busy."

"But if you're serious, if you really want to change your image, I'll give you one evening after work. But you'll have to trust me and agree with whatever I suggest, or else I'm walking. I just don't have time for games. Okay?"

"Okay!" Chelsea's face brightened and for a moment, Anna thought there might actually be hope for the girl. Or maybe Anna had seen *Pygmalion* and *My Fair Lady* one too many times. Whatever the case, Anna figured she could afford one night. Besides, she still needed to get wedding gifts and could use some time at the mall.

"Fine," Anna told her. "I'll call my hairdresser and see if she can squeeze you in tonight. I'll tell her it's an emergency. You meet me at my car in the parking lot right after work."

So it was that Anna booked an appointment with Vivian, dropped Chelsea off at the mall salon with instructions to make Chelsea look business-appropriate yet chic, then headed for Macy's, where she would start lining up things for Chelsea to try on. "We have to move swiftly," she'd told Chelsea. "As soon as Vivian's done, call me and we'll meet up."

Anna had never considered herself a fashion expert, but she had learned a few things from her housemates, and her sense of style was far more evolved than poor Chelsea's. She headed straight for the career section, found a salesgirl, and soon filled a fitting room with suit jackets, blouses, skirts, and trousers.

"You say she's a size ten," the girl said to Anna. "But is she a big ten or a small ten?"

Anna thought for a moment. "She's taller than I am. But then everyone is. I guess she's a big ten."

"Then I'll put some twelves in there too."

"I need to go get some wedding presents," Anna told her. "If you find anything else that seems to work, go ahead and put it in there. I'll be back in about half an hour."

The girl seemed impressed. "You really are multitasking, aren't you?"

Anna nodded. "I figured I could be getting the gifts wrapped when I come back here to help Chelsea try things on."

Fortunately, Anna already had printed out lists from the wedding registry online and knew what she wanted to get for both couples, so it didn't take long. For Kendall and Killiki, she picked up a set of tropical-colored sheets that Kendall had admitted to sneaking onto her wish list behind her mother's back. And for Gil and Lelani she chose an elegant crystal pitcher and stemware set. She arranged to get the gifts wrapped, then returned just as Chelsea was going into the fitting room.

"Chelsea!" she exclaimed. "I almost didn't recognize you."

Chelsea patted her short, feathery haircut, complete with some kind of highlighting. "What do you think?"

"It's perfect. Do you like it?"

"Like it? I love it!"

Soon they had Chelsea trying on garment after garment. When something worked, they tried to pair it with something else until finally, between the three of them, they had selected two jackets, one sweater set, two skirts and a pair of trousers.

"Are you okay with these?" Anna asked Chelsea quietly as they were sorting through the clothes one last time. "I mean they're on sale, but they're not exactly cheap."

Chelsea just laughed. "I haven't exactly invested much into my wardrobe."

"That's for sure." Anna chuckled. "But you still need to get shoes and some accessories."

"I set aside some accessories for you up front," the salesgirl told Chelsea, "just in case you were interested."

Anna never heard the total for all of Chelsea's purchases, but before they were done, they had hit the shoe department, then got some help with cosmetics. Anna knew that Chelsea's credit card had to be feeling the heat.

"Honestly," Anna said as they loaded all their things into the back of her car, "if I encouraged you to buy anything you can't afford, it will not offend me in the least if you return it."

"Are you kidding?" Chelsea carefully laid out the garment bag on top of the others. "This is an investment in my career, and I should be thanking you."

"The way you can thank me," Anna said as she drove Chelsea to her apartment, "is to start acting like you really are a professional. Someone once told me that you dress for the job you want, not the one you have. But I think you also need to act like you have the confidence for the job you want as well. First of all that means no gum chewing. No slang. No slumping. No—"

"Stop, stop!" cried Chelsea. "Let me write these things down."

Anna waited for Chelsea to extract a notepad from her slouchy looking bag. "Another thing, Chelsea, you need a briefcase. We should've—"

"I have a briefcase," Chelsea said happily. "My brother got it for me for graduation, but I always felt silly carrying it ... before."

"That was the old Chelsea."

"Right." Chelsea had her notepad ready. "Now continue."

Anna tried to remember where she was. "Okay. No putting yourself down or playing the dummy. No asking stupid questions. If you don't know the answer to something, try to figure it out before you speak.

Always use your head before you open your mouth. And always use good manners. And come prepared for meetings. Do your homework. Know what your boss needs before she even asks for it."

Anna had to repeat things a couple of times, but before long Chelsea got it all down. "Wow, Anna, how did you learn all this?"

Anna thought about it. "I guess I'd have to give my parents some of the credit, when it comes to things like manners and not chewing gum. But some things I had to learn the hard way."

"Well, I owe you big time," Chelsea told her as Anna dropped her off.

"Then make me proud," Anna said. She almost added, "And don't lose your job," but that would have sounded a little insensitive, not to mention self-serving. Anna just hoped that tonight's *Pygmalion* routine would benefit Chelsea in some positive ways. Really, that would be enough.

The next day, Anna was pleased to see Chelsea walking through the building like she was a new person. She even wore a pair of small, dark-framed glasses that looked like they'd increased her IQ by about twenty points.

"New glasses?" Anna asked quietly as they both waited for the elevator.

"I decided to ditch the contacts," Chelsea replied. "I haven't worn these since college days, but the prescription still works."

"Nice look," Anna said with approval.

They were both on their way to the same meeting, and Anna watched Felicia's eyes light up when she saw her reinvented assistant.

"My goodness, Chelsea, what happened to you?" she asked right in front of everyone. Anna held her breath, hoping that Chelsea wouldn't have a meltdown and say something dumb.

"I decided it was time to dress like a grown-up," Chelsea said calmly.

Felicia smiled. "I like it."

"Thanks." Chelsea sat down at the conference table and pulled out her notebook and pen. When she looked up, Anna gave her the slightest little wink, as in, "Go girl!"

Anna couldn't help but feel the glow of satisfaction over Chelsea's transformation. But it didn't seem to be making any difference in the Lucy department. During the meeting, Felicia asked Lucy's opinion over several things, and it was clear that Felicia continued to be impressed with Lucy's "youthful" views. Anna tried to read Edmond's face while Lucy was in the limelight. But he might as well have been playing poker. Not that she expected Edmond to be making goo-goo eyes at Lucy or anything so blatant as that. But she did remember times when Edmond openly flirted with her at times like this. Finally, the meeting ended, and Anna was relieved to get back to her desk and the happy distraction of work.

She'd barely sat down when, to her surprise, Edmond planted himself right in front of her desk area and stared at her with a troubled brow.

"What's wrong?" she asked politely.

"We need to talk." His voice was quiet, almost throaty.

She didn't know what to say, and it was hard to hold eye contact with him for more than a split second. Didn't he know how painful this was for her? Besides, hadn't they already done the breakup conversation, the one that always started with those four words? What did he want from her?

"Seriously, Anna. Can we talk? *Please*?"

"About what?" She kept her words calm, but her heart was pounding.

"About us."

Anna glanced around to see if anyone was listening, but thankfully no one was around. "What about us?" she asked in a hushed tone.

"Well, we can't talk here."

Anna pressed her lips together and looked down. Why was he doing this?

"After work?" he asked. "Can we talk then?"

"Not for long," she said without looking up. "I have to help Megan with some shower stuff."

"Okay. I'll take what I can get."

Anna still didn't look up. When he was gone, she felt like she could almost breathe again. It was hard to focus on work, though, and she began to resent his visit. What did he want from her? Everyone in the office seemed to know that he and Lucy were a couple now. Did he think that Anna would be willing to play "the other woman" against Lucy? No, that was ridiculous.

At noon, Anna wondered why Edmond hadn't simply suggested they talk during their lunch hour. As she hurried out to her car, she discovered the reason. Because there, sitting in Edmond's car, he and Lucy appeared to be engrossed in an intense and intimate conversation.

Anna turned around and went back into the building. She was glad they hadn't seen her, but she wasn't willing to risk starting her car and drawing their attention. Instead, she just kept walking, exited the front door, and went across the street to the local deli, where she ordered a bowl of soup, then sat there and watched it get cold.

Why was he doing this to her? Why? Somehow she managed to pass the hour and, despite not wanting to, she returned to work. There, to her surprise, a vase of yellow roses was dominating her desk. Assuming there had been a mistake, she checked the card. Her name was printed in block letters on the envelope. But all it said inside (again in the same block letters, which may or may not have been written by Edmond, since she'd only seen him write in cursive before) was, "Anna, you're the best!" She read the card several times, trying to interpret what it meant. Was it: "Anna, you're the best sport—as in, you'll forgive me for marrying Lucy"? Or, "Anna, you're the best choice—as in, I like you better than Lucy"? Or was it even from Edmond? And why was she obsessing over it?

Anna waited until five fifteen. Edmond didn't show. Hadn't she told him that her time was limited? She considered going up to his office but remembered the last time she'd done that and knew she wouldn't survive another similar encounter. She finally decided to leave and gathered up her things, as well as the roses, which would be nice for Lelani's shower, when suddenly Edmond appeared.

"Oh, I thought you'd forgotten," she said as they stood face-to-face, the roses like a shield between them.

"Sorry, I got tied up."

"Right." Anna tried not to look disgusted as she imagined him literally tied up with Lucy. Meanwhile, he just silently stared at the roses, and she started to get seriously irritated. "I thought you wanted to talk," she said finally.

"I did."

"But now you don't?" She knew her voice sounded harsh, but she couldn't help it. Why was he jerking her around? Didn't he know how much she'd been hurting, how she had finally started to get over him? And now he was trying to rip off the scab?

He continued to stare at the stupid roses, a puzzled frown across his brow and his lips pressed tightly together. Still, he said nothing.

"Look, Edmond, I told Megan that I'd be home early tonight," Anna said. "We have a lot to—"

"Yes, I'm sorry I wasted your time, Anna." Then he turned and walked away. She started to call out his name, to ask him to come back. But it felt as if her voice was frozen inside of her.

Lelani

"That shower was absolutely lovely," Lelani told her housemates after the guests had gone. "Perfect." She hugged each of them. "Thank you all so much."

"Don't thank me," Kendall said as she picked up a stack of used paper plates. "Megan and Anna did everything."

"It's your house," Lelani reminded her.

"Speaking of the house," Kendall said, "I've started calling around about in-home health care. It's kind of expensive. But one social-services lady told me there's a way that Nana's house can help to pay for it. First, though, I need to know for sure that you guys, I mean Anna and Megan, are serious about wanting to do this."

"I'm in," said Anna.

"Me too," said Megan. "And I could even help out with her care this summer, since I'll probably be jobless as soon as school ends."

"You could have free rent," offered Kendall. "I mean, that's not much. But it might help."

"It sounds like things are working out," Lelani told her. "I'm impressed that you're able to figure out something like this with everything you've got going on—the wedding and all."

"How do your parents feel about this idea?" Megan asked Kendall.

Kendall just shrugged.

"You haven't told them?" Anna looked slightly suspicious.

"Shouldn't you discuss it with them?" suggested Lelani. "I mean, Nana is your dad's mom. I would think he'd want to be in on something like this."

"Good idea." Kendall nodded. "I'll call my dad." She dropped the plates into the garbage, then looked at the clock and jumped. "Uh-oh, I almost forgot tonight is our marriage-counseling session. Gotta go."

"Tell Killiki hi for me," called Lelani as Kendall disappeared up the stairs. Then she turned to Anna and Megan. "Now, you two do me a big favor and go put your feet up while I finish cleaning this up, okay?"

"But this was your shower—"

"My shower and my turn to clean it up," Lelani commanded them. "Seriously, you guys did a great job; now go have a break, please!"

"If you insist." Megan sighed. "I won't deny that I'm tired."

"See." Lelani nodded. "Now go."

Megan turned and left, but Anna continued clearing the table and Lelani decided not to argue with her. Anna had been a little moody these past few days, and Lelani was starting to get worried. Was it possible she was feeling pushed out by all this attention on the wedding? Lelani was glad all that would soon be over.

"Anna?" asked Lelani when they were both washing up things in the kitchen. "Are you okay?"

"Sure." Anna made a good attempt at a smile. "I'm great."

"Seriously, Anna, have I done something to offend you?" Lelani dropped some silverware into the dishwasher. "I mean I know your mom's been giving me a lot of attention lately and there's still the Saturday-night shower that—"

"No, no," Anna just shook her head. "That has nothing to do with it."

Lelani studied her for a moment. Just by saying "it," Anna made Lelani feel that her instincts were right.

"Look, Anna," she said gently, "we're going to be sisters, right?"

Anna just nodded as she rinsed a pitcher, then sat it on the drainer to dry.

"And sisters should share things, right?"

Anna didn't say anything.

"Please, tell me what's bothering you. Maybe I can help."

Anna turned to Lelani with tear-filled eyes. "You can't help, Lelani. No one can help."

Lelani wrapped her arms around Anna, stroking her hair like she would stroke Emma's. "How do you know I can't help unless you try?"

Anna started crying harder. She pulled away from Lelani and used a dish towel to blot her tears.

"Go into the living room and sit down," Lelani told her. "I'll make us both some tea. You go ahead and have a good cry, and then we're going to talk. Okay?"

Anna mumbled, "Okay," then with dish towel still in hand, she shuffled out into the living room. When Lelani joined her with their tea, Anna had stopped crying, but her eyes were still sad and red-rimmed.

"Tea and sympathy," Lelani said as she handed a cup to Anna.

"There's really nothing you can do to help me," Anna said quietly.

"Sometimes it helps to just listen."

"But I didn't want to tell you." Anna sniffed. "This is your time to be happy. Yours and Gil's. And I didn't want to do anything to rain on your parade."

"Gil and I have so much happiness, Anna. Really, you don't need to worry. Just tell me what's wrong."

"Only if you promise not to tell Gil or Mama or anyone in the family, okay?"

"You have my word."

Anna began to pour out the sad story of Edmond and a silly girl at work named Lucy, explaining how just this week Edmond had wanted to talk to Anna and had perhaps even sent her roses, but then Anna said something stupid and it had all gone south.

"And now Edmond won't even talk to me or look at me or anything, and I'm so unhappy that I want to quit my job. But I can't afford to quit my job without going home to live with my parents. And I can't stand to do that. I just feel totally hopeless."

Lelani shook her head. "I'm so sorry."

"I know I'll be okay. But it just hurts." Anna tapped her chest. "Deep inside, it hurts. And I want it to go away."

Lelani considered this. "Can I ask you a question, Anna?"

Anna shrugged. "Why not?"

"Do you think it hurts because your pride's been hurt? You know what I mean. Like, your feelings are hurt and you're embarrassed. Is it that kind of hurt? Or is it something more? Does it hurt like your heart is broken? Like you really loved Edmond and perhaps you didn't realize it fully before?"

Anna nodded, but fresh tears were spilling down her cheeks now. "The second one."

"So you really did love Edmond?" Lelani was slightly surprised to hear this. Anna had always been slightly offhanded about Edmond before. She would say they were good friends. And when they broke up, she had seemed to take it in stride. Or else she'd been hiding her true feelings.

"I did love Edmond, and I still do." Anna made a little gasping sound. "How do you stop loving someone, Lelani? How do you simply shut down because he stops loving you? How do you tell your heart to stop thinking about him? To stop wanting him back? How?"

Lelani sighed loudly. "That is one of the big unanswerable questions of the universe. I don't know how. I could say that time helps. And it does, I know that personally. But who knows how much time? I could say that growing up helps, which I also understand firsthand. I could even say that eventually finding someone new helps. But I doubt any of that would make you feel better."

Anna wiped her face with the dish towel.

"I haven't been much help, have I?" said Lelani.

"Actually, you have." Anna stood now. "I remember how heartbroken you were last fall. I didn't understand it then. Sometimes I thought you were just being dramatic. But I do understand now. And knowing that you survived it, Lelani, well, that gives me some hope."

Lelani smiled. "Not only did I survive it, Anna, but I'm marrying the most wonderful man on the planet."

Anna's face lit up a little. "And knowing that gives me hope for my situation too."

"Now you go to bed and I'll finish cleaning up," Lelani told her firmly. "And I will not take no for an answer."

✂⊂⊃✂

Normally, Lelani did not like to interfere in the lives of others. But something about Anna's story—the idea of Edmond falling for a girl like Lucy and dumping Anna like that—well, it just didn't ring true. Not that she thought Anna was being untruthful. She simply thought that Anna must be mistaken or confused. And because Anna was soon to become her sister, Lelani felt she had the right—no, make that the *responsibility*—to intervene. Or at least to get to the bottom of this.

As she waited for Edmond to meet her for coffee at Starbucks, she vowed to be very discreet.

"So how are you doing?" Edmond asked as he set his coffee on the table where Lelani was already seated. "Getting any pre-wedding jitters yet?"

She smiled. "Not really. But I am counting the days."

He sat down and just looked solemnly at her.

"I know you're curious as to why I asked you to meet me," she began.

"A bit." He took a sip of coffee and waited.

"It's about Anna. I realize that it's probably none of my business, except that I love Anna and I know that she's in a lot of pain right now."

Edmond seemed surprised by this. "Anna's in pain?"

Lelani gauged his reaction, then nodded. "She and I had a long talk last night. She didn't want to tell me what was going on, but I sort of forced it out of her."

He leaned forward slightly. "What *is* going on?"

Lelani wondered how much to say. Out of respect for Anna, she didn't want to throw all the cards on the table. On the other hand, she wanted to be honest and find out the truth. "Anna told me about you and Lucy."

"And what did Anna say?" His voice was tinged with defensiveness.

"That you and Lucy are dating and—"

"We are not dating."

"Really?"

"I know that some people assume we're dating, and I realize we have been seen together, even by Anna, but I swear to you, we're *not* dating."

"Okay. You're not officially dating. But Anna said that she saw the two of you together in your office in what looked like a … well, a compromising position."

He looked slightly disgusted. "Anna walked in just as Lucy had me practically pinned to my desk. But honestly, I didn't start it."

"According to Anna, you'd been enjoying Lucy's attention."

He nodded. "I suppose that's true. Lucy is an attractive girl, and it was fun being pursued by her. At first."

"But what about Anna?"

"That's a very good question." He looked perplexed as he adjusted his glasses. "And it was something I was always asking myself. *What about Anna?* I move forward and she moves back. I tell her how I feel and she clams up. I felt she was sending me a message."

"What?"

"Obviously that she wasn't as interested in me as I was in her."

"You truly believe that?"

"Yes." He took another sip of coffee.

Lelani didn't say anything. She knew it wasn't her place to proclaim Anna's love for Edmond. That would be going too far. "And so you allowed this … whatever it was with Lucy, to continue?"

He laughed in a sarcastic way. "It wasn't like I could stop it. Lucy is, shall we say, a persistent young woman. To be honest, she was starting to feel like a stalker."

"Was?"

He nodded soberly. "I told her this week that she had to stop chasing after me, that I wasn't interested in her, and that if she refused to leave me alone, I would have my uncle cancel her internship at Erlinger Publishing."

"Really, you told her that?"

"I did. I tried to tell Anna about this on that very day. I suspected she'd heard the rumor that Lucy and I were seriously involved. Lucy must've started that one herself. But Anna didn't seem the least bit interested in speaking to me. And I suppose that made it easier for me to believe what I'd heard about her."

"You heard something about Anna?"

"I dismissed it as idle gossip at first. But the way Anna was treating me—and then that bouquet of roses—it all seemed to add up. Anna's involved with someone else."

"I think you're mistaken."

Edmond actually looked hopeful for a moment. Then he just shook his head. "No, I think it's true. She's been in a good mood. And then there was that huge bouquet of roses."

"Anna thought maybe you'd sent them."

"Me?"

"She wasn't sure. The message on the card was a little unclear, but she thought it might've been your way of saying you were sorry."

"But I didn't send the roses."

"Then I'm sure Anna is still in the dark over who did."

Edmond looked clearly puzzled now.

"So there's really nothing between you and Lucy?" Lelani studied him carefully.

"There is absolutely nothing on my end. Like I said, if Lucy continues to pursue something, she'll be sent packing. I've already told my uncle that I'm fed up."

Lelani finished off her coffee, then looked at her watch. "I'm sorry, but if I don't get going, I'll miss the bus and be late for class."

"How about if I give you a ride?"

"What about work?"

"Some things are more important than work."

As Edmond drove, they continued to talk. Lelani didn't divulge all that Anna had told her, but enough to let Edmond know that Anna still cared. A lot.

"What should I do?" he finally asked as he was about to drop Lelani off.

She considered this. "First of all, Anna needs to know that there really is nothing, and that there never has been anything, between you and Lucy. And that might include an apology."

"An apology?"

"Yes. Although you say you weren't involved with Lucy, you allowed it to appear as if you were, and you even admitted that you enjoyed Lucy's attention. That hurt Anna deeply."

He nodded. "When you put it like that, I get it."

Lelani gathered her bag. "And, once you regain Anna's trust, I suggest you be honest with her. Encourage her to be honest with you. Don't play games."

"Right."

She opened the door. "Thanks for the ride."

"Thanks for the advice." He grinned. "Hey, am I still invited to your wedding?"

"Of course." She stopped herself from adding, "After all, you're almost family." Because the truth was, she had no idea how this thing between Edmond and Anna would play out. Love was tricky that way.

As she walked to class, she felt optimistic for both of them. And yet, she felt a bit concerned too. She had said a lot more than she intended. Mostly, she hoped that Anna wouldn't feel betrayed by any of this.

Twenty-five

Megan

"So how goes life in the art department?" Harris asked Megan after school on Friday.

She retrieved her reusable lunch sack from the break-room fridge, then sighed. "One more week. Just one more week."

"That bad, eh?"

She forced a smile. "No, it's actually gotten a lot better. I did take your advice about music, and I even brought donut holes several times. But the kids are so antsy. It's like they're literally climbing the walls." She shook her head at the memory of how she'd caught Jackson doing some kind of cartwheel on the cement wall in the art room. But she had not sent him to detention for it.

"Don't take it personally. They're always like this at the end of the year."

"Well, next week, I plan to take the class outside. We're going to sketch trees and whatever we can find on campus."

"Sounds like a good idea."

"Unless they decide to run away."

He nodded. "And that could happen."

"I figured."

They were both heading out the door now. "So, how is that MIA boyfriend of yours? Any word from Africa?"

"The guys have sent messages via our church," she admitted. "Not much information, really, but they're alive and the well is coming along, and they seem to be making some good connections with the locals."

Harris nodded, but with a knowing sort of look.

"Okay, you're probably wondering what kind of a boyfriend goes halfway around the world and doesn't even communicate with his girlfriend."

"The thought crossed my mind."

"Marcus is a good guy."

"Uh-huh."

Megan was at a loss for words. She knew she was expected to say something like, "And I know our relationship is rock solid and when he comes home, we'll still be together, yada yada yada, blah blah blah." But she also knew that wasn't really true. For all she knew, Marcus had moved on. Not only geographically, but romantically as well. Still, she wasn't about to admit this to Harris.

"Have a good weekend," she said as she turned down the hall toward the art room.

"You too," he called out cheerfully. "And if you ever get lonely or need to talk, my number's in the book."

"Thanks," she called back. Not that she would take him up on this offer. She was only being polite. Besides that, she had a full weekend planned, so full that she had begged out of the family reunion her mother was attending. Tomorrow her church was having a rummage sale to earn money for Zambia. And later that evening was Lelani's big shower at the Mendezes'. As for Sunday, well, Megan planned to crash and prepare herself for her final week as a middle-school art teacher.

She went into the art room and looked around. Despite the crazy kids and the trials they had put her through (perhaps were still putting her through), Megan really liked this job. She especially liked it when she connected with a student, like today. when she'd complimented Morgan Franz on her charcoal sketch and then witnessed the quiet girl's eyes spark happily. Suddenly they were engaged in a real conversation about light and shadow and how it was kind of like life.

"It's all about contrasts," Megan told her. "If we didn't experience darkness, we might not appreciate light."

"I suppose the dark times do make the light times seem brighter," Morgan admitted.

"And everyone has to go through some kind of darkness at least once in a while," Megan told her.

"Sometimes it seems like the darkness never ends."

Megan nodded as she placed a hand on Morgan's shoulder. "I know exactly what you mean."

And then there were students like wild-child Jackson, who had tried her patience again and again, but it seemed that his attitude toward her had changed ever so slightly. Maybe it was because she'd been trying to show her students that she cared, not just about their performances in class, but about their lives as well. That felt good.

She loaded the last of the ceramics into the kiln then turned it on to fire. By Monday these pots would be ready for their final glaze. She liked to think this wasn't really the end of a very short career. But so far, no one had made mention of Megan being at Madison next fall. As far as she knew, Heather would return to teaching art and Megan would be job hunting. Still, she was trying to keep a positive outlook. And she was trying to trust God for her future, even though, as Morgan had said, the darkness seemed endless.

Megan swept up the pottery dust and dumped it into the garbage can, then turned off the lights. If she hurried, she could catch the next metro and make it home by five. Not that she had anything to look forward to particularly. As she gathered her bag, she remembered how she used to look forward to Friday nights and doing something with Marcus. Now those memories seemed as remote as Zambia.

As she rode the metro, Megan thought about Kendall's idea to bring Nana back to Bloomberg Place. Megan's first reaction had been to say no. But after giving it some thought, she looked forward to helping care for Mrs. Weis. She liked the old woman and could understand Kendall's concern for her being shut away in the nursing home. If nothing else, it might make for an interesting summer. And it would buy Megan some time to figure out her life, which felt as if it was being turned completely upside down.

She remembered how life had been last June. Her father had just been diagnosed with cancer, and then, too quickly, he was gone. She felt a lump in her throat. It had only been a year. So much had happened since then, both good and bad. Yet, just this past spring, she had felt that her life was falling neatly into place, almost as if she finally had some kind of control. Now that seemed laughable. She thought of all the pieces of her life that were spinning farther and farther away.

Her mother's house was on the market and would probably sell before summer ended. Her friends were getting married and leaving. Her boyfriend was quite likely not her boyfriend any more. She would soon be unemployed. And, unless this thing worked out with Kendall's grandmother, Megan might just find herself homeless. Oh, she knew her mother would welcome her back, but that wasn't the same as being on her own.

Megan didn't particularly like the idea of having her little pity party on the metro, and yet it did seem a fairly good place to feel sorry for oneself. Until she looked around.

She saw others who seemed even more down and out than she was. There was a mother with two small children and a vacant, lonely expression in her eyes. And a man with his head hanging down, reeking of alcohol and hopelessness. Megan made an effort to smile at people like this. She had no idea if it made the slightest bit of difference in their world, but it helped her to feel better about hers. She was determined not to give in to despair. Instead, she would put her hope in God. Really, what else was there?

After getting off the metro, Megan always enjoyed walking the last few blocks toward Bloomberg Place. The walk helped to clear her head, and the weather had been spectacular lately. They were all hoping and praying that it would continue like this for next weekend's weddings, both of which were planned for outdoors, although they had backup plans for rain since this was, after all, Oregon.

So far, things had fallen into place for Lelani and Gil's wedding. Megan gave God the credit for most of this, since it seemed somewhat miraculous. Or maybe it was the result of keeping things simple. Kendall's wedding, on the other hand, seemed to be all over the boards. Her mother changed her mind constantly and, as a result, the plans became layer upon layer of complication. Megan felt sorry for Kendall, but at the same time she was amazed at how Kendall seemed to go with the flow, keeping her focus on the fact that she and Killiki were going to live happily ever after. Megan sure hoped that would be the case.

But when she entered the house to find Kendall on her knees with her face buried in the cushions of the sectional and sobbing her heart out, Megan didn't know what to think. She dropped her bag and ran over to Kendall's side. "What's wrong?" she asked.

Kendall turned around and threw her arms around Megan and sobbed even harder.

"Is it Killiki?" Megan asked urgently. "Is he—"

"No," Kendall cried. "Killiki is okay."

"The baby?"

"No, not the baby." Kendall pulled away now, wiping her wet face with her hands.

"What then?"

"Nana!"

"What happened?"

"She—she died!" Now Kendall started to cry even louder.

Megan wrapped her arms around Kendall again. "I'm sorry, Kendall. I'm so sorry. I know how much you loved her."

Kendall cried for a while longer and then finally started to hiccup. "I—uh—I just feel so—uh—sad."

"Let me get you some water." Megan hopped up and hurried to the kitchen, returning with a glass of water and a box of tissues. "Here, drink this." She waited as Kendall gulped down the water.

"Thanks." Kendall took in long, ragged sigh. "I'm sorry to be such a basket case. But I just can't believe it."

Megan patted Kendall's back in soothing way. "I understand."

"I wanted to take her dress shopping to—tomorrow. I—called her nursing home to see—to see if she was better—she'd been sick. And they told me she died." Kendall's chin started to tremble. "Just like that."

"That seems a bit harsh."

She nodded. "So I called Dad. And he had already heard about it. But he—he didn't even call me to tell me."

"Maybe he didn't understand that you and Nana were close, Kendall."

She sniffed and Megan handed her a tissue. "But Dad acted like it wasn't a big deal. He said she was old—that she'd had a good life—and that I shouldn't let it spoil the wedding." She was crying again. "But I wanted Nana to come to my wedding!"

"I know you did." Megan sighed. "And maybe she will. You know. Maybe she'll be watching from someplace else."

"I don't know." Kendall wiped her eyes. "I don't even think she was a Christian, Megan."

Megan didn't know what to say.

"What if she wasn't?" Kendall looked intently at her.

"What if she was?" Megan said kindly.

"But how?" Kendall frowned. "She never went to church or anything."

"A lot of people find God outside of a church. Didn't you?"

Kendall nodded. "Yeah. I guess so."

"There are some things we just have to trust God to take care of, Kendall. Things that are out of our control. This might be one of them."

Kendall blew her nose loudly, then looked up with a hopeful expression. "Do you think it's possible to pray in reverse?"

"Pray in reverse?"

"You know, pray backward. Instead of praying for something in the future, you pray for it in the past? Like could I pray for Nana to be okay with God now?"

Megan considered this. "Well, God isn't limited to our earthly clocks and calendars, so it might be worth a try."

"Will you pray for her too?"

Megan thought this sounded a little strange, not to mention childish, but then she remembered a Scripture where Jesus tells his disciples to have childlike faith. Maybe that was what Kendall had. "Sure," she told her. "I'll be happy to pray."

"Right now?" Kendall asked eagerly.

"Why not?" Megan reached for Kendall's hands and they both took turns praying "in reverse" for Nana to have come to faith before her life ended.

"Amen," said Megan when it seemed their backward prayer had ended.

"Thank you so much!" Kendall hugged her again. "I still miss Nana, but I feel better. And now I better get over to Kate's house. My dad mentioned they're having some kind of a family meeting regarding Nana. Not that I was invited, but that's not going to keep me from going."

Megan laughed. "You know, I think you and your Nana had a lot in common, Kendall."

"Really? How so?"

Megan considered her words carefully. No way did she want to insult Kendall or her deceased grandmother. "Well, you both have very resilient spirits. You're both witty. And you both have style."

Kendall stood a little straighter as she patted her tummy. "Thank you."

✄

Kendall had just left when Anna came home. Once again, she was carrying a large, elegant bouquet of roses. Only these were red.

"Are those for tomorrow night's shower?" Megan asked curiously.

"No way." Anna shook her head. "These are *my* roses."

"Who sent them?"

"Edmond."

Megan blinked. "Really?"

"But he didn't send the yellow ones." She set the bouquet on the dining room table. "Those were from Chelsea, a friend at work. I'd helped her with something."

"Okay, I get that." Megan studied Anna. "But *Edmond* sent these? I assume you know what red roses symbolize, right?"

Anna nodded with a big smile, then began to explain how Edmond had kidnapped her from her desk and taken her to lunch at a very nice restaurant, where he explained everything and apologized for hurting her, then swore that Lucy meant nothing to him.

"He said he wants us to start all over again." She sighed. "Then these roses showed up at my desk this afternoon, and the card simply said, 'To Anna with love, your Edmond.'"

"And how do you feel about all this?" Megan asked, although judging by Anna's expression, she was over the moon.

"I told him that I'd like to start over too." Anna beamed at her.

"That's fabulous news. I'm really happy for you."

"I'm still kind of in shock."

"Kendall's had a bit of a shock too." Megan used this segue to break the news about Kendall's grandmother.

"Oh, no!" Anna put her hand over her mouth. "Poor Kendall—and right before her wedding! How is she doing?"

Megan filled in more details, even mentioning the praying-in-reverse thing. "I wasn't really sure, but it seemed like it couldn't hurt. And Kendall felt better."

"That's kind of like lighting candles at church for people who've passed," Anna said thoughtfully. "I think it makes perfect sense."

Lelani and Emma came in, and Megan and Anna took turns sharing both the happy and sad news with them.

"Wow," Lelani said as she sat Emma down on the floor to crawl around. "That's overwhelming. I don't know whether to celebrate or sob."

"For now we should probably focus on Kendall," Anna suggested. "Having a family member die just a week before your wedding—it won't be easy."

"What can we do to help her through this?" asked Lelani.

"Just be her friends and love her." Megan felt Emma tugging on her shoelace and bent down to pick her up. "What could be better than that?"

"Nothing that I can think of," said Lelani.

"I agree." Anna nodded.

Megan felt exceedingly thankful for her friends, but she was also aware that the death of Kendall's grandmother probably meant that she and Anna would each need to find other places to live at the end of the month. In fact, she suspected that the family meeting Kendall had just crashed was related to her grandmother's estate, including the house on Bloomberg Place, which would probably be sold now for sure. Really, it seemed this was the end of an era. Change was roaring down the railroad track like a freight train, and there was no way Megan could stop it.

In her room, Megan flopped down on her bed and closed her eyes. She took a deep breath and consciously pushed away her doubt and fear as she imagined herself lying in the hand of God ... trusting him to care for her ... believing that he could keep her safe ... and that he would keep her from falling.

Kendall

"Oh, Kendall," Kate said as she opened her front door with an empty pitcher in her hand. "We didn't expect you to come."

"Why not?" Kendall made her way past Kate and into the house. "She was my grandmother too."

"But this is more of a business meeting." The implication was clear—no children allowed. When it came to Kate, Kendall would always be treated like a child

Kendall just shrugged. "Don't worry, I think I can handle it."

"Fine," Kate turned away. "Everyone is in Eric's den. I'm just getting some more iced tea."

Kendall reminded herself of what Megan had just said—about how she and Nana were similar—as she opened the door to the den. "Hello, everyone," she said with more confidence than she felt.

"Kendall," said her dad, "I didn't know you were—"

"So this is Kendall," said a man who was seated at Eric's desk with a folder of papers in front of him. "I'm Darren Walberg." He stood and extended his hand. "Your grandmother's attorney."

"Nice to meet you." She forced a nervous smile.

"I'm sorry for your loss."

She swallowed hard. "Thanks. I'm going to miss her."

"Have a seat, Kendall," her dad said as Kate began refilling glasses with tea. "Mr. Walberg was just starting to go over some legal things."

The attorney cleared his throat and picked up a piece of paper. "And now for the actual will."

As Darren Walberg read, Kendall's mind wandered. She remembered all the times she'd spent with Nana as a child—times when her parents and older siblings had been eager to get rid of her, in essence dumping her with her grandmother so they could go off to do things she was considered too young for. But what they hadn't realized was that she and Nana formed a bond that the rest of them missed out on. They had played cards and watched goofy TV. Nana had let Kendall dress up in her old clothes and jewelry, and sometimes they'd go into the kitchen and cook something totally crazy, inedible actually, mixed up from a wild bunch of ingredients. Then Nana would let Kendall stay up as late as she liked and sleep in even later. And the next day they would go shopping and Nana would buy something that her mother and sisters would say was in bad taste. Not that Kendall would care.

"Why does Kendall get the house?" Kim was asking now. "I mean, we all knew that Nana allowed Kendall to occupy it, since Kendall didn't really have any place else to live. But to leave that property to Kendall alone? I don't understand."

"The house has actually been in Kendall's name for more than a year now," Darren Walberg told Kate.

"It has?" Kendall frowned at him. "You mean officially and legally? Not just that I was getting to use it?"

"I mean officially and legally."

Kendall shook her head. "No one told me."

"Your grandmother didn't think it was necessary to tell anyone. She had given the property to you through a trust that was set up with me.

It was just her way of cleaning some things up before she went into the nursing home."

"Oh." Kendall tried to absorb this information. The house really did belong to her. It had for some time. Oh, she had sort of pretended it was hers, and she had wished that it was hers, but in her mind it still belonged to Nana. Perhaps it always would. "So I can do what I like with the house?"

He held up what looked like a deed. "It's your house, Kendall."

She nodded. "So I can keep it if I want? It won't have to be sold? And my friends can continue living there?"

"Like I said, it's your house."

The others began to talk among themselves now, questioning Nana's mental faculties, discussing the fairness of Kendall getting the house, as well as some of the other portions of the will—things that Kendall had missed while daydreaming. Kendall stood and walked out of the room. No one really seemed to notice.

But by the time she reached the front door, Darren Walberg was at her side, handing a business card to her. "Let's set up an appointment for next week," he told her. "I know you're getting married soon, and it might be wise to take care of this first."

"Thank you." She forced a smile through her tears.

He smiled as he placed a hand on her shoulder. "Your grandmother was quite a woman, Kendall. She thought the world of you. And no matter what anyone might try to tell you, she was of sound mind when she signed the house over to you. There will be no way to dispute that."

"Thanks." Kendall tucked his card into her purse, then left. Part of her felt hurt and betrayed by her family, but another part wasn't terribly surprised. Besides, she reminded herself as she drove back toward Bloomberg Place, she had another kind of family to go home to now.

❈

Kendall tried to wear her party face at Lelani's big shower on Saturday night, but underneath it all she felt sad and tired. When Mrs. Mendez began to serve refreshments, Kendall quietly let herself out and drove to the RV park where her parents' motor home was parked. She wasn't sure if they'd be there or not, but she wanted to talk to her dad.

She parked in the guest parking area and walked over to the spot where her parents had set up camp. She was about to knock on their door when she heard loud voices through the open window. "She was my mother," her dad declared, "and if I want to feel bad, it's my business."

"Fine!" her mom shouted back. "Go ahead and be a big baby. See if I care."

"Sometimes you are made of ice!" he yelled.

"Go to—"

"Shut up! Shut up!"

Kendall backed away from the trailer, turned and ran to her car, got in, and leaned her head into the steering wheel. She could remember times when her parents had fought like this before. Often, she felt responsible for those fights. If only she were more mature, more responsible, more grown-up, she'd always thought, perhaps they wouldn't fight so much. Was that why they were fighting now? Or were they upset, like Kate had been, to learn that Nana had given her house to Kendall? If that was the case, they could have the house. Kendall didn't want it. She reached for her phone and dialed Killiki's number.

"How are you doing, sweetie?" he asked kindly. "Did you go to Lelani's shower?"

She tearfully told him about what she'd just heard and how upsetting it was. "I don't want to be the reason my parents are fighting anymore," she sobbed. "I just want it to stop."

"Oh, Kendall," he said gently, "you can't make them fight and you can't make them stop. Don't you see that?"

"All I see is that they're unhappy and it feels like my fault."

"It's not your fault. You have to accept that. Remember what our last counseling session was about? How we have to take responsibility for our own feelings? That means you can't blame someone else and you can't take the blame either."

"I know that in my head, but it doesn't *feel* true."

"I wasn't going to tell you this, Kendall, but I changed my flight."

"You changed it?" Kendall felt alarmed. Was he going to cancel the wedding?

"Yes. I'll arrive tomorrow afternoon at four. That way I can be with you for your grandmother's funeral on Monday."

"Oh, you did that for me?" She wiped her tears with her free hand.

"Of course, Kendall. I want to be there for you. Don't you know that?"

"Thank you!" she cried. "I'll be waiting for you at the airport, Killiki. At four?"

"That's right."

"I love you!" she said happily.

"I love you too. And remember, you're not the reason your parents are fighting. They're fighting because they choose to fight. Understand?"

"Yes." She nodded eagerly. "Thank you!"

⋈

It was just past noon on Sunday when Kendall called her dad. "I don't know if you want to talk to me or not, but I—"

"Why wouldn't I want to talk to you?"

"Well, I was feeling kind of like the misfit at the family meeting on Friday, and I sort of assumed—"

"Oh, Kendall, don't you know what they say about that *assume* word?"

"Yeah, I've heard that one."

"Of course I want to talk to you."

They agreed to meet for ice cream, and when Kendall was sitting across from her dad, she started to realize that some of her assumptions, at least about him, were a little off base.

"I couldn't be happier that my mom gave her house to you, Kennie. And I'm not a bit surprised. You were always her favorite."

"So there are no hard feelings?"

"Of course not. Not with me anyway. I can't speak for anyone else."

"Like Mom?"

"Oh, your mom might've expected some sort of inheritance, but we don't need it, Kennie. We're doing just fine."

"What about the rest of the family?"

"I'm sure some of your siblings are jealous. Not much we can do about that."

"I guess not." She looked down at her ice cream.

"Let's see a smile on that princess face," he urged.

She attempted a small smile for him. "I'm still missing Nana. Remember how she loved going out for ice cream?"

He held up his ice cream cone now. "Here's to my mom and your grandmother, Kendall. She was a little quirky, but she was a good woman, right?"

"Right." She held up her cone and clicked it against his. "Here's to Nana."

"You know, Kennie, of all the grandkids, you're probably the most like her."

"That's what one of my roommates said too."

"Did they know her?"

"Sure, we had her over a few times."

"Good for you." He shook his head with a sad expression. "I was surprised at how hard it hit me when I heard she died."

"Yeah, me too."

"And I've been feeling guilty."

"Why?"

"I never visited her at the nursing home. Not once. I'm sure she was lonely there, and I feel terrible about that."

"But she had lots of friends there, Dad. I met a lot of them."

"Did you go there much?"

"I wish I'd gone more." She bit her lip to keep from mentioning how Mom had kept her from going there recently. "But really, she did have friends there, Dad. And I think she was fairly happy most of the time. She did get tired of being cooped up now and then."

"Who wouldn't?"

"Nana was actually kind of unhappy the last time I saw her, Dad. She was sick and weak and they were sedating her—"

"They sedated her?"

Kendall nodded. "I felt so bad for her about that. I mean, I realize she was a little upset, and the nurse said she'd get well sooner if she rested and everything. But it bugged me a lot. In fact, I wanted to figure out a way to bring her home, you know, to live in her house. I started talking to live-in caregivers, and two of my roommates were willing to help her in exchange for rent."

"You tried to put all that together?" He looked truly stunned.

"Yeah. I even talked to a social-services person, who was going to send some papers for Nana to fill out so that her house could be used to pay for her care."

"Wow, Kendall, that's impressive."

She frowned. "Except that it never happened."

"Still, that you would even spend time and energy trying to help Nana is wonderful. And here I thought all you had on your mind was your wedding."

Kendall actually laughed. "Trust me, Dad, I am not nearly as into this wedding as it might appear." She glanced at the clock over the ice cream counter. "Which reminds me, I have to pick *someone* up at the airport."

"Let me guess? Could this *someone* be Killiki?"

"How did you know?"

"You should've seen the way your eyes lit up."

"I'd invite you to come along"—she grinned—"but I kind of want to see him by myself first. It's been awhile."

"I understand totally."

"Besides, you can meet him tomorrow." She reached for her bag. "At Nana's funeral."

He nodded somberly.

"I wish Nana could've met him."

"I'm sure she would've loved him, Kendall."

"Yeah. I know."

Her dad hugged her and warned her not to speed on the way to the airport. Despite her excitement to get there fast, she took his advice seriously, focused on her driving, and tried not to daydream along the way. Then she parked her car and went to baggage claim, where she waited, thanks to a flight delay, for what seemed like hours but was actually only thirty minutes. Then suddenly Killiki was right in front of her, and he took her in his arms, and she clung to him and felt like everything was right with the world again.

"I wish we could drive through a time warp so that today would become one week from now," she said as Killiki drove them away from the airport terminal. "We would turn around and catch our flight to Maui."

"You'd skip the wedding?"

"Oh, yeah. In a heartbeat." She laughed. "I mean I'd want us to be officially married, but finished with the actual wedding."

"I know what you mean. But we don't want to offend your family, sweetie, and one week isn't all that far off."

"Now that you're here, it's not." She reached over and ran her hand through his hair. "Oh, Killiki, I have missed you *so* much."

Kendall gave Killiki a tour of the city, including a walk through the Rose Gardens, and eventually they enjoyed a sunset dinner at a riverside restaurant. Just before dessert came, Killiki reached into his shirt pocket. "Hey, I almost forgot something."

"What?"

"I know it's a little late." He held out a small blue velvet box, "But it took longer than I expected, and then I decided to present it to you in person."

"Oh, Killiki!" She anxiously opened the box, then gasped to see a diamond set above three smaller blue stones and surrounded by what looked like a wave of platinum. "It's beautiful," she told him. "Is the setting a wave?"

"Exactly." He grinned. "I had a friend design it. The diamond represents you, my drowning mermaid, and the lapis lazuli below it is me catching you."

"The day we met," Kendall said, remembering how he'd pulled her out of the ocean after her surfing fiasco.

"We're both caught in the wave ... that represents our love."
She handed it to him. "You put it on my finger."

He looked into her eyes. "I love you, Kendall."

"I love you too!" Then they kissed and he slipped the ring onto her finger, but he struggled to get it over her slightly swollen knuckle.

"Does it fit?" He watched anxiously as she finished pushing the ring all the way on. "Lelani told me your ring size."

"It's a little tight right now, but that's just because of my pregnancy. My other rings are tight too."

"It won't hurt your finger, will it?"

"No, of course not." She stared at the gorgeous ring. "I love it, Killiki. And I love you even more."

⋙◉⋘

It was hard to say good night to Killiki, but since Gil had offered him a room, they didn't want to get back too late. Plus there was the funeral service in the morning. For the time being, Killiki would use her car and perhaps get a rental car in a day or two.

The house was quiet as Kendall went to the kitchen for her regular glass of bedtime milk. She suspected everyone had gone to bed by now. But she felt too happy to sleep. In fact, she felt so happy she wanted to sing and dance and jump up and down and scream. But she controlled herself. She remembered that tomorrow was Nana's funeral and decided to go to bed.

The service was scheduled for ten o'clock Monday, and Killiki came by to pick her up at nine thirty. Kendall wished she had something more funeral-like to wear, but thanks to her oversized tummy, combined with her commitment not to shop, she was forced to wear a coral-colored sundress that she'd gotten for their Maui vacation, back when she'd just started to show and needed some roomier clothes. This morning it was feeling a little snug. To camouflage this, she topped it with a little white cardigan and decided it would have to do.

"Are you okay?" Killiki asked her as he drove them to the church that Kendall's family had attended for holidays, weddings, and funerals. "You seem awfully quiet."

"Sorry." She sighed. "Guess I was thinking."

"Missing your grandmother."

"Yeah, that and I'm still feeling like an outcast in my family. I mean they'll all be there, but none of them will be glad to see me."

"What about your dad? You had that good talk with him yesterday."

"That's true." She nodded and wished that the rest of her family were as congenial as Dad. Maybe a funeral would soften them a little. But when Kendall entered the church, which wasn't terribly crowded, she noticed that no one in her family had saved spaces for her and Killiki up in front. But to her surprise and relief, all of her housemates as well as Gil and Edmond were seated together just two rows behind the family, and so she and Killiki joined them.

The service was less than impressive. It was clear the young pastor, who surely meant well, didn't actually know Nana. He bumbled along until he seemed to be out of words, then he invited people to participate. "I welcome you to come on up and share fond memories of Gertrude Weis as we celebrate her life."

An uncomfortable silence followed, but after a couple of minutes, Kendall's dad stood and made his way to the podium. He cleared his throat and began to tell a story about when he was ten years old and how his mother had shown up at his school and told the office that he had a dental appointment.

"I was a little surprised," he said with a small smile, "because I didn't recall any appointment. But once I was safely off the school grounds, Mom explained that we were going to the circus." He chuckled. "The circus had come to a town a couple hours away. Mom got us lunch, then drove us all the way over there, and even though the circus hadn't started yet, we walked all around and saw everything, and when it was finally time for the circus to begin, we had front-row seats." He dabbed his eye with a handkerchief. "That was one of the best days of my life."

Dad made his way back to his seat, and the sanctuary got very quiet again. Kendall stood up. With shaky knees, she walked to the front of the sanctuary and, despite her thundering heart and the distinct feeling that she might actually faint, she told everyone about how she and Nana had "gone to Paris" a couple of weeks ago.

"Of course, it wasn't Paris for real," she explained, "but it was still really fun." She told them about how Nana spoke French and how they had pastries and espresso. And how they window-shopped, then had French onion soup. She even mentioned the pretty red shoes that had caught Nana's eye. "Unfortunately, they were two sizes too small, but we couldn't have afforded them anyway." Some people even chuckled.

"My nana taught me a lot of things," Kendall said finally. "Best of all, she taught me to use my imagination and to enjoy life. And I will always be thankful for her."

Kendall stepped away from the podium and walked past the family section, where some, like Dad, were smiling and others looked completely blank. She returned to her friends. Anna nodded approval, Lelani did a silent mini applause, and Megan gave her a thumbs-up. Kendall sighed as she sat down, and Killiki leaned over and kissed her cheek. Kendall smiled and knew that Nana would've appreciated that her friends had come.

Twenty-seven

Anna

"Looks like the kids decided to play hooky this morning," Lucy said in a condescending tone as Edmond and Anna returned to the office at one o'clock sharp. They'd grabbed a quick lunch following the service, then hurried to make it back at work on time. Several other employees were coming in at the same time, and for Lucy to speak like this was more than a little disturbing. Anna felt certain Lucy wouldn't dare pull this stunt if Felicia or Rick were around to hear. Apparently, she wasn't worried about Edmond's authority.

"We were at a funeral," Edmond said stiffly. Anna controlled herself from responding at all but exchanged a glance with Chelsea, who had entered in time to witness Lucy's little display.

"Oh, right." Lucy directed a knowing look to Crystal, the receptionist. "The old funeral excuse. Bet you never heard that one before, huh?"

Crystal suppressed a giggle, then quickly diverted her attention to the ringing phone. "Erlinger Publishing, how may I direct your call?"

"Not that it's any of your business," Chelsea said quietly to Lucy. "But they really were at a funeral and—"

"Who asked you?" Lucy shot back.

"I was just saying—"

"Well, you're right, it's *not* any of your business, little Miss Frump Muffin." Lucy chuckled. "We all know what they were *really* up to."

Chelsea's brows arched high above her glasses, but Anna was thankful to see that she simply shook her head and continued walking toward the elevator. *Good move, Chelsea.* Anna would commend her later.

"Lucy." Edmond calmly tilted his head away from the reception area as he walked over to a more private niche near the restrooms. Without even thinking, or perhaps simply to be a witness, Anna followed him.

Lucy followed too. Then she stood in front of Edmond with that same old flirty look on her face, almost as if she were challenging him. "What?"

"I want you to collect your things and—"

"Collect my things?" Her blue eyes flashed.

"Your services are no longer needed here."

She laughed. "Yeah, right. Get serious, *Ed.*"

"I'm *dead* serious, Lucy." Edmond's cheeks flushed now. Anna knew he hated to be called *Ed* by anyone.

"News flash." Lucy waved a French manicured fingernail under his nose. "You're *not* my boss, *Ed.* And FYI, Felicia has offered me a full-time position in the marketing department as soon as my internship ends."

"Your internship ends today."

"Oh, good. Then I can start my new job and actually be on the payroll." She grinned victoriously at him. "And I can get benefits."

Anna stared at Edmond in horror. What had he gotten himself into?

"I'm sorry to disappoint you, Lucy," he said firmly. "But you really do need to be on your way. Your work is finished here."

"Maybe you should take this up with Felicia." Lucy remained planted right in front of him. "She might have a different opinion."

"There's no need to speak to Felicia," he told her. "In case you didn't know, Rick Erlinger is Felicia's boss."

"So?"

"Rick and I discussed your termination earlier this week. He wanted to give you one last chance, and you just blew it."

Lucy's eyes got big. "But I—"

"Please collect your things and be on your way," he said crisply. "The sooner the better."

"But I was only *joking* with you," she said sweetly. "You know that. I like to kid around. That's part of my charm."

Edmond ignored her as he slipped his hand beneath Anna's elbow, then guided her out of the reception area and down the hallway toward her desk.

"Wow." Anna set her purse on her desk. "What a showdown."

He took in a deep breath. "Did I handle it okay?"

"Perfectly." She studied him. "But what you said was true, right? About Rick backing you on this?"

He nodded. "Rick and I met about this earlier this week. Remember that day when I wanted to speak with you, and you saw me talking to Lucy in my car?"

"Yes."

"That was right after my meeting with Rick. He asked me to warn Lucy privately that she had to back off from stalking me and act more professionally, or she would be let go with no recommendation for her internship."

"Guess she didn't take you seriously."

He sighed. "To be honest, I'm glad she didn't. Good riddance to Lucy."

"What about Felicia?"

"She'll get over it." He chuckled. "Besides, she's always asking me to exercise more authority around here. Guess I did that today."

Anna beamed at him. "You sure did."

✀

"Guess who's staying in my guest room?" Anna's mother asked Anna on Wednesday afternoon.

"I have no idea," Anna told her with impatience, "but unless this is an emergency, you're not supposed to call me at work, remember?"

"Oh, *mi'ja*, don't be such a spoilsport. I thought you'd want to know."

"The pope?"

"No, don't be silly. It's Lelani's father. Mr. Porter is our guest for the next week."

"He came?"

"Yes. Lelani doesn't even know about it yet. So don't tell her. Mr. Porter set the whole thing up with Gil. I have Emma today. Right now she's playing with Grandpa Porter, and when Lelani comes by after her final, we will surprise her."

"I'm happy for Lelani, but really I need to—"

"Yes, yes, and I suppose you and Edmond are too busy to come over here for a little family dinner tonight."

"A *little* family dinner?" Anna laughed.

"I already promised Gil I would keep it small, Anna. Only our immediate family, Mr. Porter and Lelani and Emma, of course, and I thought you might like to bring Edmond."

"Okay, I'll ask him. What time?"

"Gil is bringing food from the restaurant. I am too busy to cook."

Anna laughed. "Since when has that stopped you before?"

"You be here by six," her mother commanded.

✀

"Uh-oh," Anna said as Edmond turned onto the street to her parents' house.

"What's wrong?"

"I see cars, too many cars. This was supposed to be a small family dinner."

Edmond chuckled. "Does your mother do anything in a small way?"

"Apparently not. I hope Gil isn't too disappointed."

As it turned out, Anna's grandparents had arrived a day early and were also houseguests at her parents' house. Naturally, that meant some of the aunts and uncles couldn't be left out. Consequently the "small" dinner had grown into a gathering of close to thirty guests.

Anna and Edmond went directly to Mr. Porter, shaking his hand and welcoming him. "I see you're getting to meet some of Lelani's soon-to-be in laws," Anna told him. "I hope you don't feel too overwhelmed."

He nodded. "Yes, I've had the pleasure of meeting your grandparents."

Anna frowned. "I hope my grandmother didn't say anything too regrettable."

He winked at her. "She actually reminded me a bit of my wife."

Anna suppressed a giggle. "Yes, I can see that."

"Unfortunately, Lelani's mother was unable to make the trip." His expression was slightly grim, but Anna could tell he was trying to be polite. "She expresses her regrets."

"Here's your grandpa now," Lelani said as she brought Emma to join them. "She's just had a change and is as fresh as a daisy." Lelani handed Emma to her dad.

"How's my little princess?" Mr. Porter grinned at Emma. She looked adorable in the pink ruffled dress that Lelani had wanted her to wear for her birthday. Apparently Anna's mother hadn't gotten the final say in Emma's wardrobe tonight. Soon Gil joined them, Mr. Porter handed him the baby, and the five of them visited pleasantly about the weather in Maui and snorkeling. Mr. Porter was just telling them that his guesthouse was always available to Lelani and her friends when Anna noticed a worried expression cross her brother's face.

"Warning," he said quietly. "Trouble this way comes."

"Oh, Gil." Lelani laughed. "It's only your grandmother."

"My point precisely." He whispered something in Emma's ear and she just cooed.

"So here is the happy couple." Abuela Castillo directed her attention to Lelani and Gil. "And the pretty baby." She nodded. "You make a lovely picture."

"Thank you," Lelani told her.

"But a picture doesn't always tell the whole story, does it?"

"You remember Edmond, don't you, Abuela?" Anna attempted to redirect her grandmother's conversation. "I think you met before."

"Oh, yes. I see you two are still together." She sighed as if this was just more bad news.

"It was lovely for you to make this trip for our wedding," Lelani told her with a big smile. "It means so much to us to have family here."

Abuela's frown lines deepened. "Yes. I hear your mother has boycotted the wedding."

"I wouldn't say boycott—"

"Is she coming or not?" Abuela interrupted Lelani.

"No, but—"

"So she does not approve?"

Mr. Porter put his arm around Lelani's shoulders. "Lelani's mother has some health issues," he said solemnly, "that make travel difficult."

"So she approves of the marriage?" Abuela persisted.

"Who wouldn't approve of this marriage?" Mr. Porter said amicably. "Isn't it obvious how much these two kids love each other?" He smiled at Gil. "Who could argue with that?" He looked directly at Abuela now. "You can be assured that I back my daughter wholeheartedly."

"That's right." Gil nodded. "Mr. Porter has been incredibly supportive."

"And I see Tia Elisa looking for you, Abuela." Anna pointed across the room. "I'll bet she hasn't even seen you yet."

"Don't let us keep you," Gil added.

To everyone's relief, Abuela moved on.

"Does Mother really have health issues?" Lelani asked with concern.

He pointed to his head. "Just mental-health issues."

Lelani laughed and the others did too. But before the night ended, just as Gil and Lelani were preparing to leave, Abuela made yet another attempt to rain on their parade. "Lelani was certainly lucky to find such a hard-working young man to play father to her child. I hope she appreciates her good fortune."

Mr. Porter had been talking to someone else, but when he heard this remark he stepped next to Lelani and turned toward Abuela. "Perhaps you heard that Lelani will be finishing up her medical degree. She plans to be a doctor, Mrs. Castillo. She's a very hard-working young woman too."

"I couldn't be more proud of her," Gil added.

"And I second that, Mama," his mother said to Abuela.

"But I agree with you, Abuela," Lelani told her. "Both Emma and I are very lucky and blessed to have met Gil and to be welcomed into his family." Then she leaned over and kissed Abuela's cheek. "And I hope you will welcome us too."

"Good night," Gil called out as he opened the front door for Lelani and Emma. As the little family of three made their exit, Anna watched the expression on Abuela's face and realized that her mouth was actually gaping—ever so slightly. Perhaps even more amazing, she appeared to be speechless!

⤛⬭⤜

"So that's what you do at a bar mitzvah," Anna said as she and Edmond left the synagogue slightly before noon on Saturday.

"Are you disappointed?"

"No, but it wasn't as big of a deal as I'd expected. In some ways, it's not so different from when I had my first Communion. I mean, the religions are obviously different, but there are some similarities in the ceremonies."

"I wouldn't know, since I never did a first Communion or a bar mitzvah. But you're wrong in thinking it's over now. That was just the religious part of the ceremony. There's still a big dinner to attend, and Philip said to come hungry, because there'll be a ton of food. I guess it's almost like a wedding reception."

"I'll probably need to fast all next week," Anna told him. "Between wedding rehearsal dinners—don't forget there are two before the day ends—and wedding reception meals—and there are two of those tomorrow—someone will have to roll me into work on Monday."

Edmond laughed. "I hardly think so, but if that should happen, we can roll in together."

"This is going to be one long weekend," Anna said as they entered the ballroom where the bar mitzvah celebration was continuing. Already a band was playing, some of the kids were dancing, and long buffet tables were being loaded with trays of food.

Edmond grabbed Anna's hand. "First we'll dance to work up an appetite, and then we'll eat."

"And after that we'll dance again to work off what we ate."

"And then we'll eat again."

She laughed. "And then we'll dance!"

Megan

Megan had been startled to hear her cell phone ringing at nearly one in the morning. She immediately thought of her mom, who had driven alone to the family reunion last week and should've been on her way home yesterday. But what if there'd been an accident? With shaking hands, Megan grabbed up her phone. "Hello?" she cried urgently into the crackling static of a bad connection.

"Megan, it's me!"

"Marcus?"

"Yes!"

"Where are you?"

"Iceland," he seemed to say.

"Did you say *Iceland*?"

"Yes!" And then he said something that sounded like he was clearing his throat.

"What?"

"Never mind. I'm on my way home."

"Home?"

"Yes. Did you forget that it's Hannah's wedding tomorrow?"

"No, but—"

"We had a date, remember?"

"Yes."

276

"I can barely hear you, Megan, and we're about to take off."

"Bye!" she yelled, and just like that the connection was broken. She eventually went back to sleep, but when Saturday morning came, Megan wondered if she'd simply dreamed the whole thing. Seriously, why would Marcus be in Iceland?

Megan sat up in bed and looked at the two bridesmaid dresses hanging on her closet doors. She groaned. The satin, fuchsia, strapless monstrosity was for Kendall's wedding, and the more subdued pale aqua dress for Lelani's. Was it possible that those two weddings were really just one day away? She climbed out of bed and looked at her date book. She knew that today was Marcus's sister's wedding, but just to prove it, she read her notation. *Hannah Barrett Wedding, Five o'clock, dinner reception to follow.* Just yesterday, Megan had decided to skip the whole thing. There was too much going on. She'd planned to send her wedding gift with an apology.

Now she wasn't so sure. What if Marcus really had called last night? And yet that seemed impossible. And Iceland? That was nuts. It had to have been a dream. Just to be sure, she picked up her cell phone to check the call history and, sure enough, there was a strange number logged in at 12:56 a.m. Maybe it was Marcus. But Iceland?

Megan returned to her date book. Lelani's wedding rehearsal was set for six thirty at Megan's mom's house, followed by appetizers that were being provided by Gil's parents' restaurant. Kendall's rehearsal was to follow at seven thirty, at a location ten minutes away, and would be followed by dinner at a restaurant that Killiki had discovered. Today promised to be long, but tomorrow would be even longer.

At least she wouldn't be going to work on Monday. Okay, that was kind of a bittersweet thing. On one hand, she would miss the kids; on the other hand, a break would be most welcome. What happened after that? Megan knew it was time to stop worrying. Even if it was hard to trust her future to God, she needed to let go of some things—things that were out of her control. Really, what else could she do?

><=<

Megan wore a pale yellow sundress and espadrilles. Lelani had helped her to pick the outfit at Nordstrom, but suddenly Megan wasn't so sure. She wasn't sure about much of anything. She paced nervously as she waited for Marcus to pick her up.

She'd been in the shower when he called earlier and left a message that simply said, "Hey, Megan, I made it home about an hour ago. I'll sleep for a few hours and be by to pick you up at four." She knew the message by heart, because she listened to it over and over, trying to detect whether there was anything she'd missed. Was he getting ready to tell her that it had been great being friends with her, and now she should go have a good life?

"You look gorgeous," Kendall told Megan.

"Thanks." Megan frowned at Kendall. "Wish I could say the same for you." Kendall's face was covered in green goop. She had hot rollers in her hair, her tummy was actually bulging out of her bathrobe, and her bunny slippers looked pretty fatigued.

Kendall laughed. "Hey, this is the calm before the storm."

"Meaning it's going to get worse?"

"Hopefully not." Kendall looked at the clock. "Now, you tell Marcus to get you to the rehearsals on time, okay? Otherwise, you should borrow my car."

"If I have any problem, I'll call a taxi, okay?"

"Promise?"

Megan nodded.

"Are you nervous?" Kendall looked concerned.

"Yeah, a little."

"Just hold your head high," Kendall told her. "And remember, you are a princess."

Megan laughed. "Is that what you tell yourself?"

"I used to, back when I was having a bout of insecurity."

"And now?"

"Now I remind myself that Killiki loves me. Just as I am, he loves me." Kendall grinned. "And God does too."

"That works for me."

Kendall frowned. "The part about Killiki?"

"No, the part about God. And I guess that kind of does make us princesses, doesn't it? I mean because God is king."

Kendall was peering out the window now. "It looks like your prince has come."

"Thanks." Megan grabbed up her purse, then, remembering Kendall's advice, she held her head high as she opened the door.

"Megan!" Marcus exclaimed as he swooped her into a big bear hug. "Man, is it good to see you!" Then he held her at arm's length and let out a low whistle. "You look fantastic."

She couldn't help but giggle. "You look great too, Marcus. Nice tan. But is that what you're wearing to the wedding?" He had on a tank top, stained cargo shorts, and flip-flops.

"Nah, my tux is at the church. And that's why we need to get moving."

"What happened to your car?" she asked as they headed out to an older silver Buick, which kind of looked like a grandma car.

"I sold it." He opened the door for her. "This is my mom's. Classy, huh?"

She chuckled as she got in. This was a lot different than the hot little sports car he used to drive, and yet it was refreshing to see that he didn't really seem to mind.

"So tell me about Zambia," she said as he drove.

He immediately launched into one story that led into another about the people they'd met, how needy they were, and yet how happy and appreciative. "It was weird," he said as he pulled into the church parking lot. "I mean, they have so little and they've been through so much, and yet they're happy. I felt more blessed by them than I think they were by me. But we got two wells in and—"

"Hey, there's the long-lost missionary!" called out someone. Soon Marcus was mobbed by family and friends, and Megan knew she'd have to wait to hear more.

"Do you mind sitting by yourself?" he asked her as they were going inside. "I mean, since I'm in the ceremony. I kind of forgot about that part of the deal." He looked dismayed. "I'm not a very good date, huh?"

"You're just fine," she assured him, holding her head high again. "And I'll be fine."

"We can talk more after the wedding," he said.

"Come on, Marcus," one of the guys was calling him. "We need to pick the cooties off you before you put on that tux."

><><

It wasn't until they were on their way to Lelani's rehearsal that they actually got to talk again. Megan had been somewhat surprised that Marcus was willing to leave his sister's reception early, but he didn't seem concerned.

"I really missed you over there," he told her.

She didn't say anything.

"I know, I know. You're wondering if I missed you so much, why didn't I call or write." He glanced at her. "Right?"

"Yeah, sort of."

He nodded and looked straight forward. "Well, there are several reasons. For one thing, our cell phones were pretty much useless over there. And I actually tried to write to you. A couple of times."

"Tried?"

"Yeah. But I ended up saying too much, so I threw the letters away."

"Too much?" She wondered if he'd tried to write a Dear Jane letter and felt badly about it.

"It's hard to explain."

"That's okay." She pointed to the next turn, the one that led to her house—or what had been her house. Her mother already had an offer on it. "Just a few more blocks up."

He parked in the driveway. "We're actually a little early," she said. "But maybe I can help—"

"Maybe we can finish our conversation," he said.

"Sure." She turned in the seat to face him. He still had on his tux and looked very handsome in a rugged way with his tanned face and hair that was in need of a trim.

"When I was trying to write to you, I was saying all this stuff, Megan."

"What stuff?" She took in a slow breath and waited.

"It's like I wanted to say things ... things that I wasn't completely sure about."

"Such as?"

He ran his fingers through his hair. "Oh, you know, Megan. Like

I love you … like I think you're the girl … like I want to spend the rest of my life with you except that … well …"

She felt slightly dizzy. "Wh-what?"

"See, you're not even ready to hear it now." He shook his head dismally. "I knew I'd blow this. I'm sorry. I should've kept my mouth closed. At least for now. Bad timing."

"No, no." She shook her head. "It's not bad timing."

His brows lifted hopefully. "Really?"

"No. Go ahead and finish what you were saying. 'Except that' what?"

"Okay, I was saying I want to spend my life with you, Megan, except that I don't actually know what that means. It might mean living in Zambia or Nepal, or it might mean living in New York or just right here. The thing is I don't really know. I just know that I want to do what God wants me to do. And I really do want to go back to Zambia and finish some of the things we started over there. But I want you too, Megan. And I want you to be a part of all that. But how fair is it of me to expect you to go do something—"

"It's fair!" She wanted to leap across the seat and hug him, but she didn't.

"You'd really want to go to Zambia or some crazy place like that?"

She nodded eagerly. "I mean, I guess I have no idea what I'm agreeing to exactly, but I want to do what God wants me to do too, Marcus. And I want to be with you." She felt a little unsure now, but she also didn't care. "And I love you too, Marcus."

He blinked. "You do?"

She nodded.

Then he leaned over and kissed her, and she kissed him back. Then several minutes zipped blissfully by, but Megan knew it was time to shift gears. "Uh, Marcus," she said as she retouched her lip gloss. "I'm curious. Were you really in Iceland last night?"

He chuckled. "Yep. The cheapest flight home connected in Reykjavik."

"Talk about the ends of the earth." She shook her head. "Zambia ... Iceland ..."

"And you'd really be willing to go to the ends of the earth?" he asked hopefully.

"If I was with you, I would." The others started to arrive, and Megan knew this was a conversation they'd have to continue later. "Here come the brides."

He laughed. "Let the fun begin."

"Okay. If you thought Zambia was hard work," she said as they got out of the car, "we now have two wedding rehearsals and two more weddings to get through."

He patted his tux. "I'm ready to rock and roll."

She reached for his hand and gave it a squeeze as they walked up to her childhood home. "Welcome home, Marcus!" she said. But even as she said it, she knew she wasn't talking about this specific house or even any other physical location. She was talking about their relationship, and about her heart. And she knew without a doubt that Marcus was welcome there.

Twenty-nine

Kendall

"Two down, two to go," Kendall told Killiki as he drove her home the slow way. He'd put the top down on her car, and the warm summer air seemed to be caressing them.

"How are you and junior holding up?" he asked.

"Okay. Just tired." She leaned back in the passenger seat and ran her hands over her tummy. The baby was kicking again. But it felt good, like a reminder that he or she was alive and well and looking forward to the time when he or she would make an entrance. She reached for Killiki's hand. "I think junior is saying hi to his daddy," she said as she placed his hand on her abdomen.

He held his hand there for a minute or so just waiting. "Hey, I felt that," he said with excitement. "I really felt it. Very cool."

"Yeah," she sighed.

"I thought the rehearsal dinner went well," he said. "It seems like your family is starting to treat you differently, Kendall. Did you notice anything?"

She considered this. "Now that you mention it, I don't recall being teased too much by my sisters tonight. That's a little different."

"Almost like they're treating you like an equal?"

She nodded. "That would be cool. I mean, I know I'm not as together as they all are, and I've made some pretty dumb mistakes, but it would be nice if they didn't think I was a total idiot." She chuckled. "Did I tell you what I heard my sister Kim saying at my bridal shower?"

"What?"

"She didn't know I was listening and she said to Kate, 'Maybe we should check in with Bloomberg Place to see if the village is missing its idiot.'"

"Seriously? At your bridal shower?" He slowed as they approached the house.

"Oh, she probably didn't really mean it. She just thought she was funny."

Killiki nodded as he turned in the driveway, but she could see by the streetlight that his brow was creased with concern.

"It's okay. I'm used to being the brunt of jokes."

"You'll never be the brunt of a joke from these lips." Then he leaned over and kissed her. "Tomorrow at this time, you will be my wife, and anyone who makes jokes at your expense will answer to me."

She smiled and kissed him back, "I can't wait."

⋙●⋘

Kendall was surprised at how little she actually remembered of her wedding. There were the beautiful green lawns and the vineyard, combined with a blur of fuchsia satin, the smell of orchids, the sound of a stringed quartet playing something classical. She vaguely recalled her bridesmaids' faces, mostly the smiles of her housemates. And there was her dad's smile as he escorted her down the aisle, then kissed her cheek.

After that, it was all about Killiki … and her. The rest of the people and all those concerns over decorations and menus and gift registries and shoes and everything … It all seemed to float away.

Kendall remembered the warm feeling she got as she gazed into Killiki's sincere brown eyes, almost like she was looking directly into his soul. She recalled repeating vows and the realization that she was entrusting Killiki (and God) with her life and her baby's life and their future, until death parted them. It just felt right. Amazing and wonderful and right. No regrets.

The lunch in the vineyard seemed to go fairly well. According to her mother, there'd been some mistakes in the menu, but Kendall didn't care. The cake hadn't been quite what her mother expected either, but Kendall thought it was fine. The best part of the reception, in Kendall's opinion, was the dancing. Finally, she and Killiki danced the last dance, then Kendall threw her bouquet, aiming at Anna, but one of her leggy teenage nieces jumped up and snagged it just before Anna could.

Then, still dressed in their wedding clothes, the happy couple made their getaway in her convertible, which had been tackily decorated (she suspected her brothers' hands in this). Fortunately, Killiki had prearranged to drive her car only a short distance before he exchanged it for a rental car that they would leave at the airport when they caught their flight to Maui. Megan would pick up the Mercedes later and use it while Kendall and Killiki were in Maui.

Both Anna and Megan planned to continue living in the Bloomberg house for at least the remainder of the summer. They would all figure out the rest of the details later.

Once they were in the rental car, Killiki drove them downtown, where they checked into the swankiest hotel in Portland. They kissed as they rode the elevator to the top floor, and then Killiki carried Kendall through the door to an amazing bridal suite complete with a Jacuzzi and a river view.

The newlyweds didn't emerge for several hours, wearing an entirely different set of wedding clothes (and smiles) as they prepared to go to their second wedding of the day.

Thirty

Lelani

If anyone had told Lelani a year ago that she could be this happy ever again, she would have thought they were crazy. Yesterday the forecast had called for afternoon showers, and although the sky was getting cloudy as Lelani slipped on her wedding dress, she knew that a deluge of rain wouldn't dampen her spirits.

"You look gorgeous," Megan told Lelani as she secured a halo of white orchid flowers in Lelani's hair.

"So elegant," Kendall said from behind.

"I can't wait to see Gil's face," Anna said, "when you're coming down the aisle."

Lelani turned around to look at her bridesmaids now. "You all look exquisite," she told them. "That shade of aqua looks equally beautiful on everyone."

"And doesn't it remind you of the Maui ocean?" Megan said as she did a twirl to spin out the shimmering fabric.

Anna held out the skirt of her silky tea-length dress. "You know, I think this might be the one bridesmaid dress that I really can wear again."

"Me too," Megan agreed. "We just need to be sure we're not going to the same function."

Kendall laughed as she rubbed her round midsection. "I plan on wearing this sweet number again in Maui."

"Speaking of Maui …" Lelani went over to the large white box that was laid out on what used to be Megan's bed and carefully removed a white orchid lei, which she took to Kendall and slipped it over her head.

"*Mahalo*," Lelani said, kissing Kendall on both cheeks. "Thank you for participating in my wedding, and *pōmaika'i* as you make your home in Maui."

The next lei she put over Anna's head, kissing her cheeks and saying, "*Mahalo*," again. "Thank you for welcoming me into your family. I'm honored to be your sister."

Finally she put a white orchid lei on Megan. "*Mahalo*," she told her. "Thank you for all the beautiful preparations you did for my wedding." She kissed her cheeks. "*Aloha au iā 'oe*," Lelani said quietly. "I love you."

With tears in her eyes she said to the three of them, "*Aloha au iā 'oe* to all of you. I love you all like sisters. *Mahalo* to each of you." They did a group hug, and then they were all crying.

"I'm glad I wore waterproof mascara," Kendall said as she loudly blew her nose.

"Maybe I should borrow some of that," Anna said as she cleaned the black smudges from beneath her eyes.

A knock sounded on the bedroom door. Megan opened it, and Gil's mother came into the room with Emma in her arms. "She just woke from her nap," she was saying, "and my sister and I got her dressed and I thought you might—" She stopped speaking and just stared. "Oh my goodness, Lelani, you look so beautiful."

"Thank you." Lelani reached for Emma. She was wearing the turquoise dress that Lelani had bought especially for the wedding. "She looks perfect. Thank you."

Gil's mother continued to stare. "You really do look stunning, Lelani. I am almost speechless."

Anna laughed. "And that doesn't happen much."

"Anyway, I thought you'd want to see Emma before the wedding. Doesn't she look sweet?"

Lelani gazed into her daughter's dark eyes. "You look lovely, my sweet girl." Then she walked Emma over to the box on the bed and removed the smallest lei, this one made of pink rosebuds, and slipped it over Emma's head. "*Mahalo*," she said as she kissed Emma's cheeks. "*Aloha au iā 'oe.*" Emma reached for the lei, immediately putting it into her mouth.

Lelani laughed. "I checked to be sure it's nontoxic and found out that roses are actually edible." She went to Megan now. "Would you hold my little darling for a moment?"

"Of course." Megan reached for Emma. "Hey, good looking," she said. "You're going to steal the show out there, I can tell."

Lelani went back to the box on the bed and removed a lei of mixed orchids, some pink, some white, some purple. She took this over to Gil's mother and, careful not to mess her hairdo, slipped it over Mrs. Mendez's head. "*Mahalo*," she said as she kissed both cheeks. "Thank you for accepting me and Emma into your family."

Gil's mother nodded, but there were tears in her eyes. "Now, I better take Emma and head on down there. It's almost time, you know."

When it was just the four of them again, Lelani asked Megan to say a prayer for the ceremony, and they all joined hands as Megan prayed. "God, we ask your blessing on today's wedding. We pray that you bless Lelani and Gil as they make their vows before you and their family and friends. We pray that everyone attending this wedding would support and honor Gil and Lelani. And we pray that you not only bless this wedding, but that your blessings would continue throughout their marriage. Amen." They all echoed the amen.

Megan handed Lelani her bouquet of white orchids and roses. It was time to go downstairs and wait inside the house until the music cued them to begin.

"Lelani," her dad said as he joined them in the great room. "You look beautiful." He kissed her cheek, then held out another white orchid lei. "I don't know if you want to wear this or—"

"Of course I'll wear it." She tipped her head so he could slip it on, and even though she hadn't planned to wear a lei, she was touched that her father had thought of this. "Thank you."

"I have something else." He looked uncomfortable as he reached into his pocket and retrieved what looked like a slip of paper.

"What is it?"

He handed it to her. "From your mother."

Lelani blinked. "My mother?"

He nodded solemnly.

Lelani unfolded the paper and stared at the perfect cursive handwriting. She knew it belonged to her mother.

> Dear Lelani,
>
> I know I am a selfish woman. Your father has told me this many times. But something happened last week that helped me to see myself for what I am. And I didn't like what I saw, but I won't go into that now. I asked your father to give you this note before your wedding. I want to tell you that I'm sorry. I hope you will find it in your heart to forgive me someday, although I realize I don't deserve it. I

hope that you and Gil and Emma will be very happy. Maybe someday we will be able to work out our differences. Until then, I hope you know that I love you.

Mother

Lelani's eyes were blurry as she handed the note back to her dad. "Will you keep that for me for now?"

He nodded. "I hope that wasn't too upsetting. I told your mother that I'd have to read it before giving it to you. I didn't want to spoil your day."

She hugged him again. "No, Dad, that didn't spoil my day. It actually made it better. Thanks."

It was time for the bridesmaids to begin the processional. Kendall led the way, followed by Anna and then Megan. Lelani watched as they took their turns going down the aisle that led from the deck into the garden, where the flowers and foliage looked spectacular thanks to the filtered light that was coming through clouds just before sunset. Lelani had heard a photographer call that "God light" before, and it seemed a perfect description.

"Are you ready?" her father was asking her.

"Absolutely."

They began their walk across the deck and down the stairs. All of the guests were on their feet now, but one guest caught Lelani's eye. She blinked and looked again. Because there in the back row, on the bride's side, which was mostly filled with Gil's relatives, stood a tall, beautiful woman wearing a pale blue dress.

"Mother," Lelani gasped as she continued to walk.

"What?" her dad glanced at Lelani.

"She came."

Her dad looked as stunned as Lelani when he saw his wife, but when Lelani paused next to her mother, handing him her bridal bouquet, he seemed to understand. Then Lelani stepped away from him, removed the lei he had just given her, and placed it over her mother's head, kissing both cheeks. "*Aloha au iā ʻoe,*" she said.

"*Mahalo.*" Her mother nodded with moist eyes. "I love you too, Lelani."

Now Lelani returned to her dad and, blinking back her own tears, they continued down the aisle until she saw Gil. He wore the lei she had asked her father to give him as well as the most enormous smile. Suddenly it seemed she couldn't get to him quickly enough.

Her father paused as the pastor asked, "Who gives this woman to …" But Lelani's eyes were locked on Gil as he took her free hand.

"Her mother and I," Dad said solemnly, then he kissed Lelani and released her to Gil.

The ceremony was sincere and simple, and when Gil and Lelani repeated their vows, she knew that they both meant every word. She prayed that they would honor the promises. As the sun was going down and the sky was painted in glorious shades of pink, coral, and purple, they were pronounced "Mr. and Mrs. Gil Mendez," and the couple kissed and the audience cheered. Truly, this was the happiest day of her life!

><><

The final wedding reception was winding down as the last of the guests trickled out. Everyone had eaten and danced and visited and laughed, then eaten and danced some more. It seemed that their crazy rollercoaster ride was finally coming to an end, and yet it was hard for the four young women to say good-bye.

"What a whirlwind weekend this had been," Anna said as the four ex-housemates gathered in the back of the restaurant. "Two weddings and a bar mitzvah." She sighed. "I hope I never have to do that again."

"And I had *three* weddings," Megan added. "I'm exhausted."

Kendall suppressed a yawn. "I only had two weddings, but I'm pretty wiped too."

"I think I'm just getting my second wind," Lelani admitted.

"Which you'll need for that red-eye flight to Maui," Megan reminded her.

Lelani frowned. "I'm still not sure about leaving Emma behind."

"You don't take a baby on your honeymoon." Kendall laughed as she patted her tummy. "Well, unless that baby is incognito."

"Between my parents and your parents," Anna assured her, "Emma will be well cared for."

"You have to admit, it's really a great setup," Megan pointed out. "You and Gil will have a few days to yourself, then your parents will bring Emma over with them on Thursday."

Lelani nodded. "Yes, it does seem perfect."

"I can't believe we're saying good-bye," Megan said sadly.

"Not good-bye," Kendall said. "Aloha—and that's both *good-bye* and *hello*, remember? Lelani and Gil will be back in two weeks, and I'll be back by the end of summer to figure things out with the house and everything."

"And to show us your baby," Lelani reminded her.

"We'll have a baby shower!" exclaimed Anna.

"Even so," Megan said slowly, "it's good-bye to sharing a house together."

"That's true." Kendall sighed. "Who knew when I put that crazy ad in the paper that everything would turn out so great!"

"Like it was meant to be," Anna added.

"Like God knew just what we all needed," Lelani said with tears in her eyes.

"Each other," Megan said. And suddenly they were crying and hugging all over again.

It was true. Their relationships with each other really were meant to be. God had known just what they needed, and through all the ups and downs of life and heartache and growing up, God had used their friendships to touch them. He had truly knit their hearts together.

... a little more ...

When a delightful concert comes to an end,

the orchestra might offer an encore.

When a fine meal comes to an end,

it's always nice to savor a bit of dessert.

When a great story comes to an end,

we think you may want to linger.

And so, we offer ...

AfterWords—just a little something more after you

have finished a David C. Cook novel.

We invite you to stay awhile in the story.

Thanks for reading!

Turn the page for ...

- **Discussion Questions**
- **A Conversation with Melody Carlson**

Discussion Questions

1. Would you have counseled Lelani or Kendall to elope? How would that decision have affected their friendships? Their family dynamics? Their romances?

2. Lelani and Kendall had to deal with the "interference" of Mrs. Mendez and Mrs. Weis in their celebrations and plans. What did you admire about how they handled these challenges? What would you criticize?

3. How did you feel when Gil suggested Lelani move their wedding to Maui for her mother's sake? In what ways did the idea help or hurt Lelani? Do you think Alana's apology was connected to this gesture?

4. What gave Kendall the strength to overcome her sisters' condescension and exclusion?

5. If you were Lelani, would you have agreed to a face-to-face meeting with Ben? How would you have handled that encounter?

6. Megan observed that Kendall and Nana had a lot in common. What were their best common qualities? Do you have a friend or loved one who is both very different from you and a lot like you? What does this relationship mean to you?

7. What do you think was the root cause of Anna's and Megan's "man trouble"? Could it have been prevented? Why or why not?

8. Was Anna's makeover of Chelsea selfish or altruistic?

9. Compare the ways in which each character's mother influenced her choices and self-confidence. Identify examples of how a negative action on the mother's part nevertheless led to a positive result in the daughter's life.

10. Over the course of the series, which character's journey most closely mimicked your own? What lessons learned by this character connected most personally with you?

A Conversation with Melody Carlson

Did anything about the characters or events of 86 Bloomberg Place surprise you as you wrote the series?

Because I never outline my stories, I'm often caught off guard by my characters. I was shocked when Kendall slept with Matthew Harmon and even more shocked when she went down to LA to stalk him. When it turned out she was pregnant, I wondered, *What's it going to take to get to this girl?* Then I was surprised to unravel Lelani's story and why she'd left Emma with her parents in Maui. I was almost as surprised when Lelani stood up to her mom and fought to get Emma back. Then I was shocked when Kendall almost drowned, and there was a brief time when I thought she might lose her baby. Instead, she found her faith—and Killiki. That was fun. So, yes, you could say I get surprised all the time.

How much of your own life is represented in the lives of these four women? Do you identify more with Megan, Lelani, Anna, or Kendall?

I feel like I have a bit of all of them in me. Like Megan, I tend to be fairly grounded and practical. Also, I worked for an interior designer, and I've organized/decorated for several weddings. Like Lelani, I can sometimes be a quiet observer as well as a peacemaker. Like Anna, I worked as an editor for a small publishing house. Kendall is probably least like me, although I have to admit to having done some pretty impetuous things in my lifetime.

Which one of these characters ended up being your favorite in the series?

Kendall, for sure! At first she made me crazy and I wanted to shake her. But at the same time, I loved her childlike qualities. She was fun and impulsive and slightly naïve in a worldly sort of way. But she was also on a path to self-destruct. Still, it was fun to see a character go through all that and finally find God in a big way that totally transformed her life. I believe in those kinds of miracles.

You've written so many novels for and about young women. Why is this audience so close to your heart?

Partly because I came to faith as a teenager and am fully aware of what a huge impact that had on my life. But besides that, I think it's really hard being twenty-something these days. Romantic relationships are tricky to navigate, friends come and go, careers don't necessarily stay on track, parents can be difficult, and what happens when you make a bad choice? My hope is that readers will live/learn vicariously through these characters and be encouraged to live their best life.

If your readers could take away one idea, promise, or hope from the 86 Bloomberg Place series, what would you want that to be?

I'd like them to feel hopeful that all things are possible when you let God be the major influence in your life.

Other Fiction by Melody Carlson

Spring Broke

(David C. Cook)

Let Them Eat Fruitcake

(David C. Cook)

I Heart Bloomberg

(David C. Cook)

These Boots Weren't Made for Walking

(Waterbrook)

On This Day

(Waterbrook)

Ready to Wed

(Guideposts Books)

Crystal Lies

(Waterbrook)

Finding Alice

(Waterbrook)

Looking for Cassandra Jane

(Tyndale)

Notes from a Spinning Planet series

(Waterbrook)

The Secret Life of Samantha McGregor series

(Multnomah)

Don't Miss the Rest of the 86 Bloomberg Place Series

Catch up with Kendall and the girls as their lives take unexpected twists and turns in the rest of this great series.

I Heart Bloomberg • *Let Them Eat Fruitcake* • *Spring Broke*

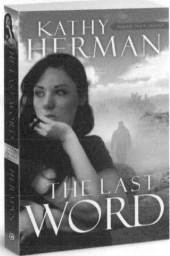
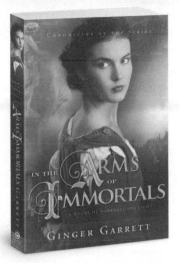